ALSO BY RAFFI YESSAYAN

8 in the Box

2 IN THE HAT

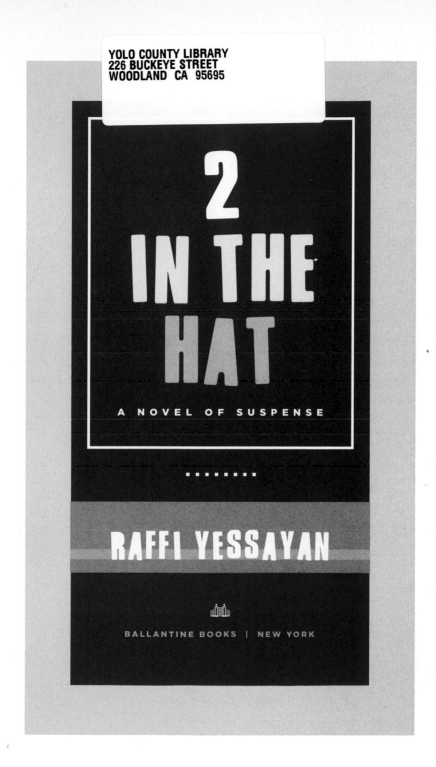

2
IN THE
HAT

A NOVEL OF SUSPENSE

· · · · · · · ·

RAFFI YESSAYAN

BALLANTINE BOOKS | NEW YORK

Copyright © 2010 by Raffi Yessayan

All rights reserved.

Published in the United States by Ballantine Books,
an imprint of The Random House Publishing Group,
a division of Random House, Inc., New York.

BALLANTINE and colophon are registered
trademarks of Random House, Inc.

LIBRARY OF CONGRESS CATALOGING-IN-PUBLICATION DATA
Yessayan, Raffi.
2 in the hat : a novel of suspense / Raffi Yessayan.
p.   cm.
ISBN 978-0-345-50263-6 (hardcover : alk. paper)
1. Detectives—Massachusetts—Fiction.   2. College students—
Crimes against—Fiction.   3. Serial murders—Fiction.   4. Serial
murderers—Fiction.   5. Fortune cookies—Fiction.   6. Boston
(Mass.)—Fiction.   I. Title.   II. Title: 2 in the hat.
PS3625.E87A615   2010
813'.6—dc22   2009043933

Printed in the United States of America on acid-free paper

www.ballantinebooks.com

2 4 6 8 9 7 5 3 1

FIRST EDITION

Book design by Barbara M. Bachman

For Hayrig and Mama

PART ONE

· · · · · · · ·

Sleep, and Death, his brother,
dwelt in the lower world. Dreams
too ascended from there to men.
They passed through two gates, one
of horn through which true dreams
went, one of ivory for false dreams.

—EDITH HAMILTON, *Mythology*

PROLOGUE

He lifted another plank and carried it toward the fire, the heat scorching his face. But it felt good, cleansing. The plank disintegrated as soon as it hit the blue flame in the glowing steel tank.

He saw the old man watching him from under a stand of trees, the farmhouse off in the distance, his eyes milk white, not really seeing anymore.

"And God looked upon the earth, and behold, it was corrupt; for all flesh had corrupted his way upon the earth," the old man shouted.

It occurred to him that he could throw the old man into the flames. No one would care. But it was better this way. Trapped in a body that had given out on him, a prisoner with a life sentence.

He gathered an armload of rotting planks and tossed them into the flames. A sudden burst of red, yellow and blue exploded into the air, a beautiful sight, the Phoenix rising from the ashes. A new life, a new purpose, a new beginning.

CHAPTER 1

George Wheeler felt around with his right foot until he found solid ground. He swung his left foot out of the minivan and tried to stand. It was impossible without the use of his hands, and they were tied behind his back. How many times had he ridden in a minivan with his boys—a newer model with the sliding doors on each side that they'd had some dumb white girl rent from a dealer in New Hampshire so it couldn't be traced back to them—ready to do a drive-by, never thinking that he would end up in a spot like this?

He was lifted out of the minivan by his shirt and forced to walk. The gun was pressed hard between his shoulder blades as he stumbled along on what wasn't hard like a sidewalk or street, more like a dirt path. The pillowcase covering his head had the stale smell of an old T-shirt that had sat in the bureau for months.

When the pillowcase was finally pulled off, he could see that they were walking through woods, but where? He looked around for something familiar, a landmark, but it was useless. Too dark. The thick woods blocked out the moonlight. But it really wouldn't have mattered if it were the middle of the day. For someone who grew up in the projects, woods were woods. You had your choice of the Arboretum or Franklin Park. He had no idea where he was. Just before the pillowcase, the last landmark he'd seen was Sun Pizza. He'd spotted the familiar big red canopy as they drove along Blue Hill Ave. They had driven around so long, he wasn't even sure if they were still in the city.

George Wheeler was scared. He didn't want to die tonight. He had thought about begging for his life, talking about his moms, trying to get some sympathy. Maybe even crying. But he had made the decision a long time ago that he would never cry or beg when this day came. He had known such a day would come, and he had sworn to himself that he would never act like a bitch. He was a thug and he would take his shit like a man.

He tried to think back to why he had started running with his crew in the first place. He couldn't even remember now. He used to do pretty good in school, before he stopped going. Maybe it was the easy money, the rush he got selling drugs for a few hours instead of working a full week at Burger King.

But once he got involved in the game, he couldn't get out. And when his crew started warring with some of the other crews, he had to prove his willingness to sacrifice everything for his boys. Most of the beefs started over stupid shit, a fistfight over a girl or someone selling a beat bag to the wrong person. Selling burn bags on the street was a sure way to bring some drama back on the crew. But once it started, no one would back down or try to make things right. When it was on, it was on.

G-Wheel was young when he had set himself out as a shooter. He had the balls to go on missions that no one else would even think about. He would walk right into enemy territory and light the place up. He had started out with the Mavericks as a crash test dummy for the OGs, the original gangstas, the older guys, doing whatever it was that they wanted done. Then he became one of the leaders of the crew. Nobody messed with him, because they knew he was capable of doing anything, to anyone, at any time.

But his reputation got around and he became a marked man himself. So many dudes wanted to take him out, to be the one that offed the great G-Wheel. At a certain point he felt that he couldn't trust anyone, even members of the Mavericks. And he was right. He had been ready for anything.

Until tonight. He'd let his guard down. Now he found himself in a situation.

He felt a hand on his shoulder. He stopped walking and the hand pushed him down to his knees. He remembered a scene from a gangsta movie he and his boys had watched. They didn't discriminate between white or black gangsta movies—they liked them all. And just like the guy in the movie, George knew he was about to get smoked.

George Wheeler wished he could go back and change all the bad decisions he had made. He wanted to undo all the blood that was shed between the Mavericks and their enemies. All of it seemed so stupid now. Fighting over what? As he knelt there in those damp, quiet woods, he accepted the fact that he was about to die. He imagined himself in a church, kneeling at the pew. When was the last time he'd been in a church?

He began to pray in a loud voice. "Our father, who art in heaven, hallowed be thy name, Thy kingdom come, thy will be done, on earth as it is in heaven—"

The cold steel of the gun pressed against the base of his skull.

He didn't waver, continuing on with his prayer, louder. "Give us this day our daily bread and forgive us our trespasses as we forgive those who trespass against us, and lead us not into temptation, but deliver us—"

He heard the explosion at the same time he felt the bullet tear into his head. It was only a momentary sensation, an instant of something like pain, then nothing.

CHAPTER 2

Angel Alves felt like a drill sergeant, watching his little athletes run in place. They were only seven- and eight-year-olds, the Mitey Mite division, and he tried not to laugh as their scrawny legs pumped up and down. But he couldn't ease up on them. They were counting on him to teach them how to win.

"Hunter," he yelled, "no time to tie that shoe. And let's get those knees up, Iris. This is football. There's no quitting in football."

He had managed that with a straight face. But he almost laughed once more, suddenly imagining the poor kids with Wayne Mooney as their coach. They'd all be in the bleachers crying to their mothers. He missed the Sarge, but he didn't miss the way Mooney rode him. Without Mooney as his boss, he had time to be a part of his twins' lives.

Alves studied Iris's running form. She kept her knees high, chest level. She was tough. If he'd tried that with little Angel, the kid would be faking an injury. He kept the kids working for another couple minutes. Then he blew his whistle, which meant they had to hit the deck. Iris was the first one down on her belly. She was back on her feet, running in place, before half the other kids hit the dirt. She had great stamina and quickness, and when he saw her doing these drills, competing with the other kids, he was reminded how good an athlete she was.

One last whistle.

"Okay, kids, that's a wrap," Alves said. "Give me one lap over the hill and you can go home. First three to make it back get to be the captains for Saturday's game."

Alves watched as Iris led the team up the hill while Angel lagged behind. He was always one of the last to finish the lap. Alves had never imagined that his daughter would be the jock in the family. Even though they were the same age, Angel was a couple of inches shorter than Iris, and a good fifteen pounds heavier. His stout legs were moving a hundred miles an hour, but not getting him anywhere. Alves hoped that football would get his son into shape and teach him discipline and toughness. So far, the only thing it had taught him was that his twin sister was a better athlete. And now all the other kids knew it too.

Alves drifted over to talk with some of the parents. A few were angry about having a practice on a Sunday night, especially with the first full week of school starting the next morning. But he had no choice. Their first game was less than a week away and the kids had to be prepared. He didn't want any of them getting hurt.

Mrs. Williams was staring him down. He gave her his best smile, hoping to break the tension. He was sympathetic, some of the mothers worked long hours like he did. She was a nurse and overprotective. The other parents were folding chairs and gathering up their things. "Same time tomorrow night, guys," he called before he lost any of them. "Trevor had a great practice, Mrs. Williams. I think we've got our center for Saturday's game."

But her smile of gratitude froze on her face as a scream cut through the air.

"Kids horsing around," someone said.

"Maybe," Alves said. He was always breaking up shoving matches, telling his players to pay attention, to stop poking each other. Raising his whistle to his lips, he turned to see who he was going to have to discipline.

A second scream, this time louder, more sustained. It was Iris. Something was wrong.

Alves began to jog across the dusty baseball diamond in the middle of their practice field, trying to make out figures on the darkening hill. Then a chorus of screams echoed across the field. There was Iris, leading the rest of the team down the hill. She had her brother by his jersey, dragging him. Alves was running at a full sprint now. When he reached Iris at the foot of the hill, her face was pale with terror.

"It's okay, honey. Daddy's here," he said, hugging her close. He reached out and grabbed Angel in his embrace.

"She's dead, Daddy. She's dead," Iris cried.

"Who's dead?"

"The woman is dead, Daddy. I know she is," Iris shouted, pointing up the hill.

"Iris," Alves said. "Listen to me, honey. I want you to lead the team back to the other parents. You and Angel can wait with Mrs. Williams. I'll be back in a minute, okay?"

He held her until she nodded.

"Everything's going to be fine. Now, run."

Then Alves started up the hill as the last of the kids staggered down. "Go to your parents," he instructed them. None of them seemed upset. Maybe they hadn't seen what Iris had.

A few of the other parents caught up to Alves. "Everything okay, Angel?" one of them asked. "You need some help?"

"Wait here," Alves said. "I'll give a shout if I need you."

Alves took his Mini Mag-Lite out of his belt holster and made his way up the hill, shining the light on the path in front of him. He was getting some extra light from the glow of the field lights, not enough to feel comfortable. As he reached the crest of the hill, the path widened out, and he emerged from the tree-lined path onto a ledge surrounding a large rock. He had never been up here before. He had only watched from the field below as the kids made their laps to begin and end practice.

Without the cover of the trees, the moonlight gave him some guidance as he navigated along the path. He scanned his surroundings, sweeping the air with broad strokes of his extended arm, the flashlight cutting into the cool night air. No signs of a dead woman anywhere. What had Iris seen?

Alves turned to go back down the hill on the other side of the rock. And, there she was, leaning up against a tree, her head tilted, gazing at him. Her face was made up for a night out. She was wearing a light-colored gown with a fancy necklace. It was her pose that set something off in him. Her back was arched, accentuating her chest, her cleavage revealed in the cut of the dress. The seductive pose, her outfit, and the makeup made her seem so alive.

But her eyes, covered in a milky film, told a different story. Alves had spent a lot of time around death in the last few years and he could sense it. If he'd wanted, he could check her pulse the way paramedics and doctors did before pronouncing death. He could attempt to revive her. But Alves didn't. She was dead.

As he got closer with his light he saw that the makeup was caked on thick, covering the discoloration of her skin. A thin black wire secured her to the tree. Her hands were tied to her hips with the same wire. Alves tried to move her head, but it was held firmly in place by the wire running through the braid in her long dark hair. Her eyes appeared to be focused on him, asking him for help. But it was too late for that. Her skin was as cold as the early autumn air.

Instinctively he reached for the radio in his back pocket. The radio was back in the car. He used his cell to call 9-1-1, telling the operator, "Detective Alves from Homicide. I've got a body at Franklin Park. In the field by the Shattuck. I need you to make all the notifications."

He had a thought. Maybe she wasn't looking at him. What had she been staged to look at before he got there? Alves bent and lifted his pant leg. He took his .38 S&W from his ankle holster. He crouched and spun around with his snubby and the Mag-Lite.

There he was, twenty yards away, against a tree, hidden by a thick shrub.

"Police! Get your hands up!" Alves shouted, staying in his crouched position.

No response.

Alves stayed low as he ducked behind the tree Jane Doe was tied to. He made his way to a tree a little closer, training the light on him. The perp hadn't moved. He was standing fully upright.

"Show me your hands!" Alves commanded, ducking behind another tree. He was less than ten yards away now. He put the light on the perp again.

In the artificial cone of yellow light, Alves saw that the figure was wearing a tuxedo.

Stepping from behind the tree, Alves made his way forward. The man stood unnaturally rigid. Not even a flinch as Alves stepped over brush and dry leaves to reach him. The man was ocean frank, like the girl. The scene was familiar. Nothing he had seen himself. But he had heard enough from his old sergeant Wayne Mooney to know what he had just found.

CHAPTER 3

The old Crown Vic screeched around the corner as Detective Mark Greene gunned the engine. Detective Jack Ahearn radioed dispatch with their location. In the back, Assistant District Attorney Connie Darget held onto the grab handles above each door. There were no seatbelts. As Greene straightened out the car, Connie ripped off the right handle. The left handle held strong. He tossed the detached U of plastic under Ahearn's seat.

Connie wasn't the on-call Homicide Response ADA tonight. He was out with the detectives, looking for a witness on a shooting investigation when BPD Operations put out the call for detectives to respond to the ball field.

Some of the prosecutors in the DA's office thought Connie was an idiot for riding with the cops nights and weekends. But Connie had picked up some pretty good cases being out at the scene.

That was how he'd picked up his first homicide, the Jesse Wilcox murder, a case that remained unsolved. Connie and Angel Alves always said Jesse was going to wind up either dead or in jail. Not six months after his last acquittal, Jesse was found shot to death. If Connie had been able to convict Wilcox on just one of his cases, he'd probably still be alive.

Greene drove down Jewish War Veterans Drive, the road that cuts through the center of the park. It connects Roxbury to Jamaica Plain, from the edge of Grove Hall to Forest Hills. They sped past the Franklin Park Zoo and White Stadium on the right, the golf course on their left. They passed a couple of marked units, one-man patrol cars, stationed to secure the golf course as a crime scene.

"Just before the rotary," Connie said. An asphalt footpath ran along-side the access road and circled the park. Beyond the path was a grassy area next to two tennis courts, which led to an opening in some trees. The baseball diamond was on the other side of the trees, flanked by hills. Everything beyond the ball field was part of the golf course.

Greene took the left turn and Connie ripped off the left handle. At least the sides matched. He tossed it under Greene's seat as they jerked to a stop. The street was blocked off by police vehicles, Boston PD and a couple of state troopers.

Seeing the staties reminded Connie that the Shattuck Hospital and the street running through the park were state property. The state police had jurisdiction over them, while the park itself was maintained by the Boston Parks Department and policed by the BPD. On TV and in movies, local and state police fought about who had jurisdiction over a crime scene. In the real world, the state police weren't so territorial. If anything, there were times when the BPD tried to dump a case on the staties to keep Boston's homicide rate down. But that wasn't happening tonight; the troopers were leaning against their cruisers.

Connie and the detectives stepped out of the car. The two detectives were an odd pair. Greene was a little guy who called the shots. Ahearn was huge, bigger than Connie.

Greene nodded to the patrolman assigned to secure the scene, and the three of them slipped under the yellow tape.

Connie caught a glimpse of the small crowd of kids and parents near the tennis courts. The kids were dressed in football gear. Pop Warner football. The crowd was growing along the access road as Connie and the detectives made their way across the field to the heart of the crime scene. It was amazing how many people were out on a Sunday night. Word of tragedy spreads fast.

The only information they had was that Detective Alves from Homi-cide had found two bodies, Caucasian, possibly teenagers, a male and a female. At first Connie was thinking OD. There had been reports of a potent shipment of heroin in the city, and those reports usually led to overdoses. But the BPD wouldn't call in every available detective for a drug overdose.

The BPD had given out intelligence of some minor gang activity amping up in Franklin Hill and Grove Hall, incidents ranging from kids in groups having fights with bottles, sticks, and bats to fatal drive-bys involving shooters on bicycles or in vehicles. But those neighborhoods were on the other side of the park, beyond the golf course and zoo. This section bordered on Jamaica Plain near Forest Hills. No real gang activity here.

"Two white kids get killed and we call in the whole force," Connie said, the sand of the baseball diamond soft under his feet. "I didn't see the same kind of attention when George Wheeler's body was found this morning."

"Wheeler was just another gangbanger. A Maverick with a bullet in his head. No need to call out the cavalry unless you're pursuing a suspect," Greene said.

From a distance, Connie could see the hill at the other end of the ball field bright as daylight. The BPD lighting crew was on scene with what seemed like all of their equipment. They must have driven their trucks off the access road and across the diamond.

"The lighting crew does a nice job," Greene said.

"They ought to," Ahearn said. "They're making enough on overtime. One of the best gigs going. They're the lighting crew, but they don't work nights. So, Connie, not only are you the only one not getting paid to be out here, some people are getting paid overtime to do their regular jobs."

Alves was up ahead, but Connie didn't recognize the men he was talking with. They looked like bosses, both older and dressed too casually—polo shirts and khakis—as if they'd been called away from a cookout. Alves was wearing a faded pair of jeans and a long sleeve T-shirt. Connie was used to seeing him at crime scenes in his tailored suits, crisp white shirts and conservative ties.

Connie'd have to wait until they broke the huddle before checking with Alves. By statute, Connie knew that the DA's office was in charge here, but in reality, the BPD detectives ran the investigation at the crime scene. Every second that passed, that scene slipped away. Some part of the killer remained at a fresh scene. Almost as though he had just stepped away and was due back any minute. Not at this scene though—the criminalists from the BPD crime lab were searching for evidence, the detectives were interviewing witnesses, the ID Unit was labeling and photographing.

Connie needed to be patient. When Alves finished up with his supervisors, Connie would see the part of the crime scene that would teach him the most about the killer.

CHAPTER 4

Luther came down the stairs of his triple decker and into the street. Like everyone else, he wanted to know what was going on. It seemed like ten solid minutes that the sirens hadn't let up. He'd watched from his window as one police cruiser after another headed toward Franklin Park. Luther walked to Columbia Road and then across Blue Hill Avenue where a crowd had gathered between the entrance to the zoo and the golf course. Officers were stationed there, blocking the park's entrance. Something big had happened and he needed to find out what.

Luther was in a dicey spot. On the one hand, he was one of the mayor's Street Saviors, a youth worker helping gang members choose a better path. Not the one he'd chosen, the one that led straight to prison. Saviors were city employees, like the police. But there was no love lost between the cops and the Saviors. Most of the cops looked at him and his partner Richard Zardino as ex-cons who couldn't be trusted.

If he was going to get the 4-1-1 on what went down in the park, it wouldn't be because he was a Street Savior, it would be because he was street. He continued down Blue Hill Avenue, avoiding the police, skirting the perimeter of the park. He turned right onto American Legion Parkway and saw a group gathered across from the Franklin Hill Projects.

This was the second time Luther had come to this section of the park today. The body of George Wheeler—that was his government name, his street name was G-Wheel—had been found by some golfers. God rest his soul. Luther had been working with Wheeler for months. Trying to sign him up to get his GED so he could take college classes. Trying to get him to go legit. But G-Wheel wasn't likely to give up the life. Too entrenched. One of the leaders of the Mavericks. They'd met in prison when Wheeler was doing a deuce on a gun. Luther tried to use their relationship to squash some beefs before they got blown out of whack and people got shot. Things had been cool. Until this morning.

Luther recognized the faces of some of the dudes. They were part of George Wheeler's crew. Maybe they had already retaliated for G-Wheel's death. That would only bring more heat on them from the police and more drama from their enemies.

Luther approached one of the familiar faces.

"What's up, Luther? You back already? You worried we stuck on stupid?"

Luther gave him some dap. "I know you're not stupid." The face in front of him was shiny with excitement. Eager, almost.

"We didn't do nothing. Yet. We're gonna chill for a while. Make sure we know who did G. Let them think about when we coming for them."

"Why's everything shut down?"

"Why you think? Po-po don't shut everything down cuz some nigga got shot."

He was right. This wasn't the response for a dead brother. That morning, police had closed off a small area while they investigated Wheeler's death. There'd been a couple of detectives and a kid from the crime lab working the case. All around them, the golfers continued their games like Wheeler's body was a squirrel dead in the street, making their way around the inconvenience of the crime scene tape as if it were another sand trap. Luther had recognized the sergeant in charge of the scene earlier. Ray Figgs from Homicide. Luther knew him from the neighborhood. Sergeant Figgs grew up in Roxbury and knew everyone on the street. At one time he was one of the top homicide investigators. Now, word was, he was more interested in Johnnie Walker than George Wheeler.

"What happened?" Luther asked.

"White boy and his woman. Dead. Now you see po-po try to catch the dude that did the shit. Already closed the park. Brought in the dogs. Next be the Feds trying to squeeze everyone."

Luther felt the heat of anger rise in his chest. He had seen this before. Feeling like this was what got him his prison time. Ten years ago, Marcus was murdered and the police did nothing. Luther had stood by, the helpless kid brother, watching his mother come to see that her oldest son's life meant nothing to anybody but the two of them. Before Marcus got shot, Luther had never been in any trouble. Never arrested for trespassing or disorderly. And, back then, everybody in Roxbury was stopped by the police and questioned. If you talked back, you had a disorderly charge for your record. Stand on school property and you got yourself a trespassing. But when Marcus died, Luther had to square things.

Marcus was not dead and buried a month when the white kid-couples first started getting themselves killed. The newspapers were all over the police to catch the killer. Prom Night this and that killer. Now, ten years later, it was as though it was happening again. No one cared about George Wheeler. Two white kids get whacked and the National Guard gets called out. Black kid gets killed and they bring in the washed up brother with a badge.

CHAPTER 5

Connie watched Alves direct the investigation, noticed how he didn't bark out orders like Wayne Mooney. Since Connie and the detectives had arrived, Alves had expanded the crime scene, closing the street and sealing off the perimeter of Franklin Park. This kept the media and spectators out. It also allowed the K-9 units to search for a potential suspect in the park without distraction. The more experienced patrolmen were taking the names of the gawkers who had gathered along the street and recording the plate numbers of the cars in the area before clearing the park.

Once Alves had the area secured, he focused on processing the crime scene. The detective would gradually work his way from the outside in, toward the most important pieces of evidence, the bodies of the victims. Connie watched as Alves took a minute to survey the area, planning his attack.

"Hey, Angel," Connie called out. This was his best chance to get Alves's attention before he got consumed by the crime scene.

Alves turned toward Connie and nodded. Then he looked back up at the hill. Even though the klieg lights lit up the area, nothing was visible beyond the woods from this vantage point.

Alves spoke with a couple of the civilian criminalists, pointing toward the hill. Then he walked over to Connie and the detectives.

"We were out looking for a witness on a shooting when we heard your call." Connie pointed to the detectives. "Mark Greene and Jackie Ahearn, they work out of B-two. This is Angel Alves."

"Nice to see you guys again," Alves said. He paused, turning back to the hill for another look.

"Anything you want us to do, just say the word," Greene said.

"I'll put you to work then," Alves said. "I've got a crime scene up there that's as close to pristine as I'm ever going to get. I don't think anyone's touched a thing, except for the killer. My daughter saw one of the bodies at the end of practice."

"Jesus," Connie said. "Is Iris okay?"

"I don't know. Marcy took her home." Alves looked over toward the street. Like he could see the twins and his wife, safe in their car, headed home. His face was creased with worry. "I got up there right after the kids. Secured everything, touched nothing. If we process this thing right, maybe we come up with something."

"Where do we come in?" Ahearn asked.

"The bodies are in about twenty-five feet from the edge of the woods. I'm treating the wooded area as the immediate crime scene. The killer had to get them in there somehow. I want to search the area between Veterans Drive and the dump site."

"They weren't killed here?" Connie asked.

"I don't think so. I'd like to know how he got them up there without being noticed."

"He must have parked somewhere close by and carried them up there," Greene said.

"Exactly. You guys are going to grab as many patrolmen and detectives as you can and walk parallel lines from the street to the edge of the woods and back."

"I'll call the DA with an update," Connie asked.

"Good. I don't need you finding evidence and becoming a witness. The DA doesn't want that either." Alves turned back to Greene. "I need you and your men to search your lanes until you've covered the area from the street to the edge of the woods. You know the drill. Look for anything that might be relevant—tire tracks, footprints, candy wrappers, cigarette butts, discarded clothing."

"Are the victims missing clothes?" Connie asked.

"They're dressed like they're going to a prom. I've got a feeling they weren't dressed like that before they were killed."

"Why does that sound familiar to me?" Ahearn asked.

Alves motioned with his hands for them to move in closer. "We're trying to keep this quiet. We think it might be the Prom Night Killer."

"I thought he was dead," Ahearn said.

"He hasn't killed anyone in ten years. Not that we know of. But the way the bodies are dressed, looks like his work."

In the unnatural glare of the lights, the concentrated silence of the men and women intent on their duties, the cool night air full of purpose, Connie knew this wasn't an ordinary murder scene. They were dealing with a serial killer. A killer who had outwitted Alves's old boss, Sergeant Detective Wayne Mooney, and the Boston Police Department for more than a decade. "Should we take a look at the bodies?" he asked, pulling a pair of latex gloves out of his back pocket.

"You and your obsession with crime scenes." Alves showed a little smile.

"You don't know the half of it." Connie laughed. "Do we get to see them?"

"I tell you what, you guys do a good job searching every inch of ground leading up that hill while I process the bodies and the rest of the crime scene, and I'll give you a quick walk-through before the ME takes them away. But don't go near them until I say it's okay. I've got to take photos, have the ME do a preliminary examination and then have the criminalists process for evidence. I don't want to miss anything."

"What are we waiting for?" Connie said to Greene and Ahearn. "You guys get started. I'll make my call."

CHAPTER 6

He *tried to fall asleep, but they called out to him. They wanted to* play. He knew he couldn't. It was against the rules. His Momma tried to stand up for him. "Let him play with his little things. What harm can it do?" But his old man had warned him. "Boys don't play with dolls." Action figures, maybe. But dolls? Never. Boys play sports, they play catch, they run, they hit. They don't care about girls in pretty white party dresses or handsome young men in tuxedos or fancy table settings.

But his Little Things coaxed him to come and play. They didn't care that he wanted to sleep. Why should they? They were selfish, making all that noise. Hadn't he put them back in the trunk? They were locked up where no one would ever look for them, under the wedding clothes, the costumes that symbolized the vows that meant nothing to the old man and Momma.

There they were again, calling his name. He tried covering his ears, but he could still hear them. They would wake the old man if they kept at it, and no one wanted that.

The boy eased himself out from under the sheets, careful not to make any sounds. He slid his feet into his slippers and moved across the floor, gracefully. If the old man knew he had kept them, fished them out of the trash and stashed them away, the boy would catch a beating. He needed to get to them quickly and play with them until they were tired. Then he could put them back to bed. They needed their sleep, just like he did.

The boy knew where to place his feet on each step leading up to the attic so they wouldn't creak. He wasn't sure that it mattered, though, with all the noise they were mak-

ing. He needed to hurry up and get to them. At the top of the stairs, he opened the door on the right, the room at the rear of the house. The room went quiet.

Absolute silence.

He closed the door behind him and listened for them. He whispered to them. There was no noise, no movement, no laughter. Where were they?

He reached to his right and felt along the wall for the light switch, but he instantly wished he hadn't. They were in the room with him. Now they were like people, bigger, bigger than his old man. Giants, with doll faces. They came toward him, not laughing or smiling. They didn't want to play. Maybe they were angry that he had left them in the trunk. But that wasn't his choice. They had to understand that. It was the old man. He was to blame. He was the one they had to hide from. He was the one that needed to be punished.

The boy tried to scream. His lungs were full, as if he were drowning. He reached for the door, but something grabbed at his arm. They were too big, too strong. Somehow he managed to shake his arm free and make a move for the door. He didn't get far, but his hand hit the light switch. Everything went black again.

SLEEP OPENED HIS EYES. There was no need to panic. He knew the dream. It was the same every time. He no longer wet his bed the way he did when he was a child.

But boy did he sweat. Sleep lay there in Momma's bed, drenched, the morning sun shining through the sheer curtains. No need to worry about hiding them anymore. The old man wasn't around. He could play with them whenever he wanted. He could leave them out, sitting at a nice café table, having a tea party or sitting on the grass having a picnic of wine, bread and cheese. But this was not the time to play.

Sleep scanned the room for the clock. It was after seven. He hadn't had much rest, but it would have to do. It was time to get up and get dressed. He needed to maintain a normal schedule, especially on the morning after the young lovers were discovered by the detective, the morning after the couple had affirmed their eternal commitment to each other.

Today would have to be the same as any other day. He wiped the sleepy seeds out of his eyes and slid out from under the sheets. He walked into the bathroom, gracefully, back arched, his body held straight to an imaginary string running down his back.

CHAPTER 7

Connie looked up from his notes as the jurors shifted their attention to the courtroom door, waiting for the arrival of the witness. Every three months a new set of grand jurors were sworn in. These jurors, seated for two months now, were a good group, very attentive. They asked the right questions and understood the big picture. Their job wasn't to determine guilt beyond a reasonable doubt like a regular jury. Their duty was to determine if there was probable cause to indict.

As a prosecutor, Connie recognized that the grand jury was one of the most useful investigative tools available to law enforcement. The grand jury's subpoena power gave prosecutors the ability to bring in witnesses, against their will if necessary, in order to lock in their testimony. His plan for today was to present the testimony of an uncooperative shooting victim, Tracy Ward, possibly a gang member himself.

Connie had been at the scene till early morning, showing the cops ways to get in and out of Franklin Park undetected. Still, they had found nothing. Now he had to focus. He was about to begin an inquiry into a shooting, a drug feud between rival gangs, he suspected. In the past year, a spate of shootings had commanded the headlines. The DA had responded by creating a Gang Unit with prosecutors who used the grand jury to help police investigations. Connie had a dozen investigations going, half his time spent trying to locate witnesses. Once he located the witnesses, the trick was getting them to cooperate.

That was the challenge he faced this morning.

He still couldn't get the image of that couple dead at the ball field out of his head. It was eerie the way their bodies had been positioned, the way the male looked like he was spying on the young woman. The way she seemed to be teasing him with her pose.

The courtroom door swung open and Detective Mark Greene led the witness into the grand jury courtroom. Tracy Ward looked like a skeleton. Connie had seen an old booking photo from an arrest about a year ago, and the guy had been beefier, solid. Ward was living proof that a shot in the gut was a great weight loss program.

The jurors focused their attention on the witness as he entered the courtroom in his orange jumpsuit, his hands cuffed in front of him and chained to his slim waist. He limped across the floor, his shackled feet shuffling along, six inches at a time. What the jurors couldn't see was that he had a colostomy bag under the jumpsuit, courtesy of the bullet that had ripped through his abdominal cavity. He was lucky to be alive.

Tracy Ward had been easy to locate for today's testimony, since he was serving a jail sentence for a probation violation. He was one unlucky bastard. Not only did he get shot, but he was out past his court-ordered curfew when it happened. The curfew violation triggered a probation surrender that landed him back in jail.

Ward's attitude was pretty typical for a gang-related shooting victim. He hadn't been overly cooperative with Connie and Mark Greene during their informal sit-down in one of the interview rooms. Connie was hoping to have more luck getting him to talk once he had him under oath, on the witness stand, in front of the grand jury.

Connie signaled to Greene that it was okay to leave Ward on the witness stand. The detective stepped out of the room, leaving only Connie, the witness, the twenty-four-person jury and the court reporter—no judge, no defense lawyers, not in the grand jury. Connie stood and approached the witness.

"Please raise your right hand, sir."

Ward reluctantly raised his hand a couple of inches above his waist, as high as he could, his cuffed left hand trailing close behind.

"Do you swear that your testimony before this grand jury shall be the truth, the whole truth and nothing but the truth, so help you God?"

"There is no God."

Great. This was not going to be easy. "Fine, then do you affirm that your testimony shall be the truth and nothing but the truth?"

Ward nodded.

"I'm sorry, sir, but I need you to verbalize all your answers so that the stenographer can record your testimony."

"Yes."

"Thank you. Now, could you state your name for the record, spelling your last name?"

"Fuck You. Last name is spelled Y-O-U." Then Ward laughed.

"That's very funny, sir. I'm going to ask you one more time, then we'll be going upstairs to see a judge who will hold you in contempt for not answering my questions. Do you know what will happen if the judge finds you in contempt?"

"Yeah. Absolutely nothing. What are you going to do, send me back to jail? I've been in the hole for two months now. You can't do shit to me."

"Please state your name for the record."

"I already did. Fuck Y-O-U."

Connie walked over and opened the door. "Detective, can you get him out of here? Just take him back to the interview room. I want to talk with him before we go to see the judge."

Ward, looking sickly in his baggy orange jumpsuit, said, "Sorry I couldn't be of more assistance to your investigation, Mr. DA. I already told you, I ain't no snitch. But thanks for bringing me to court anyway. It was nice to get out of the hole for the day." He let out another burst of laughter as the door closed behind him.

CHAPTER 8

Alves maneuvered through the parking lot pocked with mortar-sized divots, the result of decades of poorly repaired potholes. He went in the rear entrance of the bakery and scanned the shop. Half the crowd had their newspapers held so high he couldn't make out their faces. He went to the counter and ordered a coffee before walking over to the man at the corner table.

"Anyone sitting here?" Alves asked.

"Yeah," the man said.

"You sure?"

"I'm sure."

Alves took the seat across from him. "Good morning, Sarge."

"Morning, Angel." Wayne Mooney folded his newspaper and placed it on the table. "To what do I owe this pleasure?"

"Happened to be in the neighborhood on a Monday morning. Thought I'd stop for a cup of joe." Alves took a sip of his coffee. "Saw my old boss tucked away in the corner and thought I'd come over and say hello."

Mooney shook his head. "What's wrong with you? You don't come into the Greenhills Irish Bakery and order a coffee." Mooney stood and grabbed the full cup out of his hand and stuffed it into a trash barrel.

Alves sat patiently until Mooney came back with two teas with milk and sugar and two raisin scones with butter and jam.

"Irish breakfast?" Alves asked.

"This is the light version. You should see what the painters and plasterers eat." Mooney broke off a piece of his scone and chewed it. He stared at Alves long enough to make him uncomfortable. "Why are you here, Angel?"

"Double murder last night."

"I heard. Two white kids murdered in Franklin Park. Not good for the city's image. Drug deal gone bad?"

Alves shook his head.

"Funny thing. I heard that the bodies were discovered by a homicide-detective-turned-Pop-Warner-Football-coach. Angel, you're not ready for Homicide if you have time for your family."

"This is what I miss about you," Alves snapped. "You know how to lay on the guilt whenever I try to be a good father. We'll talk later about my lack of a work ethic, or, what do you call it . . . Irish guilt."

"There has to be something more to you stopping in Adams Village for a cup of coffee."

"I didn't find the bodies. Iris did. The kids were doing a lap after practice when she found the girl."

"I'm sorry," Mooney said. The ruddiness of his face deepened and Alves knew he was angry. "How is she?"

"Pretty shaken. The first full week of school starts today. She went in, but we've asked them to keep an eye on her. We deal with so many kids who witness things that no child should have to see. I tried to shelter the twins, and then last night . . ."

"This wasn't your fault," Mooney waved him off. "You moved your family to a nice neighborhood in J.P., a safe neighborhood. But you can't shelter them from the world." Mooney took a long gulp of his tea. "How did the case end up getting assigned to you? Because you found the bodies?"

"My squad was on call last night. I was on-scene, the case is mine."

"Why are you sitting here having breakfast with me? Shouldn't you be meeting with your sergeant? I'm not your boss anymore."

"I need to make a confession," Alves said. "I miss working with you. As much as I hated you breaking my chops and trying to destroy my marriage, I know you did it because you cared about the victims. You tried to make me a better homicide detective. And you always had my back."

"Your new sergeant doesn't have your back?"

Alves didn't respond.

"Who is he?"

"Duncan Pratt."

"Never heard of him."

"Exactly," Alves said. "He's an okay guy, but his heart's not in it. He doesn't know anything about homicide investigations. I'm told he found some good places to hide and study for the sergeant's exam. He had no trouble getting higher scores than the guys that were out working the streets. And he's tight with the mayor."

"How does he know Dolan?"

"Grew up together."

"Politics," Mooney said. He shook his head and laughed, an angry laugh. "No one else up in Homicide you can talk to?"

"It's not an ordinary double murder."

"I didn't know there was such a thing as an *ordinary* double murder." Mooney took another bite of the scone, brushing the crumbs into a little heap on the sheet of waxed paper that served as a plate.

"Two kids, high school or college-aged. We haven't ID'd them yet. Maybe boyfriend and girlfriend. Dressed for a night on the town. Like they were going to a black tie affair at Symphony Hall or a prom." Alves watched Mooney's facial expression change as he stopped chewing. "The male's got a bullet hole in the center of his chest. No exit wound. No signs of a struggle. Definitely a secondary crime scene. This scene was staged."

"What about the female?" Mooney asked.

"She would have looked terrific in her white dress, hair done up, but for the fact that she had been strangled, most likely with bare hands."

Mooney deliberately set his green-and-white paper cup on the small tabletop. He looked away and then back at Alves. "It couldn't be. After all these years."

"I remember the case from when I was a patrolman. And I remember what you told me about your old investigation. Everything fits."

Mooney shook his head. "Has to be a copycat."

"I don't think so." Alves paused, letting the facts sink in. "It's him, Sarge. The Prom Night Killer."

"Another stupid nickname the media came up with. They don't know shit about the case. Yet they have no problem giving the killer a moniker that leads to a cult following."

"I need your help with this one. I've got Evidence Management pulling everything from the old cases. I need you to bring me up to speed with the initial investigation."

Alves waited as Mooney stared out the window at the morning rush on Adams Street, the cars speeding, trying to beat the next light, dodging jaywalking pedestrians. This was where Mooney grew up and where he was going to die.

"I didn't tell you everything about the case, Angel."

"You told me all the major details. And that you never caught him. The killings stopped. You assumed he was dead, or in prison. Maybe that he left the area."

"He left another clue," Mooney lowered his voice. "Only a few of us close to the investigation knew about it. We can't be sure it's really him until we confirm one thing. When is the autopsy?"

"Ten o'clock. But, Sarge, you can't . . ."

Mooney stood up and put on his jacket. "You drive."

CHAPTER 9

Connie closed the door to the interview room. This was his last chance to get information out of Tracy Ward. Connie had already threatened to take him upstairs to the judge, but following through on the threat would only make things worse. The judge would appoint an attorney to represent him, and any good defense attorney would get him out of testifying by suggesting to the judge that he had a legitimate Fifth Amendment right not to testify. If the attorney was creative, he could probably find that Ward had committed some crime which led to him being shot. The court would then hold a private *in camera* hearing with the witness and his attorney, off the record, outside Connie's presence, and would probably find that Ward did have a legitimate Fifth. And that would be the end of it.

Connie surveyed the room. He had to play this right. Greene was standing by an open window smoking a cigarette, his attempt at hiding his nasty habit in the smoke-free building. Of course the smoke went everywhere except out the window. The cigarette smoke usually bothered Connie, but not today. Ward sat at the small table in the middle of the room staring at Greene, inhaling as much smoke as he could.

"C'mon, man, just a couple of tokes?" he asked the detective. "This is what they call cruel and unusual punishment, ain't it? Smoking in front of a man who's been locked up with no privileges."

Greene smiled and blew some smoke in his direction.

"Asshole."

Connie sat in the chair across from Ward. "Tracy, you want a smoke?"

"What the fuck you think, Mr. DA? Yeah, I want a smoke. And don't call me Tracy. I prefer T, or Mr. Ward from you."

"T, you know it's against the rules for us to let a prisoner smoke. You're technically in the custody of the sheriff's department even though they passed you off to the detective here. The sheriff's department doesn't like it when we violate their rules. But maybe we can make an exception for you. You promise not to tell anyone if we hook you up?"

"No problem. I already told you I ain't no snitch."

"Okay, we'll give you a smoke if you tell us what happened the night you got shot."

"What did I just tell you about not being a snitch? Why you try to play me? You just brought me into court and tried to put me on trial with no judge. That's what they call a kangaroo court, right?" He looked toward Greene.

"You weren't on trial," Connie said. "You're the victim here. You've been shot and we're trying to find out who did this so we can charge him with the crime."

"If I'm the victim, why you putting me through this shit, dragging me into a courtroom and threatening me with contempt."

"I'm not trying to put you through anything. The people in that courtroom were grand jurors. Their job is to investigate crimes and indict the people who committed those crimes. That's why there's no judge. It's a secret proceeding, and I'm the one that runs the show."

"I didn't like it and I ain't going back, not to testify, not for nothing."

"I'm not talking about testifying, and you don't need to go back. I just want you to tell me and the detective what happened that night. It doesn't leave this room. No grand jury minutes with your name on them floating around the neighborhood."

"Why should I trust you?"

"I'm a man of my word. And I ain't no snitch either. You don't tell anyone I gave you a smoke and I don't tell anyone about our conversation in this room."

"No tapes?"

Connie shook his head.

"No report with my name in it?"

"No tapes. No reports. I just want to know who you were with that night, who shot you, and what your beef is with him."

"What's in it for me?"

"You get to nail the dude who left you crapping in a bag. And you get a smoke."

"Can you do anything with my sentence?"

"No."

"Can you get me into some programs so I can earn more good time?"

"I know a deputy superintendent at the jail. I can make a call for you. No guarantees. That's it, a smoke and a phone call. And no one knows we talked."

"How about you take these cuffs off so I can enjoy the smoke."

"First we talk."

CHAPTER 18

The feeling of anxiety was the same every time Alves stepped into the sterile room. He had witnessed dozens of autopsies, but he still felt the way he did before the first one. Death was not a pretty thing, especially unnatural death. It wasn't like an elderly person dying in bed after a long life, a tired body giving out. There was something about the machinery that is the human body being stopped abruptly, unlawfully, violently, and the pathologist trying to determine which piece of the mechanism was toyed with, hindered, severed, obliterated.

Besides him and Mooney, there were three people in the room. The medical examiner, Jacob Belsky, was all suited up and preparing his equipment and a BPD photographer taking some "before" shots of the John Doe corpse. Eunice Curran, the head of the BPD crime lab, stood by, waiting to examine the body for trace evidence. At his request, she had been at the crime scene the night before, too. Eunice was the best, and Alves couldn't risk one of her newer criminalists missing an important piece of evidence.

"Find anything yet?" Alves asked Eunice.

"Nothing." She was all business today. None of the usual harmless flirting, not during an autopsy, and certainly not in front of Belsky. She walked over to another metal table where she had laid out John Doe's clothing on large individual sheets of brown paper torn from a roll. As always, she was careful to keep each item separate for further analysis and storage. "I gave these a visual inspection before I removed them. I'll go over them more thoroughly with an alternate light source when I get back to headquarters." She rested her hand on a duffel bag at the end of the table. "I brought a portable light to go over the bodies before Belsky starts cutting."

Alves watched as Mooney made his way to the autopsy table. The victim's skin was discolored, taking on a greenish-black pattern, and his face and abdomen were swollen. He looked worse than he had the night before on the hill. Other than the damage caused by decay, Alves didn't see any signs of trauma, except for the single bullet hole in the center of his chest. He hoped they'd recover a bullet inside him that wasn't too damaged. A ballistics match could be another piece of evidence linking this case to the earlier homicides and eventually to a suspect.

"Is this the kid from Franklin Park last night?" Mooney asked the obvious question, not making any assumptions.

The medical examiner nodded. "John Doe. Jane's in the other room."

Alves's BlackBerry vibrated. He removed it from his belt. "Alves," he said. He mouthed the words "Sergeant Pratt" to Mooney and headed toward the window. Pratt did all the talking and Alves listened intently. It was news that he was hoping for, news that he needed to move forward in the investigation, but news that he dreaded. When Pratt was finished, he hung up on Alves without a good-bye.

"What is it?" Mooney asked.

"They think they've got an ID on the vics. Courtney Steadman and Josh Kipping. A couple of BC students who haven't been seen since Saturday night. Their friends didn't think anything at first. But when they saw the news reports this morning, calls started coming in. Pratt sent some cars out to their parents. They're on the way to make a formal ID." It was too bad IDs were made only through photos now. Parents were deprived of the opportunity to give their children a final hug, a kiss, the chance to run their fingers through their children's hair one last time.

"Where's the girl?" Mooney asked.

"What do you need from her?" Belsky asked, not much of his face visible beneath his safety glasses and mask.

"We think these victims may be related to some homicides from ten years ago," Alves said. "Sarge was involved with the original investigation.

We need to see the female to confirm that we're dealing with the same killer."

The ME led them into the adjoining autopsy room.

"We're going to need you guys, too," Mooney said to Eunice and the photographer.

The girl looked just as bad as the boy, her body showing signs of deterioration, her eyes open and covered with a cloudy, opaque film. He wondered if she really was Courtney Steadman. He prayed that she wasn't, for her parents' sake. But then, what did it matter? Someone's parents were going to be devastated. For a moment Alves was back on the hill where he had seen her the night before, staring into his eyes, begging for help. She looked even worse now, lying naked on a cold steel table. A final indignity before being cut open, no longer human, just evidence.

Alves followed Mooney's lead and put on a pair of latex gloves. Alves helped roll her onto her side and Mooney lifted the braid of long black hair off the back of her neck. He sorted through the hair at the base of her skull. Then he stopped.

Mooney shifted his body so Alves could see the base of the girl's skull. She had been stamped with black ink.

"Is that the Yin and Yang symbol?" the photographer asked.

Mooney nodded. "It's called the Tai-ji."

"What does it mean?" Eunice asked.

"It means we're not dealing with a copycat," Mooney said as he gently lowered Jane Doe's head to the table. "I need to confirm one more thing." Mooney leaned over the girl's body, opened her mouth and looked inside.

"Angel, can I borrow your mini Mag?" Mooney said, extending his hand toward Alves. Mooney put the small flashlight in his mouth so he could use both hands to inspect her oral cavity. Then he reached in and removed a small white piece of paper.

"What is that?" Alves asked.

Mooney removed the flashlight from his mouth. "Her fortune. This is the way this guy communicated with us. A different fortune with each female victim."

"What does it say?" Belsky asked.

Mooney motioned to Eunice Curran. She carried a piece of the brown paper to him. He placed the rumpled fortune in the center. Eunice placed the sheet on the table. With her gloved fingers, she held down the two ends of the tiny strip, then smoothed out the air pockets caused by the moisture in the girl's mouth. Alves made out the black letters, all caps, on the thin strip.

Eunice read aloud, "DEPART NOT FROM THE PATH WHICH FATE HAS YOU ASSIGNED."

CHAPTER 11

Connie stepped out of the interview room and closed the door. Greene was still with Tracy Ward, smoking up a storm, building a rapport. That was a good thing. Maybe Greene could get him to testify. But if the court officers caught them smoking, Connie would catch hell for it.

The interview had gone well. Ward still refused to give it up in front of the grand jury, but that didn't matter. He'd identified the shooter as Shawn Tinsley. Even given up the names of two new witnesses to the shooting.

Now they could build a case against Tinsley. If not, they might find another way to take him off the street. Either way, they had a suspect, which was more than they had when the day started. Connie walked down the corridor toward the grand jury's main office. He'd let the grand jury chief know that he was taking the case off the list for today. No need to present any testimony now.

"Mr. Darget."

Connie recognized the voice behind him. Sonya Jordan. His old friend Mitch Beaulieu's ex-girlfriend. A defense attorney. A royal pain in the butt. He knew what she wanted. He turned and said, "Ms. Jordan, nice to see you again."

"Where's my discovery? We're on for trial in three weeks and I still don't have my client's FIOs or your ballistics expert's CV. We need to set up a time so I can look at the gun with my expert."

"I'll fax that stuff over to you this afternoon. And you can go over to ballistics any time you'd like. I don't need to be there."

"That's fine." She turned to walk away. "But if I don't have my discovery this afternoon, I'll be filing a motion with the court to impose sanctions."

"I'm sure you will, Ms. Jordan."

CHAPTER 12

Wayne Mooney ran through the Fens, past Roberto Clemente Field and onto Avenue Louis Pasteur. He was moving at a steady pace toward Longwood Avenue, the pale gray of new buildings wedged against the weathered stone of older medical buildings. He hadn't missed a noon-time run since getting launched from the Homicide Unit to Evidence Management three years ago. At first he'd been angry with the commissioner. But, honestly, he had embarrassed the mayor during a major investigation, and he had to accept his punishment. But what the mayor and the commissioner didn't know was all he'd had to sacrifice to work Homicide. His marriage, for one thing.

He had to make some decisions before getting too involved in the case. He was used to his relaxed schedule. No stress of homicide investigations, just sit around and watch boxes all day. He had the quiet of his apartment and the company of Biggie, his twenty-two-pound cat. A year or so ago he'd screwed up the courage to call Leslie. They'd met for tea and scones at Greenhills. That was something they'd always enjoyed doing together, sitting and looking out at the Eire Pub—coldest beer in the city—for a who's who of Boston's politicians, old-school guys hanging out with the working stiffs. Seeing Leslie again, without the pressures of marriage, reminded him why he had fallen for her in the first place.

He tried to pick up his pace a little as he turned down Longwood and continued across Huntington. The steady cardiac workouts were paying off. He felt like he was forty again.

He had gotten used to the idea that his career in Homicide was over. A couple more years and he could finish out his time in the Department. Then maybe he'd get a job working security at the federal courthouse— the Palace on the Pier—keep busy and put in enough quarters to collect on Social Security. Everything was planned out. Rock solid.

Now there were two more dead kids. The MO was unmistakable. This was no copycat. He couldn't let Alves handle the case alone. His old partner had come a long way as a Homicide detective, but he wasn't getting any help from his new boss, Duncan Pratt.

The victims and their families deserved to have things done right. No mistakes. Nobody getting off on a technicality. The case couldn't just be solved, it had to be gift-wrapped for the DA. And the only way that would happen is if he got himself reassigned to Homicide, reassigned to this case.

Mooney struggled down the decline of Tremont Street, watching the crowd of kids outside the Roxbury Crossing T station up ahead. They should all be in school, but he wasn't about to play truant officer.

This case was about him too. About not having any regrets when he retired. There were other cases he still thought about, cases lost at trial. But that was the system working the way it was supposed to work. If the government couldn't prove guilt beyond a reasonable doubt, then the guy walked. That was that. But someone had killed four young couples and hadn't been arrested. Hadn't been tried before a jury.

Yet.

"DEPART NOT FROM THE PATH WHICH FATE HAS YOU ASSIGNED." A simple message. Once you cracked open your cookie and fished out the fortune, read it over the fried rice and chicken bones on your plate, had a laugh, and tossed it off, you never thought of it again. Now the fortunes found in the bodies of four dead girls haunted him.

He continued past the young truants hanging out at the station and turned onto the Southwest Corridor, the final stretch, less than a mile back to headquarters. The Corridor had been built to replace the old elevated tracks that ran along Washington Street from Forest Hill to downtown Boston, supposedly making the new Orange Line aesthetically pleasing. Instead, it proved to be an excellent place for young professionals to get robbed on their way to and from work.

What was the killer trying to tell them with the fortunes? The first one, Adams and Flowers, read, "STOP SEARCHING FOREVER, HAPPINESS IS RIGHT NEXT TO YOU." Mooney remembered them all. Two months later with Markis and Riley, "LIFE IS AN ADVENTURE, FEAR AND WORRY ONLY SPOIL IT." Then Picarelli and Weston, "EVERY EXIT IS AN ENTRANCE TO NEW HORIZONS."

Mooney had just passed the Reggie Lewis Center when he started his dash, a strong kick to finish his workout. This final sprint was the most invigorating part of the run. He knew he would be sucking wind when it was over. Much better than the feeling he was going to have a heart attack jogging up a flight of stairs. When he reached the edge of the parking lot near headquarters, he walked a lap around the parked cars, a good cooldown before hitting the showers.

How did the fortunes tie together? Maybe the messages were random. Even if they were meant to throw him off, they were still clues.

Mooney wove through the vehicles parked by the evidence bays next to the ID Unit. In one of the bays was a car covered over with a massive tent, being fumed for prints. The officers from the Crime Scene Unit parked their SUVs at the end of the drive.

As he came around one hulking blue-and-white Explorer, Mooney heard a familiar voice. "Quite a run. Back in top shape?"

Commissioner Sheehan was sitting on a bench on the edge of the Corridor, a bench usually occupied by the smokers in the department. "Trying to keep up with the bad guys," Mooney said.

The commissioner pointed to the gun on his belt. "This works pretty well for bad guys. And without all the sweating."

"You taking up smoking?" Mooney asked. "Or you just out here catching rays?"

"Have a seat, Wayne."

"I'm okay." Mooney stood where he was.

"I need a minute."

"Clock's running."

"I'm putting you back on Homicide."

"This is what I remember. After I solved the Blood Bath case, it was you that shipped me out to Evidence Management, the Siberia of the Department."

"Wayne, we've got eight dead college students. Two last night. Dolan might be pissed with you, but he's not stupid."

"What about Pratt?"

"He won't be heading up the investigation. Starting today. The Mayor's promoting him to Deputy."

"A long time ago, when we both started on the job, you told me there are two kinds of people in this world, those that give a fuck and those that don't. We both know that Duncan Pratt doesn't give a fuck." Mooney turned and started toward the building, the locker room and the peace of the shower. A place he could forget for just a few minutes how incompetence always got rewarded.

"Wayne?"

"Don't worry, Commissioner Sheehan. I'm on it. And I'll try not to embarrass you or Mayor Dolan."

CHAPTER 13

Angel Alves sat alone in the anteroom at the medical examiner's office. He'd just finished up interviewing the Steadmans and the Kippings. In the two hours he'd spent with them, he'd had them ID photos of Courtney Steadman and Josh Kipping. He'd had to ask when they'd last talked with their kids and put together a list of their acquaintances. The victims appeared to be normal college kids with no known enemies, no bad habits. Before the interview, he'd had the parents sit with a victim witness advocate to talk about what would happen next, answer questions about the process, give them a Homicide Survivors pamphlet and welcome them to the club no parent wants to be a member of.

While he did that, he'd had to assign one of the district detectives to witness the autopsy of Josh Kipping.

Alves sank back in a corner chair, closing his eyes, the image of the two kids lying in the next room, their devastated parents, burned into his brain. He wasn't ready to head back into the autopsy room. He wasn't ready for any of this, especially the responsibility of catching another serial killer. He had never stopped thinking about the case three years ago that the press had dubbed the Blood Bath Killings. The surreal crime scenes, each of them the same, a bathtub filled with warm water and blood, like a suicide. The missing bodies, never recovered. The devastated families. There was no closure for any of them, especially with the killer, a man Alves had worked with, taking his own life before they could learn where he had dumped the bodies.

The BlackBerry on his hip vibrated, and he saw Wayne Mooney's number.

"What's up, Sarge?"

"What do you have? Did you get an ID from the parents?"

"I haven't even called Pratt yet."

"No need to. I'm heading up the case again. Had a brief conversation with Commissioner Sheehan out in the parking lot at headquarters. We're all set."

"You kidding me?"

"I'll update you later. Did you get a positive ID?"

"Steadman and Kipping. Parents just left. Parents spoke with their friends early this morning. I've got names. Say they were at the BC football game Saturday night. Couple left the stadium after halftime. No one saw them after that."

"What did Belsky say about cause of death?"

"Asphyxia. Steadman was strangled. No ligature marks, indicating manual strangulation. The marks from the wire were postmortem. They're trying to get fingerprints off her skin, a button on the back of her dress, her shoes."

"They won't have any luck," Mooney said.

"Kipping was shot four times." Alves stood up. He had to stay focused. "Belsky found a bunch of internal perforations. They were small caliber bullets, but they had caused a lot of damage. Death was quick. Massive internal hemorrhaging. They didn't have the clothes he was wearing when he was killed. No stippling. Belsky found tattooing on the skin. A bruise identical to a gun barrel. The killer put the gun up against Kipping and fired the shots into the same wound."

"Anything on time of death?" Mooney asked.

"Belsky should be finished soon. He thinks they died within two hours of leaving the stadium. Stomach contents consistent with their halftime meal. Rigor just starting to dissipate at the scene. Belsky figured they'd been dead about twenty-four hours when I found them."

"That's consistent with the victims in the old cases. He attacks quickly. It's not like he kills the guy and then has his way with the girl. That's not what he's about. It's all about the way he displays them after they're dead."

"That's the other thing," Alves said, pacing the small room. "Belsky wasn't sure how long they'd been up there in the woods, but it had to have been more than a few hours. Their body temp had reached equilibrium with the outside temperature. But they hadn't been put in those poses until some time Sunday morning, at the earliest, probably after it was light out."

"Why'd he think that?"

"They showed signs of lividity in the buttocks, thighs and feet, as if they'd been sitting. We found the two of them standing."

"So you think the guy had them sitting down after he killed them?"

"That's what Belsky thinks. He said that after the heart stops pumping, gravity causes the blood to pool up in different parts of the body, depending on the positioning of the corpse. Initially the discoloration caused by the pooling blood can be shifted, but after six to eight hours the discoloration is fixed."

"I understand what lividity is, Angel," Mooney grunted.

"I'm just telling you what the ME said. The bottom line is that they had been someplace else, sitting up, possibly dressed in their formal wear, before they were dumped in Franklin Park."

"It's something to think about. He may have had them sitting upright in his car, strapped in with seatbelts, while he drove around trying to decide where to dump them."

"I'm still not convinced as to how this all went down," Alves said. "Let's say he shoots Josh immediately. Why doesn't anyone see or hear it? And Courtney would have screamed. There were people everywhere. How could there be no witnesses?"

"They were drunk," Mooney said. "Maybe he tricked them into going someplace more secluded. He could have lured them into his vehicle. I could see them as good Samaritans," Mooney said. "If the guy pretends he's hurt, they walk right into his trap. Vintage Ted Bundy. He was a good looking guy, All American Boy. He'd wear a fake cast and pretend he needed help. Once the victim let her guard down, he'd attack."

"What do you think he's driving to pull off a stunt like that?" Alves said. "I'm picturing a van with tinted-out windows or a rusted-out old pickup with a cap. Every time I see something like that cruising around, I think 'serial killer.'"

"It might not matter what he's driving. Remember, he's carrying a gun, the great equalizer," Mooney said. "Guns tend to encourage people to cooperate."

"Maybe the kids saw the gun, thought they were being robbed and figured they'd be released unharmed if they cooperated?"

"Even with a gun, it would be tough to control two people while driving. Either one of the kids could have freaked out on him and he'd have to kill them in the vehicle or risk getting caught."

"What if there was more than one killer?" Alves said. "One guy to drive and one guy to control the victims until they got them to the primary scene."

"This is the work of one man."

"Okay. What if he's not driving a van. What if he's in an unmarked police car or something that looks like one? If he pretended to be a cop, he could have scooped them up without much trouble."

"What if he is a cop?" Mooney asked.

"Either way, he could have told them they were under arrest for drunk and disorderly, or that he was taking them into protective custody until they sobered up. He could have placed them in cuffs and taken them wherever he wanted. Killed them at his leisure."

"I'd like to get back out there before the next home game and talk with some of the tailgaters, see if they saw any suspicious vehicles cruising around or if they saw someone that looked like a cop riding around in an unmarked car. Problem is BC's on the road the next two weeks."

"What are the chances we'll run into anyone that was there last weekend?"

"Pretty good," Mooney said. "The same people stake out the same spots for every home game. This guy grabbed these kids. If we get lucky, one of the tailgaters saw something."

"Three weeks is a long time to wait to talk to a bunch of drunks about something they saw a month earlier."

"Read me that list of witnesses. I'm going over to BC right now."

CHAPTER 14

Mooney was tired. He crumpled into the seat of his newly assigned Ford Five Hundred. He didn't appreciate the downgrade from the Crown Vic that supervisors used to drive.

After leaving headquarters, he'd driven to Chestnut Hill. He used Alves's list of witnesses who had seen Courtney and Josh before they disappeared Saturday night. According to their friends, the couple had been tailgating along with the rest of the BC community. The game was a major event at the school, the first home game, one of only two nationally televised night games.

Their friends said that Courtney and Josh had had a few drinks. Neither of them drank often, so they were pretty intoxicated. The one thing the witnesses agreed on was that the two were in love. They went for long walks, held hands, talked, were affectionate in public. They seemed to enjoy being alone and talking. Their closest friends said their favorite spots were the area around the Chestnut Hill Reservoir and Chestnut Hill Park where they'd sit in the bleachers by the baseball field.

Mooney knew the area. At the park he pulled into one of the spots by the bleachers. When he was in high school, he had played a few games on that baseball diamond. First base for the Boston Latin Wolfpack. A few years back he'd played in a charity softball game with some cops and DAs on the same field. On the night of the murders, the area would have been teeming with people. BC was playing Florida State, one of the biggest games of the season.

How could the killer have abducted and killed the couple with so many potential witnesses in the area? Mooney believed that the woman was the killer's main target. The man was more of a prop needed to set up the scene. But the male also complicated matters. It would be harder to take two people. Probably the male victim was shot right away. The friends Mooney had spoken with confirmed that Courtney and Josh had eaten hot dogs and sausages not long before they left the game. Exactly what the ME found in their stomachs.

So how did the killer pull it off? Mooney scanned the bleachers littered with empty beer bottles and cans. The sweet smell of spilled beer was in the air. Courtney and Josh had been a little drunk, but that didn't explain why no one saw anything. Mooney stared out at the empty ball field.

Someone must have seen something.

CHAPTER 15

Sleep sat in his car in the parking lot at the far end of the field. He watched the detective walking along the bleachers and then down onto the baseball diamond. This was the detective who had read his messages and still didn't understand. Now here he was looking for clues to find out what had happened to the two lovers.

He would not find any. Because Sleep hadn't left any. He was careful not to leave evidence that would implicate him. The first time he was impulsive, careless. Not any more. Now, everything was planned perfectly. And, of course, he had made himself invisible. The cops would only find what he wanted them to find. The man and the woman. The black and the white. The life and the death. The Tai-ji. The message.

Sleep watched as the detective made his way back up to the last row of the bleachers and sat on the aluminum bench. He slumped forward, hands dangling between his knees, staring down. Body language said the detective was beat, and it was only the first day of the investigation. Sergeant Mooney would have to get used to those feelings just as he had ten years ago.

CHAPTER 16

Sergeant Detective Ray Figgs ducked into the men's room and took a swig of scotch from the flask in his breast pocket. Carefully unfolding a bar napkin, he took a small cache of peanuts and shoved them into his mouth. He'd chew them as long as possible before swallowing. Wiping the salt from his hand onto his wrinkled pants, he straightened out his tie and stepped into the corridor. Ballistics was around the corner.

Figgs rang the bell, and one of the ballisticians let him in. He picked a pair of latex gloves from one of the boxes lying on the desk top, and put them on. He took a seat and waited for Sergeant Reginald Stone. Stone had promised to do a rush job on the bullet that killed George Wheeler.

Stone came from his office carrying an envelope and a plastic vial containing a single bullet. He secured the bullet and gestured for Figgs to come over to a comparison microscope. "Ray, this is the projectile you brought me this morning. The George Wheeler homicide. Forty cal." Stone took a second vial with a second bullet from the manila envelope and secured that alongside the first. "This is from the Jesse Wilcox homicide. The number of lands and grooves gives us our weapon, the striations give us a match."

Figgs had anticipated this news, but the reality hit hard. The same .40 was being passed around all over the city. It didn't make sense that a community gun, a stash gun, was being used by so many rival gangs. It would be impossible to link it to any one suspect. "How many incidents is it tied to?" Figgs asked, dreading the answer.

"Close to a dozen, if you count everything, homicides, nonfatals, and shots fired."

"Any connections between them?" Figgs asked.

"None that I know of. But the analysts at the BRIC have mapped each incident where ballistic evidence was recovered. That'll give you a history of the gun and how it's been used."

In the old days, they used to map all that out on a chalkboard. The Boston Regional Intelligence Center was his next stop. Right down the hall. After that, after the fancy computer-generated maps and information bubbles, it was back to basic police work. Knocking on doors, reinterviewing witnesses, finding a common link. If there was one.

Time for all that after he freshened up in the men's room.

CHAPTER 17

Connie parked in the South Bay courthouse parking lot, next to the police station. He was trying to make roll call, but he was late. He grabbed his police radio from the center console. Besides the use of an office vehicle, the radio was the only thing he got when the DA named him a Rapid Indictment Prosecutor. But it was a good piece of equipment to have. He pushed the button on the side of the radio. "Bravo DA One, Ocean Nora," he said, signing on for the night.

"DA on," the dispatcher acknowledged him.

Connie stuck the radio in the back pocket of his jeans and secured his .38 in his ankle holster, the weapon of choice of some of the old school cops before they got the semis. As an assistant DA, he wasn't supposed to carry a gun at work, and he certainly wasn't supposed to carry one riding around at night with the cops. But he'd rather lose his job than lose his life.

Figures moved across the windows in the courthouse, and he thought back to the long nights he'd put in prepping cases in that building. The courthouse was still home to him. He had started his career there, working cases with Angel Alves, next door in District B-2, Roxbury.

Connie picked up his pace. He'd hoped to catch part of the four o'clock roll call. He needed to have the same information as the cops when he was on the street with them. In the main lobby, he punched in the key code and took the back stairs to the second floor and stepped into the watch room just as roll call was ending.

Connie didn't recognize the patrol supervisor giving the briefing. The sergeant stopped his update as the defective spring on the door hissed gently and then gave way, the door slamming shut. The sergeant stared at Connie for what seemed like a minute without saying a word. It was no secret that some of the cops, especially old-timers like this sergeant, didn't like having ADAs in their station. They didn't trust lawyers even if they were on the same side. They saw every young prosecutor as a defense attorney in training. He turned to Connie. "You the DA I've been hearing so much about?"

"I suppose so," Connie said.

"Name?" he barked. He had an egg-shaped head, a high and tight doing nothing to disguise the horseshoe-shaped bald spot on the top of his head.

"Conrad Darget."

"Who you riding with, Darget?"

After riding with different guys for the first few months after becoming a RIP, Connie had settled on Mark Greene and Jack Ahearn. They were the hardest working detectives in the district, destined to make Homicide. "I ride with Greene and Ahearn, sir."

"Fine. You carrying?"

He had to give an answer. "Sir, I . . ."

"Never mind," the sergeant interrupted him. "I don't want to know. You signed a liability waiver form?"

"Yes, sir. On file with the captain."

"I don't want to catch any shit if you get hurt out there. And if you are carrying a piece, don't use it. Detective Greene, make sure he has a vest. I don't want a DA getting killed on my watch." He turned back to face the officers standing before him. "Everyone. Careful out there tonight. Things have been heating up. And like I said, anyone with information on Wheeler, reach out to Sergeant Figgs." The familiar hiss and bang announced the patrol supervisor's departure.

Roll call was over.

Connie waded through the officers and found Greene and Ahearn. "What's on the agenda tonight?"

"Shawn Tinsley. The shooter Tracy Ward ID'd today," Greene said. "I pulled everything I could find on him. Checked his BOP. Not much of a record. Weed charges, a domestic. Everything dismissed. I pulled his

FIOs to see if any of the guys have stopped him, see who he's hanging with. No real bad guys in the bunch, at least not according to their BOPs. I checked with the BRIC. Not on their radar either."

"That could be a problem. They are the Boston *Regional* Intel Center. If they start asking who the kid is, next thing you know, the whole world knows Shawn Tinsley."

"I didn't tell them why I was asking about him. Otherwise they'd tell the Strike Force and half the Gang Unit would be up Tinsley's ass in ten minutes."

"Not the most subtle bunch," Ahearn laughed.

"That's their job," Greene continued. "Jackie and I used to do the same thing. Won't help us on this case. Tinsley'd know something was up and he'd lay low."

"Let's hope we get lucky and find him tonight," Connie said.

Greene said, "I think Tracy Ward's full of shit. He gave us Shawn Tinsley's name just to get us off his back."

"And to get a smoke," Ahearn added.

"His story sounded too good," Connie said. "He gave us a lot of detail about Tinsley's crew. How they've been dealing crack. How Tinsley thought Ward was moving in on his turf."

"None of that has checked out. That's why we're going up there tonight. See if there's any truth to what he gave us." Mark Greene patted his chest. "You want to borrow a vest, Connie?"

"Never wear one," Jackie Ahearn said. "I hate those things. Can't move around. I'm not afraid of bullets." Ahearn smiled. "Connie, use mine. Get it out of my locker on the way out. You know the combination. But hurry up. It's almost four-thirty and we haven't made any arrests yet."

"I'll put it on in the car," Connie said. "What about the two witnesses Ward gave us? He said they hang on Magnolia. If we find them, we can hit them with subpoenas for the grand jury. Maybe they can corroborate Ward's story."

"Or blow it out of the water." Greene said.

Sleep entered Momma's bedroom and drew the shades. It would be getting dark soon and he couldn't risk anyone seeing the splendor of what he had done with the old place. They wouldn't understand. But Momma appreciated it, he knew she did. Now she could relive those days, the happy times.

He opened the yellowed wedding album, flipped the gorgeous slip of parchment inscribed with his parents' names and the names of their attendants. Sleep loved most the photograph of his mother alone, standing before a lush fall of velvet drapery. There was a corona of light behind her, perfect as the Virgin Mary's halo, her skirts fanned out around her invisible feet. She is holding a bouquet of pale roses—probably yellow, her favorite. A cap of white artificial flowers interspersed with tiny bows of netting is perched jauntily on her head. Her hair is the deep auburn of his childhood, shining, curled and brushed away from her heart-shaped face, revealing her widow's peak. She is smiling shyly at the camera.

The photo, of course, had been taken before all the disappointment in her life, before the old man stopped loving her. Before he started blaming her for giving him a freak for a son.

This room, the house itself, was a special gift Sleep had given her. He sauntered across the darkened room and flipped the switch on the wall.

The room had a warm glow, the pink walls reflecting beautifully. His Little Things loved it. The perfect atmosphere for them.

It was also the perfect backdrop for the handsome couple as they began their lives together. Sleep walked around the room, admiring the photos he had taken of them as they sat in this room only yesterday. They looked so happy, sipping champagne, eating finger sandwiches, laughing. Then off to the park, their little Garden of Eden, away from the rest of the world. She must have been a little drunk at that point, willing to give in to him. And that was where he had to stop them. They would be frozen in time, just at that moment before she gave in to temptation, the moment before she made the decision that would lead both of them to misery. Now they could both feel the anticipation, the longing, the magic of true love. For all eternity.

He wished he could have spent more time with them at the park. It would have been wonderful to stay the night, but he could never do that. Stay too long and you leave too much of yourself. He had stood on that hill long enough to inhale the cool early autumn evening. To see stars, even with the distant city lights. Study his young lovers. Till he heard the voices of the children. Screeching. Their feet drumming the earth. Like little furies.

At least he had the pictures.

Sleep made his way around the room, stopping to admire each of the photos he had taken. Each told a different fragment of the story of these young lovers. They were a beautiful pair. He was happy for them. They had been given the gift of eternal happiness. He lay down on Momma's bed, closed his eyes and imagined himself back on the hill with them, breathing in the smell of the woods, sharing in their unbridled love.

Momma would be so proud of him, of all he'd accomplished, of who he had become.

CHAPTER 19

I love you, honey." Alves was using the phone in the conference room to get the privacy that he couldn't get at his work cubicle. "Tell Iris and Angel I love them."

"What time will you be home?" she asked. She didn't sound angry, more disappointed, frustrated.

"Late. We just came up from the press conference. The plan was to put the public on alert. And to avoid giving specifics. But the reporters went crazy with speculation. Tonight Mooney and I have to go through boxes of evidence, see if there's a connection to old cases." Alves looked at the six boxes of reports and photos stacked in the corner.

"The reporters are saying the Prom Night Killer is back."

Alves had wanted to spare his wife for as long as he could, but the reporters had pounced on the obvious connections. One after another they'd called out the name of the killer linked to six unsolved murders.

"I need you at home. Iris is up in her room. She didn't eat any dinner. She's got her brother all nerved up. Angel, she found that young couple right down the street."

"Marcy, if it helps any, he didn't murder those kids in our neighborhood. Franklin Park was a secondary crime scene, a dump site." As soon as the words were out of his mouth he realized how bad they sounded.

Not comforting to think of a killer using your local park to stage a murder scene.

"What the hell does that matter." Her voice was strained with anger. "This maniac was in *our* neighborhood, where our kids play, where we sleep at night."

"That's why I need to be here." Alves tried to talk calmly, but she had a point. His first job was to protect his family. "The only way I can hope to solve this case is to learn as much as I can from Mooney's old files. Try not to worry. I asked the captain at E-13 to make extra rounds on our street."

"We'll be fine."

"Marcy . . ." He heard the phone click. Alves placed the receiver down. He could feel the vein in his temple throbbing. She was right. He shouldn't be here. He should be home with his family, making his wife and kids feel safe enough to sleep.

He picked up a stack of photos—at the top was one of Courtney at the crime scene. Her face wasn't contorted in terror. He studied the photo, from the gentle wave of her long hair caught back in its braid to the firm line of her chin. He'd seen the look before, on the faces of other victims. A little smile almost, a kind of peace.

CHAPTER 20

Alves was starved. Mooney finally got back from BC, and he brought pizza. Alves cleared a space on the conference table and found some paper plates and napkins in a file drawer.

"No football practice tonight?" Mooney said.

"Cancelled for the rest of the week. One of the other parents is taking over for me when they start up again."

"How are the kids? How's Iris?"

"Not playing anymore. Iris won't go near the field. And Angel has never seen his sister scared before. Let's eat," he said. He didn't want to think about Marcy getting the kids ready for bed. How he wasn't there to tuck the twins in. He opened the pizza box and took a long, stringy slice. He held the box open while Mooney took one. "Learn anything about Courtney Steadman and Josh Kipping today?"

"Both decent students. Good kids. Saturday night they were pretty drunk. We know that from the autopsy. They were lightweights who got caught up in the tailgating atmosphere. At some point they slipped away."

"Probably to go fool around," Alves said.

"They didn't seem the type. They were pretty caught up in the whole Jesuit education thing. Liked to hang out and talk." Mooney's face flushed with anger. "Two goofy kids go out and have a few drinks, and this bastard takes their lives."

"Did you get a chance to reach out to the parents of the other victims?"

"I did that before I went to BC. I had to let them know what happened and prepare them for the media blitz that is sure to follow. I've kept in touch with them over the years. Six families."

"Eight now," Alves said.

Mooney paused. "I call them every summer on the anniversaries, just to let them know I haven't forgotten. I told them that we're working the cases together, that you'll look at everything with fresh eyes."

"Where do you think Josh and Courtney went from the game?" Alves asked.

"Either the reservoir or the park at Cleveland Circle."

"Not one of their rooms?"

"Their friends said that's where they liked to go to be alone. But that night there was no being alone anywhere. On top of the rowdy BC diehards, there were busloads of Seminole fans up from Tallahassee."

"Sounds like you were there," Alves said.

"I was. Working a detail. That's what makes it so hard to believe he pulled it off without being seen. He's getting bolder. And better."

"Did you ever have any real suspects?"

"We had a few guys with bad records but no evidence connecting them. The first vics, Adams and Flowers, were killed where they were found. The others were staged at secondary crime scenes. Where are the photos from the first scene?"

Alves shuffled through the stack and found the manila envelope with the photos and handed it to Mooney. Alves had spent the last couple hours organizing the boxes and looking through the files. "Reports indicate it was a nice night. Looks like Kelly Adams and Eric Flowers snuck out of their prom at the Sheraton Prudential for a walk that led them to the Fens. Next morning a runner found them dead on the grass between a park bench and some shrubs."

Mooney flipped through the photos. "My first time working a serial murder. I'd seen plenty of domestics, bar fights turned fatal, even mob hits. But nothing like this. The victims were dressed up in their prom clothes. The only victims wearing the clothes they were killed in. After that, the victims were dressed up by the killer. Flowers's shirt had a stellate pattern, a four-pointed star-shaped tear." Mooney made a rough diamond with his index fingers and thumbs. "There was also tattooing, bruising in the shape of an elongated gun barrel opening."

"A contact shot like the others."

"Eric Flowers was shot three times in the chest, one entry wound. He may have struggled a little, but he bled out quickly."

"Belsky found four slugs with one entry wound and similar tattooing on Kipping. I'll have Belsky compare the tattooing on all the male autopsy photos. I took the slugs to Stone. They're a match. That leaves us with the females," Alves said, holding up a photo of Kelly Adams, lying in the grass next to her prom date.

"She was strangled," Mooney said, "probably with bare hands, just like the other females. The thing is she had a real tattoo of the Tai-ji. After that, he started stamping the symbol on the other girls with a craft store stamper." Mooney tossed a balled-up napkin on the table. "This whole Tai-ji thing is bullshit. He's using that because he saw Kelly's tattoo and thought it would throw us off. I bet he doesn't even know what it means. He certainly doesn't know what it should look like. The last two times he's stamped it upside down."

"Does it matter if the white is on the right or the left?"

"The white side representing heat should be rising and the dark side, the cool side, should be settling. Another thing. Kelly and Eric were dragged from the park bench behind some bushes." Mooney handed a picture to Alves. "The killer didn't use any wires, and the staging was simple, but it looked like they were lying next to each other, having a picnic or something. Somewhere along the way he shoves the Chinese fortune in her mouth."

"The *Herald* always comes up with a great headline," Alves read from a cut-and-pasted headline, "PROM NIGHT, BLOODY PROM NIGHT!"

"The media were ridiculous. The city was hitting an all-time low in the homicide rate. Good for the average Joe, bad for newspapers. These first murders gave the press a jump start. They made the killer out to be the next Boston Strangler. I think he killed impulsively the first time. Pure luck he didn't get caught." Mooney pointed to a gruesome photo of the young lovers, lying in the grass. "Then the newspapers make him out to be this super villain. My theory? They *gave* him the idea to keep using the same MO. It turned into a game. He takes more victims, only now there's more work involved. He has to eat enough Chinese takeout to find a good fortune, keep a supply of clothes for his victims, buy some cheap jewelry, stamp the tattoo, transport them to some secluded spot and pose them. Now he's enjoying it. He's getting more sophisticated, using the wire."

Alves remembered the frenzy that summer. At the time he was working last halfs, the midnight shift. Newly married. Between work and court, he barely had time to read the paper. But he remembered the intense media coverage. "So you think the media made this guy a serial killer?"

"They encouraged him. So many details of the first case are coincidental. The victims happen to be dressed up. They're killed and then staged in the vicinity. I don't know why he uses the fortunes. But the Taiji stamped on the back of Kelly's neck? He didn't bring that to the party." Mooney dropped the photo in front of Alves. "He gets a boatload of attention for his crime. Next thing you know he starts killing and recreating that first scene. Where are the pictures from the second crime scene?"

Alves had separated the photos into stacks. He handed Mooney a tightly packed envelope.

Mooney flipped through the photos till he found one that showed a wide angle of the crime scene. "Daria Markis and David Riley. He left them on the Riverway, not far from the banks of the Muddy River. The scene was hastily put together. Not enough wire. David Riley's body slumped on its side. We were lucky we found him in the overgrown reeds. Daria was wired to a tree, but slouched forward. The killer was nervous someone would see him. He's gotten better at staging. He's gained confidence that he won't get caught."

Alves nodded. "Looking at these pictures, I was starting to think we weren't dealing with the same guy. Last night's scene looked like it was orchestrated by a pro. Something you'd see at a wax museum. Nothing like Kelly and Eric."

Another thing Mooney had taught him. Think of the case in terms of the victims, remember their first names, humanize them. All of it helped him focus.

"Where are the pictures from the third scene?" Mooney asked.

"Over there," Alves nodded toward the two boxes in the corner.

Mooney went over and dug out the bottom box. He removed another envelope and slid out the photos. "Gina Picarelli and Mark Weston. Found in Olmsted Park. The killer was more comfortable, taking his time to get it right, closer to what you saw last night with Courtney and Josh. He used wire to pose Gina more seductively, with her head facing her would-be suitor."

"Who is spying on her through the bushes, like a game of hide-and-seek. It's almost as if he's using the victims to act out his own voyeuristic fantasies. You think he's into bondage? S and M? That could be why he ties them up," Alves said.

"They're never put in bondage poses. And he doesn't show much so-phistication with knots. Always a simple square knot," Mooney studied the photos. "Anything from Eunice?"

"She did a rape kit. No semen or saliva."

"He never sexually assaults them," Mooney said without looking up. "So we have no motive beyond this voyeuristic fantasy." His voice was low and measured. Alves expected him to pound the table, snap a pen in half, the usual Wayne Mooney anger and frustration response, but this quiet intensity was different.

"Eunice is comparing the wire he used in this case to the wire in the old cases," Alves said. "Same with the clothes. I'll check with her in the morning. We don't know if he's had this stuff stored someplace or if he buys things when he needs them." Alves reached across the table and took the last slice of pizza, stiff and cold. It didn't matter. Good pizza could stand the test of being eaten cold.

"The clothes are a good angle. I spent a lot of time trying to figure out that end of it. They were always used outfits, but they didn't belong to the victims. Either too big, bunched up with safety pins, or too small, left unzipped and unbuttoned."

"Same thing last night," Alves said. "Josh's pants were at least six inches too long. Pinned up. Courtney was busting out of her dress in the back. You couldn't tell until she was cut loose from the tree."

"I always figured the clothes might have come from thrift shops, Sal-vation Army or Goodwill, but I could never prove anything. He could be buying the stuff at yard sales. Tough to trace. But we've got to check it out anyway. Maybe he made a mistake this time."

"Most thrift stores don't have security cameras. They usually take cash only. We might find a receipt where someone bought some evening gowns and tuxes, but we'll have no way of IDing the person. I'm hoping a male buying dresses sticks out in someone's mind."

"Give it a shot," Mooney said. "Leslie used to work with a theater company. People used to go out to Goodwill to buy up gowns for their productions." He looked back down at the photos he had arranged on the table. "It's good to be working with you again, Angel."

CHAPTER 21

Ray Figgs switched off the lamp and sank back in the upholstered chair. Most of the furniture in the small room was from the old house. Dad's TV chair. His metal snack tray. Dad's lamp with a base of carved pine—two wood ducks on a log. Always reminded his dad of fishing holes down South. All of it to make the old folks feel comfortable in their new digs. They weren't called nursing homes anymore, they were rehabilitation centers.

Figgs watched his father breathe—like a baby, irregular blips and bubbles. His dad had been a police officer too—retired more than twenty years. Used to love to listen to Ray's stories, give him advice. Ray wished he could talk to his father now.

Lately, all his cases were gang shootings. He spent his time out talking to a bunch of people who had witnessed the shooting, and they all basically told him to go pound sand. If those cases didn't get solved in the first couple of days, they were not going to get solved. Not until someone with information got jammed up on a drug or a gun charge and started looking to cut a deal for their testimony. That was the only way those cases got cleared. It didn't matter how many hours were put into the investigation. It all came down to someone willing to rat someone else out to save his own hide.

His father would understand what he was up against. Ray used to process every crime scene according to protocol. He'd follow up on leads and talk with witnesses, lean on them, haul them in to the grand jury if he needed to.

His father's skin was ashy in the semi-dark. He'd have to remember to pick up more of that lotion his father liked. The one that smelled like almonds. Ray could rub it on his father's hands, his forearms. His father seemed to like that.

All he could think about was that .40. At least two kids killed with the same weapon. Evidence from shots-fired in different parts of the city linked to the same gun. A stash gun. He needed to clear his head. He needed to connect the dots.

CHAPTER 22

Mooney put down the stack of reports and stood up from the table. He walked to the window and looked down at the few cars passing by on Tremont Street. It was after ten o'clock. They had gone through most of the old files. He'd had enough of sitting around reading reports and looking at pictures. He had missed being at the crime scene the night before. A Sunday night, and he'd been home watching the opening games of the football season. Only twenty-four hours ago, he'd been assigned to Evidence Management. Working days. "Let's go," he said. "I want to see where he left Courtney and Josh."

It was great working with Angel Alves again. He was young enough to believe he could solve every case and had the energy to follow through. His energy was catchy, but Mooney had to keep him focused. Mooney was primed for the long night ahead.

"Any idea how he picks his victims?" Alves asked as he started the Ford.

"After Kelly and Eric? I don't know. This city's full of college kids. He could have run into the others, walking after dinner, outside a club, after a party. We had some info that one of the couples—Daria and David—used to go parking up on Chickatawbut Road in the Blue Hills."

"Mostly gay guys cruising up there, and it's outside the city."

"The staties helped us. We sat on it for a few weeks. Kept an eye on some of the regulars and stopped a few to FIO them, get their names and addresses. They must have spread the word. Within two days we were watching squirrels and raccoons. Six murders, bodies at three different sites, and we had nothing."

"Just like we have now," Alves said.

"Did you know there's a website devoted to this guy? Prom nightkiller.com. A bunch of conspiracy theorists speculating about who the killer is and why he stopped killing. Most of them think he's still out there. Like the Jack the Ripper theorists—they believe the killer is some powerful politician's relative and the police are covering it up. The website must be buzzing tonight."

"I'll talk to the guys at the BRIC about monitoring the site," Alves said. "They track everything going on in the city. A great resource on shooting cases. It's not just intel, they've also got the Shot Spotter. Within seconds of a gunshot, the system pulls up aerial images and uses triangulation to show where the shots came from. The cameras set up around the city tie into the system and provide video of that area at the time of the shots. It's a great way to get an ID on a suspect or to eliminate someone as a suspect."

"Sounds good on paper." Mooney was staring straight ahead.

"It's not perfect. They're still working out the kinks. And there aren't enough cameras set up around the city yet. Remember how we used to pull the jail tapes and listen to phone calls of guys in custody? The BRIC working with the Sheriff's Department can set it up so that my cell phone will ring whenever a person of interest makes a call from jail. I can listen to the call live. Pretty amazing stuff."

Anything was worth a shot. "So you think these guys at the BRIC can monitor the website?"

"They can. They might be able to tell if this guy's trying to communicate on it. Maybe there are hints that he was going to kill again."

"It's worth a try, but I don't think this guy is one to communicate. We tried to draw him out, but he never left any messages outside of the fortunes."

"We need to get him in a dialogue. Maybe we can have someone at the BRIC get involved in an online chat on the website. Have him say that he thinks the recent killings are the work of a copycat. That this guy is an amateur, not the real Prom Night Killer."

"So we piss him off and get him to convince us he's the real killer." Mooney recognized the sound principle behind this gambit. Serial killers always thought they were smarter than the cops. They wanted the last word.

"What if he tries to convince us by killing two more kids?" Angel asked.

"That's always a possibility." Mooney lifted a photo of Courtney Steadman and Josh Kipping, studying it. "But that's a risk we have to take."

Alves parked along the access road, near the tennis courts. The park was dark. A blanket of grass led to the baseball diamond and, beyond that, the fairway. A darker sweep led to a hill, rising against the night sky, ragged and forbidding.

CHAPTER 23

It had been quiet. No arrests. They'd spent most of the night looking for Tinsley, circling the streets of Grove Hall, an area of Roxbury with old mansions with widow's walks and stained glass, a neighborhood now plagued with drugs and violent crime. Connie had been to crime watches and community meetings. He'd met families living in the same houses for generations who refused to give up their neighborhood to a few bad actors.

"What are the names Ward gave us?" Ahearn asked.

"Michael Rogers and Ellis Thomas," Connie said. "You know them?"

Ahearn shook his head, focusing on the dark road ahead.

Greene said, "I ran their BOPs. Thomas is clean. Never been arrested. Rogers is another story. Looks like he's putting himself in the mix, cafeteria-style offenses. Little of this, little of that. Possession of weed, shoplifting, disorderly, resisting, that kind of crap. Next thing you know he's sticking kids up at school, stealing cars. Had a gun charge dismissed. Backseat passenger in a car that belonged to the driver's girlfriend. Gun in the glovy. I'm thinking he's a crash test dummy, trying to earn some respect, get himself a reputation on the street."

"If this kid wants to keep building his résumé, then he's got to establish himself as a shooter," Connie said.

"Jackie," Greene said, "If we see anyone hanging out, we'll stop and

FIO them, get their personal info, see what they're up to. Don't let on who we're looking for or why. We don't want anyone going after Ward for being a snitch. If we find Rogers and Thomas, we'll pull them aside and see if we can get anything. If not, we'll hit them with the subpoenas. Sound good, Connie?"

"That's a plan."

Ahearn turned the car at a ninety-degree angle to the curb, lights on the sidewalk. Connie followed them out of the unmarked cruiser. They walked toward a group standing in front of them. A small shrine of burning candles flickered in the night. A pile of teddy bears honored the most recent homicide victim. Not ten feet away was another shrine, the toys washed out from sun and rain, the votives filled with old rainwater. On the corner was a small store, the brick façade painted with a mural dedicated to the "fallen heroes" of the neighborhood. Connie recognized the faces, gang members that had terrorized the area. Now they would be remembered as innocent victims of gun violence, the familiar RIP painted over their images.

There were eight of them gathered there, mostly teenagers. And two older guys. One of them was dark-skinned, maybe thirty. Maybe one of the OGs. But he was dressed too sharp. Buttoned-down oxford shirt, sports jacket, slacks, and spit-shined shoes. Connie had seen him before, but he couldn't place the man's face.

Then there was the white guy.

He *really* didn't fit in the picture. He was short, a little over five feet, dressed in jeans and a windbreaker. At first, Connie thought he might be a junkie looking to make a score, but he looked too clean to be a fiend. If he wasn't there to buy drugs, what was he doing on Magnolia Street in the middle of the night?

They were outnumbered almost three to one. Connie focused on everyone's hands as he'd seen Angel Alves do. He laid back as the detectives approached the group.

"What's going on tonight, gentlemen?" Greene asked.

"We didn't do nothing," one of the teenagers protested.

"You din' do nothing?" Ahearn asked, bending over and picking up a half empty forty-ounce bottle of beer in a paper bag. "This feels cold. Whose is it?"

Jackie Ahearn was someone you didn't want to mess with. There was a story about when Ahearn and Greene first made detective and got transferred to B-2. One of the neighborhood gangs kept telling them they weren't shit without their guns and badges. Ahearn took off his gun and badge, laid them on the hood of his car, and offered to have a fair one with anyone willing. There were no takers.

"It's our boy's. He likes his beer cold," one of the kids said. He was young, a small, skinny kid, maybe sixteen or seventeen.

"Which boy?" Ahearn asked.

"The one whose memorial you're disrespecting," the kid said, pointing to a guttering candle at Ahearn's feet.

"All you guys been drinking tonight?" Ahearn asked.

Silence.

"Anyone have anything we should know about?" Greene asked. "Liquor, weed, weapons?" Ahearn started patting them down, and Greene joined him. Connie stayed back and let them do their jobs. The kids stood with their arms out. They knew the drill. Keep your mouth shut, let the cops do what they had to do, and they'll let you go.

"Please, do not lay your hands on my body, unless you have a warrant." The words were spoken with an unexpected formality.

"Excuse me?" Ahearn said to the sharply-dressed, older black man.

"You heard me officer," the man said. "I do not mean to be disrespectful, but I have done nothing wrong. I can not condone being searched under these circumstances."

"What's your name?" Ahearn asked.

"I do not believe I need to answer that question, but I will. My name is Luther."

"Luther what?"

"Just Luther."

"You only have one name, like Madonna or Usher?"

"I only have one name, like Luther."

"Well, Luther Last-Name-Unknown" Ahearn said, "what exactly is a grown man doing hanging on a corner with a bunch of teenagers? Teenagers with beer. You wouldn't happen to be the one who bought the beer, would you? Because it is illegal to contribute to the delinquency of a minor, and you would be subject to arrest and a search incident to arrest. You still think I can't search you?"

Luther slowly put his hands out toward Ahearn, palms up. "I did not do anything illegal. I am an outreach worker, a mentor with the Crispus Attucks Youth Center."

Ahearn smirked. "You got to be kidding me. Is that why you're out here? Trying to save America's youth?"

"I also work for the mayor," Luther said. "We come out a couple of nights a week to talk with the kids."

Now Connie remembered who he was. And the white guy, too. They were two of Mayor Dolan's Street Saviors. It was their job to make relationships with kids in gangs and help them out of the so-called "life." Connie had seen them at gang intelligence meetings sponsored by the BRIC at police headquarters every other week. Ahearn hadn't made the connection.

"I don't care who you are," Ahearn said. "Working for the mayor doesn't give you a free pass to buy beer for kids so they'll think you're cool."

"I did not buy them any beer. It is my job to counsel these young men. They are grieving because they lost a friend. They wanted to share libation with him." Connie had seen this before. Kids passing around a forty-ounce beer and pouring some of it over the spot where a friend had been killed. "I do not fully agree with what they are doing, but I have not come here to judge. I want to help them find ways to deal with their anger without seeking revenge and retribution."

Ahearn shook his head. "So you figured you'd buy them some beer to help drown their sorrows. Is that what the mayor's paying you to do?"

"We did not buy the beer." Luther pointed to the white man. Connie turned to look at him more carefully. The man was short and stocky, thick with muscle, prison muscle. The kind of guy you wouldn't want to get into a scrape with. His dark hair was neatly combed, slicked back, the wet look. He wouldn't have been bad looking but for his right eye. The eyelid was half closed and the eye itself drooped. "My partner and I came out here tonight, without weapons, knowing that violence could erupt. But we have faith in these young men. We can help them choose a better path."

"Why don't you pass a joint around with them while you're at it?" Ahearn asked.

"I am not encouraging any of this behavior, officer. Nor am I condemning it. I am a man who has broken no laws, and I will not be searched by you or anyone else. You should not be searching any of these young men either."

"They are minors in possession of alcohol," Ahearn said. "Another one of those little laws that you don't seem to think matters."

"No one was in possession of that bottle. It was on the ground, part of a shrine."

Connie could see Ahearn's face tensing with anger. He watched as Greene stepped between the two men. He must have realized that they couldn't win this battle.

The mayor would take Luther's side if this thing blew up. The Street Savior Program was his baby, giving him credibility in minority communities. It was a crime prevention effort to point to whenever he and the commissioner were criticized for overaggressive policing. Nothing would look worse in the press than two cops and an assistant DA acting like cowboys rousting the mayor's Street Saviors. It would be powerful ammunition for the mayor's critics. The DA wouldn't be too happy about Connie being in the middle of it either.

"Jackie, come here for a second," Greene said. He led the big man back toward their cruiser. Connie could hear Greene's Irish whisper as he told his partner to calm down. It would take some work, but Greene would handle Ahearn.

"Can I speak with you?" Connie said to Luther and his partner. He walked toward the corner, away from the group of kids, the two men following.

Connie extended his hand. "Luther, I'm Connie Darget. I'm with the DA's office."

"We didn't do anything wrong, Mr. Darget." His voice was calm, as it had been throughout the exchange with Ahearn. When Connie shook the man's hand, he could feel a ripple of anxiety.

"I know," Connie said. He turned to the white man and extended his hand. "I didn't get your name."

"Rich Zardino."

"Haven't I seen you guys at the gang intel meetings?"

The two men nodded. Not overly talkative. Upset by the exchange with Ahearn.

"I want to apologize for what just happened," Connie said. "Maybe you can help me. I'm investigating a shooting and these detectives offered to help me find a couple of witnesses. They weren't trying to give you a hard time. We just want to find these kids. We're concerned they may have guns."

"We understand, Mr. Darget," Luther said.

"Connie."

"We don't want trouble with the police, either. But we'd lose our street credibility if we allowed the search. I didn't want to show up the officer in front of the young men, but I had to stand my ground."

"Understood. These witnesses I'm looking for are not in any trouble. Do you know Michael Rogers or Ellis Thomas?"

"Sorry, I do not," Luther said, maintaining a tone of formality.

Zardino shrugged his shoulders.

"Thanks for your help. Here's my card. I'll let the detectives know I'm all set. You can get back to doing your job."

Connie shook their hands. Hopefully there wouldn't be any complaints filed with the Police Commissioner or with the DA.

CHAPTER 24

Rich Zardino's hands were clenched as they walked back to the car. He didn't trust cops. He didn't trust anybody. Serving eight years of a life sentence had taught him that he had no friends. After his release and some bad press for the city, the mayor had offered him this job, a "sorry we took eight years of your life" peace offering. Both he and Luther had done their time, innocent or not, and now they were committed to working for peace.

Zardino didn't want to throw it all away because of a confrontation with a couple of yahoo dt's. The dt's would badmouth him and Luther to other cops. Say they were teaching kids their constitutional rights, helping them become better criminals. He knew the cops didn't trust them. To them, he and Luther would always be thugs, one bad decision away from a life sentence.

"You okay?" Rich Zardino asked Luther. Luther seemed startled by the question, like he was a million miles away. It had taken Luther awhile to warm up to him, an Italian guy from East Boston who had done state prison time for a murder he didn't commit. What would a guy like that have in common with the kids they were servicing, black and brown kids from Roxbury, Dorchester, and Mattapan? But they both knew it made for great press. A former gangbanger, a convicted felon who had found

Christ teamed up with a wrongly-convicted white guy. The kind of stuff they made movies about.

Turned out he was pretty good at communicating with the kids. He was real, and that was all he needed for the kids to trust him, no matter the color of his skin.

"I'm upset those cops put us in that situation," Luther said. "The big guy could have shown us a little respect and it wouldn't have gone down like that."

"Don't sweat it. It's over," Zardino said. "The police have a lot to lose if they file a report."

"Maybe I should have handled it differently, let them search me, let them see that I'm clean."

"Bull." Zardino spat in the street. It was a dirty habit that drove his partner crazy. "You did the right thing. How else are they going to learn to stand up for their rights?"

Luther was always stumping about setting an example. But tonight, no one had learned anything from the beef with the cops. Once the police left, the kids started imitating the pissed-off cop, trying to high-five Luther for how he had handled them. That drove Luther nuts.

"Maybe I *am* making them better criminals," Luther said. "But so are the police, by treating *everyone* like a criminal. They're teaching them to distrust the police, to disrespect authority and to turn to the streets for support. At least what happened tonight was witnessed by a prosecutor."

"I don't trust that guy," Zardino said.

"You don't trust any lawyers. I can't say I blame you after what you've been through."

"I was watching him," Zardino shifted and got comfortable against the car. "He wasn't going to say nothing while the cops did their thing. When he found out who we were he realized it wouldn't look good. I saw the light go on in his head. That's the only reason he stepped in."

"Maybe."

"Definitely. I know guys like that. He had no problem with what the cops were doing until he thought it could come back and bite him. Then he's a peacemaker. Screw him. He's a lawyer. No, he's a prosecutor, an officer of the court, sworn to uphold the Constitution. He shouldn't be letting dt's do things like that. He's as bad as they are."

"He extended the olive branch to us. We might as well use him as an ally."

"We need to watch our backs."

"You really are one suspicious dude."

"That's what happens when your friends set you up and send you to jail for a crime you had nothing to do with. I don't trust anyone except my mother."

"Truth told, my boys forgot about me when I was upstate. No visits. No money in the canteen fund for chips, sodas and snacks. In the end, Richard, it's always just you and your mom. And the Lord."

CHAPTER 25

*A*lves saw her standing at the bus stop. She was always at the bus stop.

She wasn't too far away. Maybe a hundred yards. If he hurried, he could get to her in time. But his feet were heavy. He tried moving faster, his legs weren't responding. He had to close the gap between them.

Then the bus came around the corner, smoke billowing behind it. It was loud, without a muffler. He called her name, but she couldn't hear him over the roar of the bus.

He had to get to her.

He was running now, but the bus was moving so fast. He called her name again. This time he couldn't even hear his own voice.

He watched as the bus stopped to let her on. He could see the driver and the passengers.

He shouted her name one last time.

Alves stopped running. The driver watched Robyn Stokes, Alves's childhood friend, dressed in her hospital whites, as she climbed the steps. When she turned to find a seat, the driver looked over at him. It was a familiar face, the face of a former colleague, a man he didn't know too well, but had respected. The man who had murdered Robyn Stokes. The driver, Mitch Beaulieu, former assistant district attorney and murderer, pulled the bus away from the curb with Robyn and the rest of his doomed passengers. Alves felt his hip, his back pocket, for a phone, a radio, his gun. Nothing. There was no way to stop the bus. Then he heard a loud bang.

Alves jerked forward in his chair. It took a moment for his eyes to ad-just to the bright sunlight streaming through the conference room win-

dows. The noise Alves heard must have been a door out in the hall slamming.

It was getting harder to sleep. Whenever he closed his eyes, he
thought about his old friend Robyn. Killed three years before by a killer
the press called the Blood Bath Killer. Left tubs full of water and blood.
No bodies. He and Mooney had caught Robyn's killer, Mitch Beaulieu,
but they never found her body. He owed Robyn and her mother one last
thing. A Christian burial. A final resting place, a grave to cover with
flowers.

Propped in front of him against a pile of folders was a note written on
a sheet torn from a detective's notebook. *Quick shower then off to ballistics. You
check in with Eunice Curran. WM*

CHAPTER 26

Mooney stepped out of the Homicide Unit and turned down the corridor toward the gym. The city had spared no expense when they built One Schroeder Plaza. Their new headquarters had everything from a state-of-the-art crime lab to a gym as good as any private health club in the city.

Mooney stepped into the gym and took his first left into the locker room. He wasn't looking for a workout. No time. He needed a quick shave and shower.

Within a half hour he was banging on the glass doors of the Ballistics Unit with his knee, a cup of coffee in each hand. He knew Sergeant Reginald Stone would be in early; like Mooney, he was a Marine. He gave it a minute before kicking the baseplates of the heavy doors.

A few seconds later Stone emerged from an office door at the far end of the Ballistics Unit. He didn't look happy that someone was trying to kick in the door.

"Open up, Reggie," Mooney shouted through the heavy glass doors.

Stone looked down at Mooney's hands. "Cream, no sugar?"

"What am I, an idiot?"

Stone smiled and came over to let him in. Mooney went to put the coffees down on a table so he could shake his friend's hand, but he was greeted with a firm hug instead. It was awkward, since Stone was so much shorter. He had quite a bear hug for a little guy.

"Ease up there, pal. You're going to be wearing two cups of coffee if you're not careful," Mooney said.

He released Mooney from his grip. "Great to see you, Wayne."

"I haven't had a chance to congratulate you on the promotion, Reggie. The first black officer to head up the Ballistics Unit."

"I don't look at it like that. I'm just another sergeant given the honor."

"Bullshit," Mooney said. "This is big. You're a groundbreaker. It's important to the other officers coming up in the department."

"There are some people out there saying I only got the job *because* I'm black."

"Give me the names of the bozos talking smack, and I'll crack them over the head. You got the position because you're the best man. This ballistics unit has been messed up for years. How many guns have been secured here as evidence and turned up missing?"

"My first priority is to inventory, box up, and bar code everything for the evidence management system."

"You're the best. And you're going to prove it by helping me out with a case." He handed one of the coffees to Stone.

Stone led Mooney back to his office. "What case?"

"Josh Kipping. Alves brought you four slugs and some autopsy photos yesterday."

"The Prom Night Killer." Stone sat behind his desk and removed the lid from his coffee. "Interesting case. Multiple shots. One entry. Angel told you I matched the projectiles to the evidence from ten years ago?"

"That's helpful." Mooney flipped the cover off his coffee and took a sip. "But I already knew it was the same guy. What's your theory on the single entry wound and the number of shots fired?"

Stone took a sip. "I think he's using a machine gun."

"A machine gun?" Mooney almost coughed up his coffee.

"Not a regular machine gun. Not something that was manufactured as such." Stone put his cup down and got up from his chair. "Come with me. I want to show you something."

Mooney followed him down the hall to the Secure Firearm Evidence Room where the guns were stored. Stone walked down the rows of shelves and came out with an evidence box. He led Mooney to the test firing room.

"What do you have there?" Mooney asked.

Stone placed the box on a table and removed the gun. "It's an interesting case from a few years back, before I made sergeant, when I was just a detective examining firearms and testifying in court. It's a twenty-two caliber Berretta semiautomatic, altered to fire fully auto."

"I'd like to see how to do that."

"Let me show you." Stone took a stack of photos from the box and spread them on the table. "I had a second gun that was in pristine condition. Took the two of them apart and took some comparison photos. You can see in the pictures that the trigger bar arm has been cut by about a third in the altered firearm. You know how this type of weapon is supposed to work."

Mooney nodded, focusing on the photos.

"When the gun is fired, the slide is forced back, loading the next round from the magazine and resetting the hammer. The bar arm's supposed to hold the hammer in the cocked position until you pull the trigger again to fire the next round. With the bar arm cut short, the hammer doesn't stay in the cocked position. The weapon keeps firing as long as you hold the trigger. It keeps firing until the clip is empty. Nine rounds. Unless it jams."

"Does it jam?"

"Every time. I've never gotten it to fire the full nine rounds, but it always manages to pump out three, four, even five rounds."

"Like we've found in each of the victims."

"Correct. Let me show you." Stone opened a file cabinet drawer, shuffled through some boxes and took out some .22 caliber ammunition. He fed nine rounds into the clip and slid it into the handle of the gun. He put on his sound-deadening headphones and handed a pair to Mooney before making his way to the projectile recovery tank. He put on his safety glasses. "Watch carefully, Wayne. It's going to come out in one burst. To an untrained ear it would almost seem like one shot, but you'll see and hear that it isn't. The first time I fired this thing, I almost had a heart attack. I didn't know it had been altered. I was just testing it to see if it was a working firearm and it took off on me."

Stone positioned himself, the gun in his right hand, supported by the left. Then he squeezed the trigger. Mooney saw the flash from the barrel of the gun. He could hear it was multiple shots, but he wasn't sure how many. He tried to count the shell casings as they were ejecting, but it happened too fast, the casings scattering on the floor.

Stone removed his ear protection. "I think that was five. That's what it felt like." He bent over and picked the casings up off the floor. "Confirmed. Five."

"The bullets that killed these kids are also twenty-two cal. Were they fired from a Berretta?"

"I think so. Six lands and grooves with a right twist. Consistent with a Berretta. But I'd want to see the weapon to make a positive match. If this killer has a gun like this, altered in the same way, it would explain why you have multiple shots, but never the same number, and only one entry wound. And tattooing consistent with this gun barrel." Stone placed the gun down on the table. "Wayne, you know this gun serves only one purpose. It's a hit man's weapon. Small caliber, so it doesn't make too much noise. When you pull the trigger, it sounds like one round being fired instead of four or five. It fires so fast that the last round would be fired before the first casing hits the ground. And you know from experience that small caliber rounds can cause more internal damage to the victim."

Stone picked the gun up again. "And this gun would be useless in a gunfight. You basically get one pull of the trigger and you discharge all nine rounds at once or the gun jams up. Either way, if you miss your target, you're out of luck. The fight's over and you're a dead man."

CHAPTER 27

Alves rang the buzzer outside the crime lab. He was tired. Putting his head down on a conference room table for a couple of hours didn't qualify as a good night's sleep. Having nightmares and picturing your sleeping family alone in a dark house didn't help.

"Can I help you?" Alves heard the pleasant voice behind him. A young woman opened the door to the crime lab. He had never seen her before. Blond hair, pulled back in a ponytail. She looked like a teenager, but she was probably a new criminalist, straight out of college with her biology degree. The new hires seemed to be getting younger.

"I'm looking for Eunice Curran?" Alves said.

"And you are?"

"Detective Alves. Homicide." He had his gold badge clipped to his belt.

She left him at the reception desk and went back to check with Eunice. Following protocol. Good for her. Once she'd cleared everything with the boss, she let Alves enter the inner sanctum of the DNA lab and the evidence examination rooms. Eunice Curran was in one of those rooms, laying out the evidence she had recovered over the last couple of days.

"Hi there, handsome," she said. "I've been expecting you. Like clockwork, you always show up the morning after . . . an autopsy, that is. But you're usually not this early."

"Never made it home last night."

"I saw your buddy Sergeant Mooney across the hall," she said. "That's two days in a row I've seen you guys together. People are starting to talk."

"Nothing to talk about. Mooney's back in Homicide."

"Good to hear. Let me show you what I've got . . . the evidence, that is." She brought over two paper evidence bags. He could see the change in her face, in the tone of her voice. She was discussing her work now, so no more fooling around. "Here's the wire that was used to secure the victims. I've kept them separate. It's all identical black telephone wire, one of the fine, multicolored wires you find inside a telephone line. I pulled the evidence from the old cases. It's a match. It looks like he's taking ordinary telephone line, slicing off the outer casing and using the black wire inside. He probably likes it because it's less visible to the naked eye than the colored wire, the reds, greens and yellows. It definitely serves its purpose. Thin, but sturdy."

"Any idea where he got it?"

"Manufacturer's a company called Teletech. They've been around forever. Seeing that it's a match with the wire from the earlier crime scenes, I'd say he got a good supply of the stuff somewhere. Kept it on hand over the years."

"Maybe he works for a phone company or a company that installs security systems," Alves said. "He might be an electrician. Any one of those jobs would put him in regular contact with this kind of wire."

"He could have bought it at Home Depot, like everyone else. Paid cash for part of a roll and kept it on hand. I don't think it's any indication of what he does for work."

Alves shook his head. "Have you ever been to a mason's house, Eunice?"

"You mean like a Benjamin Franklin, George Washington type Mason, or a tradesman who lays bricks?"

"Works with bricks." He avoided the word lay. He figured she was through with the flirting, but why give her ammunition?

"I can't say I have, but if you know one who's not married, feel free to give him my number."

"I'll get on that." He smiled. "If you ever get lucky enough to see a mason's house, you'll notice that all of the home improvements involve masonry work. New walkway, brick. New siding, brick. Garden edging, old bricks. Kitchen and bathroom floors are tile, never linoleum."

"What's your point?"

"My point is that people like to work with a familiar medium. If a guy works with concrete, he'll put in a concrete walkway with a concrete apron around his house. My next-door neighbor is an electrician. If he gets bored on weekends, he changes light fixtures, puts in new circuit breakers and transformers. Once he even dug a trench in his front yard and ran PVC pipe underground so the power and phone lines running to his house wouldn't be visible."

Eunice tried to interrupt him, but Alves held his hand up.

"The most important thing I've noticed about this neighbor is that he uses pieces of that heavy Romex electric line—the kind with the positive, negative and grounding wires in the white casing—to tie things up. He uses it instead of rope. If he puts a ladder on the roof of his van, he secures it with a couple of pieces of Romex. Rolls up his garden hose for the winter and ties it with Romex. His wife plants a sapling in the back yard, he keeps it upright with a piece of rebar and Romex. He uses it for everything because that's what he's familiar with."

"So your next-door neighbor is the killer because he likes to use electrical wire to tie things."

"What I'm saying is the killer didn't just choose this type of black telephone wire. It chose him," Alves said. "Maybe that's the case with everything he uses. Mooney brought this up last night and it got me thinking. What if this guy is with a local theater group? What if he does lighting and electrical work for them? That would give him access to the wire, the makeup, and the clothes. Working in theater would give him a reason to go to thrift shops, yard sales, and flea markets looking for used formal wear for men and women. No one would question it."

"Problem is the makeup isn't that heavy theatrical makeup. He caked it on the best he could so the victims looked good from a distance, but it was inexpensive makeup, like Revlon, the kind that's sold in pharmacies and supermarkets."

"This is the first time he's used makeup," Alves said.

"I noticed that. I guess he just wanted to add a new touch to his creation. Another thing. I'm not sure if this tells us anything, but the clothes smelled like naphthalene."

"What's that?"

"Mothballs. Old school mothballs. They still make them, but most mothballs today are made with dichlorobenzene. Less flammable."

"So it makes sense that he could have had the clothes in an attic."

"Or he just bought them at a flea market," Eunice said. "Stuff someone else had stored away. So it doesn't tell us anything, really."

"I can't help but think this guy has this stuff packed up and ready to go. We know he's got a supply of the wire. We know he's had the same gun all these years. I'm willing to bet he's done the same with the clothes. What about the jewelry?"

"The first victim had a gold necklace, real emeralds."

Alves had read in the reports that Kelly Adams's mother loaned it to her for the prom.

"After that, costume stuff. Similar, but cheap glass beads. I can't tell you if he bought the jewelry last week or ten years ago."

"Eunice, are you familiar with the BTK Killer?"

Eunice nodded. "Bind. Torture. Kill. Dennis Rader."

"Rader lived what most people would call a normal life, aside from the fact that he was a murderer. He was involved with his church, Boy Scouts, a regular family guy. But he had a 'hit kit' with pistols, knives, venetian blind cords, plastic bags, duct tape, electrical tape. He kept it all hidden in a closet until he went out on one of his 'projects.' Sometimes he shoved the stuff he needed into a coat pocket, sometimes he'd carry it in a black bag or a briefcase. Maybe our guy's had his 'kit' stored somewhere over the years. I'm checking the local storage facilities. There weren't that many ten years ago."

"The next safest place would be with a girlfriend or wife, if he had one," Eunice winked.

"Exactly. He had to have been living somewhere, with someone he could trust. Problem is we're not going to find that person until we find the killer." Alves felt a sudden surge of tension run from his shoulders up into his neck. He could expect a headache if he didn't get some fresh air soon.

Alves needed to get back out on the streets. He'd had enough of sitting in offices and conference rooms, reading through old case files. Courtney and Josh were his latest victims, and that was where Alves needed to focus his attention. "Thanks, Eunice."

"Any time, handsome."

He went for the door, then stopped and turned back to Eunice Curran. "You'll let me know if you come up with anything else."

"I always do."

CHAPTER 28

I found a broken meter," Zardino said. "Never pass up a broken meter."

"What good is it if it's in Cambridge?" Luther asked.

"Stop crying." But Luther was right. It had been a long walk in the hot September sun. As they rounded the corner onto Huntington Avenue, the Northeastern University campus came into view. "We're going to be here for a few hours. I needed a good spot. Finding the perfect parking spot is one of my many talents."

"You could have dropped me at the door."

"If I'm walking, you're walking." Zardino smiled. "The good news is that you get to look forward to walking back."

"Not today. I have a meeting with a client at the Youth Center. I'll take the T when the conference ends."

Zardino picked up the pace. "The mayor doesn't like it if you show up late for one of his events."

Luther lengthened his strides, and Zardino had to jog to keep up with him. Today was the mayor's Annual Peace Conference, held every year around the time school started. Everyone would be there: elected officials, law enforcement, social services, professors, some students. The place would be packed, and he and Luther were speaking.

"We're sitting on another panel today, Luther. Just follow my lead. I'll talk a little bit about my life, my background and my experience in the criminal justice system, how I was framed and wrongly convicted. And you can talk about your experience."

"As a real criminal, someone rightly convicted?"

"As someone who got caught up in a bad situation and made some mistakes," Zardino explained patiently, "but who's turned things around. You know the spiel. The same pitch we use when we talk on the street."

"I don't mind telling people about the mistakes I've made," Luther said. "But why should I humiliate myself in front of a bunch of suits, cops and white women social workers from Wellesley?"

"Because Mayor Dolan pays you to. Could you survive on the money you make at the Crispus Attucks?" Zardino didn't wait for a response. "Of course not. That's why it's nice to have that steady income from the Street Saviors. Did I mention the health insurance? We can't lose sight of the big picture. We just need to play the game and sometimes that involves being Dolan's poster boys. Today could be good for your career. A lot of those white women from Wellesley are college professors. You impress them, they might have you back to talk to their classes or to professors at a faculty training."

"Sounds like you've got the routine down."

"You know my lawyer, the one who got me out of jail?" Zardino asked.

"The one from Harvard Law School? Sonya Jordan?"

"When I first got out, she used her connections to get me speaking gigs—conferences for lawyers and judges, college and law school classes. I even did some TV and radio interviews. She's not just some ham-n-egger trying to make a quick buck. She wanted to let the world know that there are people who have been wrongly convicted. It was a way for me to tell my story. That's why the mayor hired me."

"And you get paid for all these gigs?"

"Sometimes. Usually I get a sandwich and a bag of chips. But I let people know this can happen when people abuse the system. It's everyone's nightmare, getting convicted of a crime you didn't commit. I'll tell you something else. You should see how the women act after I tell my story. At least one good thing came out of my nightmare. My plight is a chick magnet."

"I'm all set with the chicks. I want to know how I'm going to follow your act. My story's not heartbreaking. Remember, I *did* commit the crime. I hurt someone, Richard. I put him in a wheelchair. I went to prison. A lot of people don't think I was in there long enough. They figure the man in the wheelchair is trapped in sort of a prison, so I should be there, too."

"Your message is that you made mistakes. You did your time. And now you're trying to keep kids from making the same mistakes. The people at this conference will want to know what it was like for you growing up in a tough neighborhood, losing your big brother the way you did, and then turning to crime yourself."

"You have put a lot of thought into my life and the decisions I've made." Luther smiled.

"See who comes to these things. See what people are interested in. You've got a unique story and people want to hear it. You just need the right way to tell it. The kids on the street are a tougher audience than these creampuffs." Zardino spotted a packed Student Center just ahead of them. "These people have no idea what it's like to grow up in a poor neighborhood, with gangs, guns and drugs. You know more about it than any of the so-called 'experts' in the room. You'll be a rock star with the students, especially the *Chiquitas*."

Luther stared straight ahead at that comment. He didn't have much of a sense of humor about women. "I don't want to embarrass myself in front of these people," Luther finally said.

"You'll be fine," Zardino said.

CHAPTER 29

They were crammed in a small interview room on the sixth floor of the courthouse. Lydia Thomas was in Connie's face, shouting. "I don't care what kind of subpoena you served my son with. He's not going into no grand jury!"

It was too early for this. It had been after midnight, after dogs at Simco's for dinner, when they'd found Ellis Thomas hanging out in front of an apartment building on Magnolia Street. His crew took off when they spotted the unmarked car. But Ahearn got to Ellis and served him with a subpoena in front of the whole neighborhood.

Fatigue from his late nights and crazy mornings with uncooperative witnesses was starting to set in. Connie and Mark Greene hadn't counted on Ellis Thomas showing up this morning with his mother. His angry mother. But since she was there, he knew it was best for her to let it out. Then, maybe he could reason with her.

"I'm sorry, ma'am, but he has to go in there and tell us what he knows about this case," Connie said.

"He doesn't know anything. He didn't see anything. He wasn't there." Ellis was slouched in his chair, sullen and silent. Mrs. Thomas reached over and pulled her son by his red-and-black Avirex shirt, forcing him to sit up straight. "Tell them, Ellis."

Connie spoke up before Ellis could say anything. "We have a witness who says he was there."

"Your witness is lying. Ellis was home with me that night."

"Ellis admitted to us last night that he was there."

"He was mistaken."

"No one's mistaken. Our other witness is not lying," Mark Greene interrupted her. "Your son saw everything."

"Who the hell are you?" she took a step toward him.

"Mark Greene. I'm the detective investigating this shooting."

"Well, *detective,* we're not in a police station, are we?" She stood over him. She was a tall woman, imposing. "We're in a courthouse. So, unless you're a lawyer, I suggest you stay out of this conversation. I don't even know why you're in this room."

"Because I asked him to be here," Connie said.

"Well, Mr. Darget," she said, her voice heavy with sarcasm, "my son was subpoenaed to testify before a grand jury. You've been trying to interrogate him in this room all morning. Why haven't you brought him to the grand jury so he can tell *them* he didn't see anything?"

"Because I don't want him to make the mistake of going in there and lying. Miss Thomas, I want us all to talk this through first. If you'd take a seat we can try to figure out what to do here." Connie pulled out the chair next to Ellis.

"I don't need to sit. And I don't need to figure nothing out."

"Please, ma'am?" Connie tried a soothing tone. "I need to know what he saw. Then we can make sure he's safe."

"You can't do anything to keep him safe. You gonna ride the bus with him every day? You gonna walk him to the corner store when he want a bag of chips? These kids are vicious. They kill you for no good reason."

She was right. There really wasn't much he could do for her son. If these gangbangers wanted to get to her and her son, they could.

"My office has access to witness protection funds," Connie said. "It's nothing like federal witness protection, but we can help move you to an apartment or a housing development in another neighborhood."

"So you want *us* to pack up and move out because of these thugs? You think that will make the neighborhood safer? You be giving them the power. You think they don't have ways of finding us? No, Mr. Darget, I lived in that neighborhood my whole life. We are not moving."

"What do you think it does when people hide in their houses and pretend they didn't see anything? These kids know that the adults are scared of them. If you really want to change the neighborhood, someone has to be the first to stand up."

"I know that, Mr. Darget. I'm no fool. I know what it will take to bring these kids down. If I witnessed the incident, I would be testifying in front of that grand jury right now. But this is my only child. From the day he was born, it was just the two of us. I swore I would protect him. I will not let him bear the burden of saving our neighborhood. He's too young to carry that responsibility."

"Miss Thomas," Connie said, "the grand jury is a secret proceeding. It's not open to the public like a regular courtroom. No judge sitting, no defense attorneys. It would just be me and Ellis in there. I would ask him questions and he would answer them. He'd only be in there ten, fifteen minutes, and it would be over."

"Mr. Darget, I know there's one more person in that courtroom. Nothing is secret in there. There's a court reporter who takes down every word. Am I right?" Lydia Thomas asked. "And she type it out for the world to see. She put my boy's name on the first page. She write his name before every word he speaks."

"No one will have access to the grand jury minutes."

"Don't try to play me. I seen your 'secret grand jury minutes.' I seen them plastered on doors and hallways and telephone poles in my neighborhood. The kids call them black and whites. They pass them around whenever they get them from their lawyers."

Greene shifted in his chair. What she said was 100 percent true.

"Mr. Darget. If my son goes in there and testifies, he will be marked for death."

"We can get a protective order from a judge," Connie argued. "No one sees the grand jury minutes unless we charge someone. That's the only time I have to turn them over to the defense. Then I can ask the judge to order the defense attorney not to make any copies. I can have it ordered that he not give a copy to the defendant."

"So you want me to put my son's fate in the hands of a lawyer?" She gave a short laugh. "I'm supposed to trust that some defense attorney is going to follow a court order and not turn over a copy of my son's testimony to his client? What happen if that attorney says his secretary *accidentally* sent a copy to his client? I tell you what happen. He apologize to the court and that will be the end of it. And my son's testimony, his 'secret' testimony, will be out there."

"Most attorneys are honest and respect the court's orders. If you're worried about it, I can also redact your son's name out of the grand jury minutes that I turn over. I will black out every reference to his name before I turn anything over to the defense. We'll be covered even if we're dealing with an unethical defense attorney."

Mrs. Thomas stared at Connie. For the first time all morning it looked like he had her thinking. He needed to act fast and stay on her.

"Ma'am, this is your chance, your son's chance, to make a difference in your neighborhood, the neighborhood you grew up in. Your chance to take it back. What if we were able to rally some of your neighbors to stand behind you and Ellis when it comes time for him to testify at trial? We've done it before. I'm glad you don't want to run from these kids. It's more effective if we can get the whole community to stand up. They'll learn not to mess around in your neighborhood."

"So they just move on to another neighborhood and terrorize them?"

"If they do, we'll follow them and try to get those people to fight them the same way you did. If everyone stands up to them, they'll eventually have no place to go. The first thing we need to do is hold them accountable for shooting Tracy Ward."

"No black and whites floating around?"

"Court ordered, and redacted. And I'll get people in your neighborhood to show their support for what you and Ellis are doing."

Lydia Thomas sank into the chair Connie had provided for her. She took a deep breath. She brought her hands to her face and started to cry.

She was going to let her boy testify.

Connie felt the cold wave of responsibility roll over him. He had promised a woman he would keep her son safe. He needed to deliver on that promise.

CHAPTER 38

Massachusetts Avenue was crowded with students. Sleep savored the stroll through his favorite section of the city. He had enjoyed his visit to Boston College—such trusting youngsters there—but Chestnut Hill was so inconvenient, nothing more than a glorified section of Brighton, the forgotten stepchild of Boston. The neighborhood was tough to get to, plagued with tight, crowded one-way streets that were difficult to maneuver, and it was nearly impossible to find a parking spot—not an insignificant detail for what Sleep was trying to accomplish.

But the BC campus had served its purpose. It had pulled the police attention away from his favorite part of the city, the neighborhoods around the Fens, with so many schools, so many beautiful couples. This section of Mass Ave. near the Christian Science Park was a magnet for students from Northeastern, Berkeley School of Music, and the New England Conservatory. Even those from BU and BC managed to find their way to this Mecca of youth and beauty.

He continued on toward Commonwealth Avenue, looking in the windows of the many restaurants and bars along the way, dodging skateboarders whizzing by. Sleep was overwhelmed by the number of people basking in the sun, enjoying what was sure to be one of the last warm days before the fall settled in in earnest. All these fresh faces, young people experiencing the best time of their lives. Time could stop for them.

They could spend eternity as they were, enjoying the company of a young lover, flirting, teasing, anticipating the moment when the two would become one. He could give them that gift.

Sadly, there were too many for him to attend to. He had to be selective, careful. Sleep would never just take them off the street, not without a plan. Not anymore. He had only done that the one time, the first time. It was a foolish risk he had taken. He was lucky he hadn't been caught. But he didn't regret having done it. Now he understood that he needed to know more about them, to study them, to learn their habits, prepare and patiently wait for the right moment, just as he had done at the football game last weekend. That had seemed risky, but he had planned. He was prepared to drive away if things weren't perfect, but everything had worked out fine.

Sleep stopped when he reached Newbury Street. The memories of that first night came back to him in a rush as he stood on the corner, and for a moment he had difficulty breathing. Then he remembered something from high school football after wind sprints. He put his hands on his hips and raised his head to open his airway and breathed. He knew why he had come, but he wanted to take his time, savor every moment. He waited for the light to turn, then crossed to the other side of Mass Ave. and began his trek down Newbury. To the spot where it all began. Maybe he would get lucky and see *her* working in the shop.

He took his time, looking in each of the store windows along the way. His favorite part of window-shopping wasn't so much the items on display, but the design of the displays themselves. He despised discount stores, the way they just threw clothes over the mannequins and stuck them wherever they found some open floor space. The boutique shops on Newbury Street were different. There was an art to setting the displays, positioning the mannequins in a way that would entice people to enter the store to learn more about these life-sized dolls, the world they lived in, the clothes they were wearing. Sleep knew that he could do this better than anyone else, even without a college degree. He had, after all, been practicing on his own since he was a little boy.

CHAPTER 31

Alves was hungry. He waited patiently as Mooney unfolded the legs of the card table and set it up in the living room. There was no dining room in Mooney's tiny apartment, so this would have to do. Mooney went to a closet and rounded up a couple of folding chairs and set them up. "Dinner is served," he said.

Alves took the sandwiches from the brown paper bag, figured out which one was the large Italian with everything, unwrapped it and used the wax paper as a plate. He forgot his manners and took a bite before Mooney had a chance to sit down.

"What do you have to drink?" Alves asked, his mouth full.

"Tap water and beer."

"I don't drink Boston tap water."

"Let me get you a beer."

Biggie, Mooney's Maine coon cat, jumped up on the card table and started rubbing his chin on a corner of Alves's wax paper plate. He wasn't sure if the cat was begging for food or looking to be petted. His head was as big as a coconut. He waited for Mooney to come back with the beer.

"I really don't like cats, Sarge."

"You're not allergic." Mooney said. "So suck it up." Mooney lifted Biggie and put him on the floor. By the time he sat in his chair, the cat was back on the table. He flopped down on the one empty spot, as if he knew he'd get tossed out if he got too close to the food. Mooney handed Alves a beer, an ice cold sixteen-ounce can of Schlitz.

"I dislike Schlitz beer more than I hate cats."

"Sorry. They were all out of that John Adams Wicked Pisser Summer Brew that you drink."

"Where do you find this stuff?"

"I have my sources."

Alves popped the top and took a sip. It wasn't so bad, but he wouldn't give Mooney the satisfaction. He made a face like he was drinking skunked beer, then cleared his palate with another bite of his sub. He watched Mooney take his time unwrapping his sandwich, folding the paper back so it wouldn't touch his tie. "What did you get?" Alves asked.

"An American with mayo."

"I forgot that hanging out with you is like going back in time. I know sub shops have Americans listed on the menu, but I've never actually seen anyone order one. What's in it?"

"Bologna, boiled ham, salami and American cheese."

"With mayo? I'd rather drink Schlitz beer." Alves chugged half his beer and made a show of wiping his mouth with his shirt sleeve.

"Eat your sandwich before Biggie gets it." Mooney took a bite and washed it down.

Alves could see the man's mind working. He could see that Mooney was not in the mood to discuss the merits of his sub sandwich. "You come up with anything today, Sarge?"

"Yeah. A headache. I told you what Stone said about the gun. Later I interviewed Eric Flowers's parents again, started digging around in his past. First time around, we spent a lot of time on Kelly Adams. I want to be sure Flowers wasn't the primary target." Mooney looked frustrated. "I have to figure out why he's started up again."

"I had a thought about that today," Alves said.

"Let's hear it," Mooney's mouth was full, a small glob of mayonnaise clinging to his lower lip.

Alves motioned for Mooney to wipe his face and he did. "I was talking with Eunice Curran about the possibility that this guy has a hit kit like Dennis Rader."

"BTK."

"Rader kept everything he needed for his so-called 'projects' in a hit kit in his bedroom closet."

"I read about that on the Internet."

"Look at our guy. The wire's the same, the cheap necklaces, the ballistics, and it looks like he may have had the clothes stored away. Eunice mentioned mothballs."

Mooney nodded. "So he's had all this stuff stashed somewhere while he was away."

"What if he wasn't 'away'? I got a list of recent releases from the DOC. Only a couple of guys live near the BC campus. Their records didn't fit. Mostly involved with drugs. No real violence or sex offenses. That got me thinking. What if this guy stopped killing because he wanted to stop. He was smart enough, or paranoid enough, to stop because he didn't want to get caught. BTK did the same thing. Just stopped killing. He had images of his victims, so he could relive the attacks as fantasies."

Mooney closed his eyes. He looked to be mulling things over.

"Just a thought," Alves said. "Maybe he has pictures or video of his victims."

"How does this help us?"

"I don't know that it does, beyond helping us understand him better. If that's what happened, if he's like Rader, just a seemingly upstanding citizen with no criminal record, who can stop killing when he wants to, then it does us no good to round up the usual suspects."

"Do it anyway. It's a nice theory, Angel, but we have no idea if it's true. It just puts more pressure on us to figure out how he came across Steadman and Kipping." Mooney downed the rest of his beer. He went into the kitchen and came back with two more. "Let's get back to the two most recent vics. If the killer ran into them at school he's probably not a student, unless they've got thirty- or thirty-five-year-old freshmen running around BC. Maybe he works there."

"Administration faxed me a list of employees, from maintenance workers to professors. I have the groundskeeper who paints the lines at Alumni Stadium and the Zamboni driver at the Conte Forum. I have the BRIC helping with that, running everyone's BOP."

"What about the bars in the area?" Mooney asked.

"I talked to the sergeant who does the licensed premises checks in the district. He's getting me a list from every bar. Bartenders, waitstaff, bar backs, bouncers, hostesses. Everyone. These two didn't drink much, but they went out with their friends to hang out, dance."

"I talked to Commissioner Sheehan. He's putting out the word to all the media outlets that anyone with information should call the Homicide Unit or the Crime Stoppers Hotline. That should bog us down with useless leads."

"I checked in with their professors, got class rosters, talked with a bunch of kids who were too busy texting and talking on their cells to notice anything."

Alves and Biggie watched Mooney pick through his sandwich and pull out strands of shaved onions. "I knew I tasted onion. I told them no onions. Tomatoes, pickles, no onions. They can't even make a simple sandwich anymore."

"Are you going to finish eating that or what?" Alves asked as Mooney fished through his sandwich fiasco. Biggie was purring so loud it sounded like a motorcycle. He had never understood why people kept cats. They were unpredictable. A cat that big could kill a baby. Maybe, just maybe, he'd let Angel and Iris get a hamster some day. "I've had enough of working in your living room with Mr. Big Cat here, staring at my throat."

Mooney took a bite of his crumbling sandwich. Typical Irish guy. Couldn't eat a couple slices of shaved onion. "Almost done."

"I got a bunch of video. BC has a decent number of cameras set up all over the campus, same with some of the bars. The guys at the BRIC are going over the footage, looking for Steadman and Kipping, see if anyone's following them. I told them to look for suspicious vehicles circling the area, unmarked cruisers that don't belong, the kind of stuff we talked about."

"Are they monitoring the website, too?"

"That, and one of the detectives has been logging on to the site and leaving postings on the message board, trying to get a response."

"Anything?"

"Nothing yet."

Mooney took the last bite of his sandwich and wiped his hands with a paper towel. No napkins in the bachelor pad. He took his time, finished off his beer, and held the last can out to Alves. Alves shook his head. Mooney opened the beer and took a savoring draft. "It's time for the same information to get leaked to the media. I don't get along with many reporters, but I've got a few who owe me a favor or two. We're going to have them tout me as the guy who caught the Blood Bath Killer. Now I've got my sights set on this guy. The press will catch me off guard, as I'm walking out of headquarters. I'll let it slip that I think he's a copycat, a fraud, that the real killer is probably dead. We need to get him to communicate. And make a mistake."

"I hope we're not making the mistake. Forcing him to kill two more kids. Shouldn't we wait on this, see what we come up with first? We haven't looked into all the people working at BC, the bars. He's not stupid. Even if he thinks we didn't find the Tai-ji or the fortune, he would assume we have a ballistics match. Which means the killer isn't a copycat."

Mooney balled up his waxed paper. He stood up and reached for his jacket. "That's what we're doing tonight. Let's go hit those bars."

CHAPTER 32

Connie pulled over when the call came in. His radio was the most important tool for keeping on top of the action in real time. It could be cleared as shots fired. Or there might be a shooting victim.

He listened carefully.

"Three callers report hearing shots from the area of Greenhay and Magnolia," the calm voice of the dispatcher anounced.

Connie thought about turning around and going to the area, but he didn't want to waste time. No point unless the police confirmed someone had been shot.

One of the responding officers radioed back. "Negative. I got nothing out here."

No witnesses.

No ballistics.

No victim.

Connie took his foot off the brake and continued on home. If anything turned up, a message would go out to all the alpha pagers. Like the one Connie wore on his belt, a gift from the captain at District 2. With the alpha pager, Connie got the same notification the BPD brass got whenever there was a shooting, homicide, hostage situation, any major occurrence in the city.

He was tired. He headed down Blue Hill Avenue and took a right onto American Legion Highway. He'd be home in ten, fifteen minutes tops.

The radio crackled. The call sign indicated the Rapid Response car on Magnolia. "Bravo one-o-one," the patrolman's voice rose with nervous energy. "I got something behind Nine-thirty Magnolia. An abandoned house. I need a patrol supervisor out here and EMTs. I think we need to make notifications."

They had a body.

Connie spun into a quick U-turn at a break in the island that ran down the center of American Legion Highway. The tires squealed as he put the pedal to the floor and raced back toward District 2. The heart of Roxbury.

CHAPTER 33

Alves checked his beeping alpha pager. Shooting on Magnolia. One body. Male. The good news? The victim wasn't wearing a tux.

The other good news was that Alves wasn't on call tonight. He pulled his car into the driveway. It was almost eleven o'clock, and he'd just left Mooney. The minivan was parked in the driveway ahead of him. Lights were on in the bathroom and kitchen. Marcy might still be awake.

Alves hadn't been home much since Iris had found the bodies two nights ago. He had only seen Marcy for a few minutes earlier in the day when he stopped in to shower and shave. Iris and Angel had already gone to school, and Marcy had given him the silent treatment. It wasn't the usual silent treatment, the one he got for working late and leaving her to deal with all the kids' activities. It was clear she was angry that he'd left her and the twins alone with a killer in the neighborhood.

He tried to open the front door quietly, but it stuck at the top the way it always did. He gave it a little shove with his hip, and it creaked open. Marcy was sitting at the kitchen table with a cup of coffee. She didn't look up at him. "Are you sleeping here tonight?" she asked.

"I'm in for the night," he said, taking care not to be sarcastic with his answer.

"You sure? I was just watching the news. They found a body in Rox-bury."

"God, they're quick. That just came across the pager, and they're already reporting it on TV?" He walked around the table and kissed her on the top of her head. "Mooney and I aren't on call tonight. Unless someone turns up dead dressed in formal wear, I'm not going anywhere."

She didn't smile.

"How's Iris?" he asked. "She make it through school today?"

Marcy nodded. "My mother picked them up at school. She had them all day. Said they were okay. Iris was a little withdrawn. Spent most of the day in her room reading. Mom left an hour ago, when I got home."

It hit him. Marcy was teaching three classes this semester. A full time workload for a part-time professor. She usually taught two sections, Tuesdays and Thursday in the late morning. That way she could send the kids off to school and be home in time to meet them at the bus. Her schedule got thrown off this semester when one of the full-time professors took a medical leave, sticking Marcy with two afternoon classes and a night class. They had decided that she would get the kids out the door in the morning and her mom would be there for them in the afternoon. Alves agreed that he would come home early and help out. He figured he could manage since it was only two days a week. The first day with the new system and he'd already blown it. "I'm sorry, honey. I forgot. I'll be early on Thursday."

"That's okay. You do your work," she said, her voice thick with sarcasm. "The kids will be fine. They can just eat Cheerios out of the box. And my mother loves having them for eight hours straight, twice a week. It's good for her arthritis to stay out until ten, eleven o'clock at night. And, sweetheart, it's not like anything bad ever happens in our neighborhood. We haven't had a double homicide in two whole days."

What could he say? She was right. He shouldn't open his mouth, but once he started talking it was too late to take the words back. "Honey, I understand how you feel, but I know that this neighborhood is safe."

"Don't patronize me, Angel."

"Marcy, the killer didn't attack anyone in this neighborhood. He could have dumped those bodies anywhere in the city."

"But he didn't. He left them right here, practically on our doorstep. He left them for our daughter to find. If he wanted you to find them he could have dropped them off at One Schroeder Plaza."

"Now you're being ridiculous."

"Am I? What would have happened if she had found the bodies while your killer was still tying them up?"

He didn't allow the thought. It was more than he could take.

"I didn't think you'd have an answer for that one." Marcy dumped the rest of her coffee in the sink. "I've decided to take the kids and live at my mother's for a couple weeks. Till you solve the case. Her house is not that far out of your way. You can stop by and visit whenever you're off duty."

She left him standing by the kitchen table, his head spinning with the news.

CHAPTER 34

Sergeant Detective Ray Figgs downed another shot of Johnnie
Walker Red. The Tap in Dudley Square was good for a quick drink. Or
eight of them. It was better than going home and watching reality shows
until he passed out on the couch. Or sitting with his father in the rehab.
First he needed a cigarette. Thanks to the mayor and the city council and
the freaking state legislature, he couldn't smoke in the bar. He'd have to
go stand on the sidewalk with the other holdouts, sweating in the summer and freezing their butts off in the winter. It was ridiculous how he
and the other smokers were punished for fueling the economy, spending
their money in bars, tipping the waitresses and bartenders, supporting
half the state's social programs with the cigarette tax. Not to mention
Keno.

Ray Figgs reached into his jacket pocket for his last cigarette, a
crumpled-up soft pack of the no-name brand sold at Economy Gas on
Blue Hill Ave. As he fumbled for the pack, he felt his pager vibrating. He
had five unanswered pages, three from Operations and two from Inch
O'Neill, his partner. Inchie was a good detective. Didn't need babysit-
ting, did things on his own. Figgs checked his alpha pager and saw that a
male had been killed on Magnolia Street.

He settled up his tab, grabbed a few handfuls of salted peanuts, folded them into a cocktail napkin and shoved it into his sports jacket pocket. He took another handful and tossed them in his mouth. He would chew them on the ride. He was really going to need the nuts tonight. He was the on-call Homicide Sergeant and he was already late getting to a crime scene.

CHAPTER 35

Connie hung back while Greene, Ahearn and a couple of patrolmen secured the scene on Magnolia. The house was a single-family colonial with green asphalt shingles and graffiti-covered plywood sheets covering the windows and doors. Connie had spent most of the night in this neighborhood with the detectives looking for Michael Rogers, Ellis Thomas's friend. Thomas hadn't given them much information, even after his mother agreed to let him talk. The kid was scared word would hit the street that he was a snitch. The only thing he'd told them was where to look for his pal.

The two patrolmen were setting up the crime scene tape around the property. Greene and Ahearn stood in front of the building, managing the crowd gathering in the street. Ellis Thomas lived across the street. Connie expected the kid's mother, with Ellis in tow, to show up on the scene.

As Connie moved closer, he could see that Greene didn't look good. He should have been barking orders. Instead he was quiet. Jack Ahearn, alone, minus his usual swagger, was moving the crowd back.

"Jackie, where's the body?" Connie asked.

"In back with Detective O'Neill from Homicide. He's securing things till Figgs gets here."

A car pulled up across the street. Connie and the detectives watched as Lydia Thomas—Connie recognized her large frame—struggled to get out of her car. She scanned the crowd, turning her attention to Connie and the detectives. A thin woman in a housecoat rushed to hug her.

"This is going to get ugly," Ahearn said. He pushed the button on his radio and said, "Where's the Bravo 902? We need a supervisor and some backup units out here."

"What's going on?" Connie asked.

"What do you think?" Greene asked.

Connie looked back at Miss Thomas. She lurched out of the thin woman's embrace. In an instant she went from concerned mother to angry bear. She walked toward them, quicker than Connie thought a woman her size could move. "You did this!" she shouted, pointing at Connie. "You killed my son!"

Connie turned to the detectives. He could see it in Greene's eyes. Ellis, her only son, was dead. The same son that Connie had promised to protect.

Greene tried to pull him back, but Connie was stronger. He stood his ground and waited for her. She stopped a few inches away from him. Almost as tall as he was, close to six feet, she was intimidating.

"I'm sorry," Connie said. There was nothing else he could say.

She slapped his face. He didn't turn away or try to block her hand. She was right. He *had* killed her son.

Then she started to cry. Not quietly, the way she had cried up the grand jury earlier. She was wailing. She wasn't afraid of losing her son anymore. He was lost. Her knees buckled. Connie thought of big timber crashing during a storm. Violent. Dangerous. He caught her in his arms and led her back toward her house.

CHAPTER 36

Alves lay in bed with his eyes open, watching shadows move back and forth on the ceiling, the moonlight intercepted by the trees swaying outside the window. Marcy had fallen asleep right away. Or pretended she had. The news that she was packing up the twins and moving over to her mother's—even if only temporarily—had blindsided him. He had hoped the regular rhythm of her breathing would help him sleep. It usually did. An hour later he was still awake.

Alves closed his eyes. He was getting caught up in a cycle that was going to wear him out. Trying to sleep. His mind racing. Thinking about his marriage, the case. When he did fall asleep, the alarm would sound and it would be time for another day.

He opened his eyes again. It was a shame to waste the mental energy. He knew everything there was to know about the investigation. But he knew nothing about the killer. He didn't know why he killed or how he selected his victims, the two most important pieces of the puzzle.

Alves thought about Mooney's plan to draw the killer out, to get him to communicate. Get him to make a mistake. He remembered the website promnightkiller.com. Mooney had talked about the cult following that the killer had developed over the years. How could someone have a fan club based on the murders of innocent couples? The BRIC was monitoring the site, but Alves hadn't had time to go there himself. This was as good a time as any to check it out.

Alves slid out from under the sheets and quietly made his way back downstairs. The family computer was set up in the den. He logged on and saw that the site was active. He scrolled down the long list of messages posted on the message board, wondering how many of them had come from the officers at the BRIC. The killer's groupies seemed to know quite a bit about the murders. Someone running the site must have known enough to file a request under the Mass Public Records Law, because the actual police reports were posted. Mooney had been careful to leave out any references to the fortunes and the Tai-ji from every report, so at least that information was not available to these kooks.

The people who visited the site had an unhealthy obsession with trying to discover everything about the killer and his crimes. They posted any information they could find about the victims, much of it unflattering, hoping that the more they knew about the victims, the closer they'd get to understanding the killer. It didn't seem to matter who the source of information was. The victims and their families were being victimized again.

Someone using the screen name printsofdarkness had posted the message: "The killer is known to police. Like old Jack the Ripper. A friend or relative of someone high up in the department, same old story. This is the biggest COVER UP!!! in history."

Shortnsassy wrote, "He's out there now. Waiting for the right time. Then he will begin his work in earnest."

Alves could feel the fog of a headache settling in behind his eyes.

Two days ago, the only people who thought about the unsolved murders were Wayne Mooney, the families of the victims and the losers on this website. Now everyone in the city was thinking about the killer, locking their doors.

Alves logged off. Looking at the site convinced him that the killer had to be one of the visitors to the site, maybe not a contributor, but certainly an occasional visitor. So maybe they could draw him out and get him involved in a dialogue. It had to work. So far, they had nothing else.

But for now, he would make another attempt to get some sleep.

CHAPTER 37

Connie stayed with Lydia Thomas until the EMTs arrived. They gave her a sedative and took her by ambulance to Boston Medical Center. She had wanted to go back outside and see her son, but Connie had convinced her that she could see him later, after they processed the scene. "We can't miss any evidence," he had told her. "Not if we're going to catch Ellis's killer." Even before the sedative had kicked in, she had looked at him with hopelessness in her eyes.

When Connie finally stepped back outside he could see that the scene was more controlled, a half dozen cruisers on the street, enough patrol officers to control the crowd, and supervisors giving orders.

"Is Figgs on scene yet?" Connie asked Ahearn, shaking his head. "He's had a problem with the bottle as long as I've known him. Hasn't solved a case in how long?"

"Luck of the draw," Ahearn said. "We don't decide who's on the pager."

"We need to make sure this one gets solved."

"It's his case, Connie."

"I can't let this one go. I'm responsible for that kid's death."

"You brought him up to the grand jury as a witness. He barely cooperated. It's not like his testimony was floating around in the neighborhood. He gave you nothing."

"But I promised his mother he wouldn't get hurt."

"We don't know what happened here. Would it have been your fault if he got hit by a car?"

"He died because I brought him in to the grand jury."

"You don't know that. For all we know this could have been a drug deal gone bad or a botched robbery. Let Ray Figgs do his investigation, and we'll see where it goes."

"But I'm telling you right now. I can't sit and watch Figgs do nothing." Connie walked into the middle of the street and put in a call to the DA. He would need to know what was going on. That one of their grand jury witnesses had been murdered not twelve hours after his appearance in court.

PART TWO

. . . .

If you want to understand the artist,

look at his work.

—JOHN DOUGLAS AND
MARK OLSHAKER, Mind Hunter

CHAPTER 38

Sleep vacuumed the house, the hardwood floors, the area rugs, the runner on the stairs. Then he polished all the woodwork, the piano and the mantel. That was how Momma liked it done. The house hadn't been very dirty. But it had to be cleaned every week, as Momma had taught him. He didn't want to live in a pig sty, did he? He would clean the kitchen and bathroom last, everything spic and span.

He enjoyed cleaning, bringing back order from chaos. As he cleaned, he thought about her. Not Momma. *Her.*

He remembered when she tried to push him out of her life. He was upset at first, until he realized why she'd done it. She had tried to set him free because she loved him. But he could never leave her. He was forever hers.

That summer, so many years ago—they were still teenagers—he was finally enjoying life. He was getting paid to do the work that he loved. The old man had been dead close to a year, so there was no one to criticize him. So what if he liked to play with his Little Things? That didn't mean that he was gay. How could he be gay if he was in love with Natalie?

She was the reason he had gone into the city. It was the beginning of the summer and she had left home, taking an apartment in the South End, working at one of the boutiques on Newbury Street. He had missed seeing her every day, so he'd spent hours walking, window-shopping, getting a cup of coffee, pretending to read books, hoping to bump into her.

He would use the window in the store across the street from Natalie's shop as a mirror, hoping to catch a glimpse of her in the reflection. That was how he'd met Ronald.

HE'D BEEN STARING INTO *the window when Ronald appeared and began undressing the mannequins. He remembered the way Ronald looked the first time he met him—tall, slender, with tight jeans and a silk shirt, open halfway down his chest. Sleep felt small looking up at him.*

Momma would have said that Ronald was a handsome man with his dark shining eyes and neat white teeth. A man who would take his girl for a romantic picnic. Maybe at Jamaica Pond, maybe Olmsted Park. That first time, Ronald smiled, gave him a wink and went back to work. Sleep was fascinated by what he was doing with the mannequins. For a while anyway, he'd forgotten about Natalie. He watched for close to an hour as Ronald dismantled the old display and set up the new one with a beach theme—brightly colored starfish, antique sand buckets, striped umbrellas. About halfway through the job, Ronald came out and introduced himself. Soon Sleep was working as his assistant. Lifting and carrying the things Ronald needed. Incredible, he thought. A dream. He and Ronald set up displays in half the stores on Newbury. It was perfect, getting paid to do what he loved and having the chance to see Natalie every day, the way he used to.

Then it happened. It was a Saturday, a beautiful day. He and Ronald were setting up a new display when Natalie walked in. She was angry, accusing him of watching her, following her, stalking her. He still remembered her words. "You're creeping me out," she had said. "We grew up together. Why are you doing this to me? We used to be friends." Used to be? She acted like she didn't remember how she had come to the house after his father died. How she sat with him and Momma, making them all tea. That even if they weren't together, that special bond was there. She was quiet for a second and then she mentioned a restraining order.

Ronald and their client heard every word. "I don't know what she's talking about," he told them after she'd stormed out. He was scared he'd lose his job, but Ronald understood. He said he knew that women sometimes overreacted to things. "Let's get back to work," Ronald said. "We have a busy night ahead of us." They were scheduled to change displays in a couple of stores, getting them ready for summer sales starting on Sunday morning.

Ronald picked up some Chinese food for supper, but Sleep wasn't hungry. He was too upset by what Natalie had said. He didn't particularly like Chinese food, either. The brown rice tasted like cardboard. He managed to force some noodles and rice down after

Ronald showed him how to smother the rice in lobster sauce. When he finished, Sleep tucked his fortune cookie, dessert, in his back pocket. He wanted to be alone when he read his fortune. As they started back to work, Ronald asked about Natalie. How he knew her. Why she thought he was following her.

It was none of Ronald's business.

Ronald told him to loosen up. He put his hand on Sleep's shoulder and gave it a squeeze.

"What the hell are you doing?" Sleep bent away from his touch. It felt fiery hot, and heavy like a big machine.

Ronald stepped back, startled. "I was trying to help you talk things out."

"Don't touch me. What are you, half-a-fag?" He didn't really know what that meant except that his father used to say it when Sleep played in the attic.

Ronald's face went rigid. "I'm sorry you feel that way. Maybe that girl was telling the truth. We can't keep stalkers working in boutiques."

Sleep was stunned. "You mean . . . ?"

Ronald gestured toward the door.

Sleep walked out onto the sidewalk, feeling alone and scared. In one night he had lost the woman and the job he loved.

He still had one thing. Sleep had his gun. It wasn't really his gun. He had found it in his father's belongings, and he'd been carrying it around for months. When he first found it, he took it and hid it in the trunk in the attic. As he got used to it—the way it felt in his hand, a comfortable fit—he started to carry it around. He wasn't sure why. It just felt cool, tucked into his waist, held up by the makeshift holster his father had made from a piece of heavy gauge wire, one end looped around his belt, the other stuck in the barrel of the gun. He felt invincible when he had his piece with him. No one could mess with him. He was a big man when he had the gun.

After Ronald fired him, Sleep walked to the Fens. The sun was setting. When he sat on a bench, he heard the crunch of the fortune cookie in his back pocket. He didn't know if he should laugh or cry. He couldn't do anything right. He reached back and held the cellophane wrapper with the crumbled mess in his hand. With all that had happened in one day, he needed some good news. Maybe this was his real fortune. He hoped it would be a good one. There was no rule that said the fortune wouldn't come true just because the cookie was crumbled was there? Maybe the broken cookie had broken his bad luck. He tore the cellophane with his teeth, dumped the shards of cookie onto the ground. The pigeons could have them. He removed the strip of paper and read "STOP SEARCHING FOREVER, HAPPINESS IS RIGHT NEXT TO YOU."

He closed his eyes tight. Maybe this was his fortune.

He opened his eyes. There was a young woman at the other end of his bench. She had long dark hair like Natalie. Maybe she was his true love. She was looking straight ahead.

He never had the nerve to introduce himself to pretty girls. He just needed to talk to her. His fortune said that happiness was right next to him. There was no one else around.

"What's your name?"

She said nothing.

"You come here often?" That was a really stupid thing to say.

Nothing.

"I think you're pretty."

She looked away.

"My name is—"

"Okay, Babe, you ready to get going?" A man stepped out from behind a bush, adjusting his fly. He was tall and muscular like Ronald.

"I've been ready to go since we got here. If you can believe it, this guy's been hitting on me." She laughed.

"Look, pal," the guy said. "Snow White doesn't date any of the seven dwarfs." They both laughed.

"That's not funny."

"You're right it's not." She tried to control her laughter.

"Tell him to apologize," Sleep said.

"You should be the one apologizing to her for being a creep," Ronald said. He put his arm around Natalie's waist. She buried her cheek in his chest.

Sleep reached into his waistband and wrapped his fingers around the handle of the gun.

They were turned away, starting to move down the street. Sleep sprang up and moved in front of them. As he pressed the gun into Ronald's chest, he pulled the trigger. Sleep was stunned by the force of the cool metal in his hands. Instantly, it seemed to stutter and fire again. Ronald's eyes stopped laughing. Bright red crept over his shirt like a seeping stain. His legs crumpled, like a ruined paper doll. Natalie didn't move. Like a mannequin, she stood with her arms reaching out to Ronald. Her mouth opened, and before she could make a sound, Sleep pounced on her. He had to keep her throat from making a sound.

When they were both quiet, not laughing anymore, he felt better.

The broken cookie was right. He had found happiness right next to him.

HE WENT TO THE mudroom in the back of the house and grabbed the mop and the metal pail. He had to get back to work. Enough time spent daydreaming. The kitchen needed to be cleaned or Momma would be disappointed. He couldn't have that. And if he had time enough later, he'd walk around his favorite spot. The Victory Gardens in the Fens.

CHAPTER 39

Connie took a seat near the back of the room. The second gang meeting since Ellis Thomas's death. The superintendent broke up a huddle of cops in the corner and directed them to take seats. Connie balanced the stack of papers on his knees. The analysts from the BRIC had given him a packet of information on what the superintendent called the major "impact players," the bad guys who they believed were the most likely to be involved in a shooting. Connie's packet included their criminal records, police reports from recent arrests, and FIOs showing where they'd been hanging around and who they'd been hanging with.

"It's a little after five, let's get started," the superintendent checked her watch and shouted over the noise of the crowd of probation officers, youth workers, prosecutors—all outsiders that the cops didn't trust—and cops from the Homicide Unit, the specialized units like the Drug Control Unit and the Youth Violence Strike Force, aka the Gang Unit.

The goal was for them to come together and share information. It sounded reasonable enough, but the competition between units was fierce. The din slowly faded.

Even though Connie had a grasp of what was going on in Roxbury, District B-2, these bimonthly meetings were a way for him to get intelligence from around the city, to find out who the players were in the other districts. The bad guys didn't care about district borders.

"I want to start with the homicide from last night. Shawn Tinsley," the super said. She was standing next to a podium. To her right were half a dozen analysts from the BRIC. The meeting was a way for them to disseminate intelligence, but it also gave them the opportunity to confirm, through the cops on the street, that their intel was accurate. The superintendent nodded to one of the analysts, a young guy sitting in front of a laptop. He clicked the mouse and the blue screen with the BPD shield at the front of the room faded into a mug shot of a young black kid with corn rows and a small, scruffy beard.

Connie knew the face.

The superintendent continued, "This is Shawn Tinsley. We're hearing that he might have been associated with Castlegate. A shooter. But we haven't been able to corroborate that info. He was the main suspect in the Ellis Thomas homicide a little over two weeks ago on Magnolia Street. He may have shot a kid by the name of Tracy Ward, too. Looks like he was definitely one of our top impact players."

She loved using sports terminology. Bad guys were "impact players." High crime areas were "hot spots" or "red zones."

"Tinsley didn't really have much of a record. No guns or drugs, just larcenies and Chapter Ninety violations. Then he turns up dead last night. Sergeant Detective Figgs is here from Homicide. He's looking for help." She motioned for Ray Figgs to step forward.

Figgs got up from his seat in the front row. He looked a little banged up, in his wrinkled suit, stained shirt, top button undone, and a cheap tie. He had the ashy-gray skin of someone who didn't spend much time outside. Figgs made his way to the podium, probably needing it to balance himself.

"Mr. Tinsley was discovered around sunrise this morning," Figgs said, "by a woman walking her dog on Tenean Beach in Dorchester. ME said he was dead six to seven hours before we found him. No calls for shots fired last night."

"Any hits on the Shot Spotter?" someone at the front of the room asked.

The superintendent stepped in. "Many of you know about the system of sensors strategically placed in different spots in the city. These sensors are so sophisticated they can tell the difference between a backfire, a firecracker, or gunfire. The Shot Spotter can triangulate the location of the shots within five seconds and the closest cameras will zip to that spot. To answer your question, Tenean Beach isn't exactly one of our hot spots," she said. "We don't have any sensors or cameras set up there."

The system hadn't helped much in Ellis Thomas's case either, Connie thought.

Figgs continued, "Tinsley was shot three times in the back. Looks like he was trying to get away from the shooter. Ballistics made a match to a forty-caliber semi that's been involved in a bunch of shootings over the last six months. Could be a stash gun. Last time we had a hit on this gun was the George Wheeler homicide, almost three weeks ago."

"I don't think it's a stash gun," a voice called out from the back of the room, one of the guys from the Strike Force. "A few months ago that gun was involved in shots fired at some kids who are feuding with Castlegate. It doesn't make sense for one of the Castlegate shooters to get killed by the same gun, unless he was killed by one of his own."

Figgs signaled to the young man sitting at the computer and another image appeared on the screen, a map of the city broken down into police districts. There were red dots and blue dots with names and dates written next to them, and black lines with arrows connecting all the dots. "Let me clarify. It's a stash gun that's getting passed around to different groups all over the city. The red dots are homicides. The blue dots are shots fired. Ballistics recovered, no one hit, probably kids doing drive-bys, shooting wildly, missing their targets."

Connie was surprised by Figgs's presentation. As bad as he looked, he was able to pull himself together for this meeting in front of the superintendent. Too bad he was heading right back to the bottle as soon as the meeting was over.

"What do you need from us, detective?" the superintendent asked.

"Any information you have on Tinsley or Wheeler. Anything linking Tinsley to the Ellis Thomas murder would be helpful. I'd like to know how the .40's getting passed around and who's doing the passing." Figgs stood for a few seconds to see if anyone was going to offer help, but the cops were a tough crowd. No one did any talking. "Give me a call if you think of anything."

The computer geek hit a key and Figgs's contact information filled the blue screen.

Figgs straightened his rumpled jacket and took a seat.

The superintendent took the podium again. "There's been a lot of mis-information about the Shot Spotter. I'm going to turn the microphone over to the Deputy from Operations to explain the system in more detail. He'll speak about what this technology can and can't do for our cases."

CHAPTER 48

Figgs walked toward the exit of Police Headquarters. That had been one long meeting. It was already getting dark. He needed a cigarette.

"Sergeant Figgs." He heard his name as he reached the glass door. Behind him in the cavernous lobby he saw two familiar faces. "Hi, Sergeant." The ADA stuck out his hand. "Connie Darget. I was at the Ellis Thomas murder scene."

Figgs nodded.

"You remember Detective Mark Greene from District Two. We're investigating the Tracy Ward shooting. Whatever started that beef has led to your two homicides. Ward told us that Tinsley shot him. He named Ellis Thomas as a witness. The next day we had Thomas and his mother up the grand jury. A few hours later, he turns up dead. Seems obvious that Tinsley or someone in his crew was responsible for killing Thomas."

"I know that," Figgs said. "But I don't have any witnesses putting Tinsley anywhere near Thomas. No one's talking about what happened."

"Tinsley wasn't too cooperative with us," Darget said. "We served him with a grand jury subpoena. He blew it off. I went to see the judge in the first session and get a Capias for him. Detective Greene scooped him up the next night. We had him up the grand jury a few days after Thomas was killed."

"He was a jerk," Greene said.

Darget said, "Part of the new generation of kids who aren't afraid of anything. When you're young, you do stupid things thinking you're invincible. Driving like a nut on the J-Way, jumping off a cliff at the Quincy quarries."

"What's your point, Mr. Darget?" Figgs asked.

"First, I figured Tinsley was thinking the same way. But he wasn't. Just the opposite. He decided he didn't have much time left. He was what, seventeen years old? He believed by the time he was twenty, twenty-one, he was going to be dead or in jail for life anyhow. He said he'd rather be dead."

"Got his wish," Figgs said.

"We tried to get through to him," Darget said. "I told him to think about his mother. If he gets killed, she's the one suffering for the rest of her life. If he's in prison, she'll be doing the time too."

"Tinsley wasn't buying it," Greene said.

"He told us he wanted to sow his seed to carry on the family name. Needed to back his boys. His loyalty to his crew was more important than any bond he had with his mother," Darget said.

"What did he tell you about the shootings?" Figgs asked.

"Said he didn't know anything about them," Greene said. "He had no trouble with Ward or Thomas."

"We asked if he was beefing with anyone," Darget said.

"Told us he could take care of himself," Greene said. "But we knew someone was going to retaliate against him. That's why the super ordered the Strike Force to follow him. See what he was up to. Did a day in the life, followed him around for a week."

"They come up with anything?" Figgs asked.

"No. Tinsley must have known he was being watched."

"That's one thing you got right," Figgs said. "Too bad he didn't catch on it was the bad guys following him." He opened the door to leave. He lit his cigarette in the foyer and stepped out into the night.

CHAPTER 41

Alves spotted Connie standing with Mark Greene in the main lobby of Schroeder Plaza. "Not the person I want to run into right now," Alves said. He'd taken a thousand calls from Connie trying to get the scoop on the case.

"I thought he was your bff," Mooney sniped.

"Connie's getting to be a pain. Seems to think that he can catch the killer. Since the Blood Bath case, I've been more careful about giving out information on an open investigation." Alves knew he had said too much to Connie during that case. And that Connie may have unwittingly fed that information to Mitch Beaulieu, the killer.

"Where's the third Musketeer?" Mooney asked.

"Ahearn?" Greene asked. "Got stuck with the super after the meeting."

"Hey, Angel, I've been meaning to call you," Connie said. "Anything new on Steadman and Kipping?"

"I haven't caught him yet. How's that for an update?"

"Thanks for ditching me with the super." Ahearn joined them.

"These meetings would be vastly improved by the addition of an open bar," Mooney laughed. "No one shares information. No one trusts anyone else. Speaking of which," Mooney turned to Connie, "who are those two guys you were talking to before the meeting?"

"A couple of the mayor's Street Saviors. The white guy is Rich Zardino."

"Richie Z," Mooney said. "Two-bit hood from East Boston. Convicted murderer."

"He was exonerated," Connie said. "Wrongly convicted."

"Sure he was. Once in a while a guy gets lucky enough that all the witnesses against him are dead. Then he gets some new witness to come forward and tell a different story. The next thing you know he's a big hero. 'Wrongly convicted' by a corrupt system." Mooney was winding up for one of his rants.

"His case is a little different," Alves said. "The only witness who testified against him was a federal informant. Turns out the witness lied about Zardino to give the feds someone to send to jail for an unsolved mob hit."

"I'm sure he did something he deserved to go to jail for," Mooney said.

"We had a run-in with him and his sidekick the other night," Greene said. "His buddy acts like he's a lawyer instead of an ex-con."

"He's lucky I didn't give him a beating," Ahearn said.

"Goes by the name Luther," Connie said. "He did time in state prison on a home invasion. Shot someone."

Mooney shook his head. "Luther what?"

"He only gave us Luther."

"That's not his real name," Mooney said. "He used to be a little thug. I remember the face."

Mooney had a gift for faces. He could thumb through a stack of Arrest Summary Reports and remember most of the faces.

"Darius Little," Greene said. "I looked into his background after the incident the other night."

"That's it," Mooney said. "They used to call him D-Lite. No criminal history when he was younger, but his big brother was no good. Darius went away to college down South. Played football, Division One. Great running back. He was home from school one summer when his brother lost a gunfight and ended up dead. Darius never went back to school. Then he's in the mix with his brother's old crew. Kid became a one-man crime spree, and the man he shot ended up in a wheelchair. His lawyer got him in front of the right judge. Took eight to ten on a plea deal. Only nineteen at the time."

"You know quite a bit about him," Alves said.

"I investigated the brother's death. Darius flipped out at the scene. Had to cuff him to calm him down. We never caught the killer, and Darius still holds a grudge. Said I didn't work the case hard enough. Said I was too busy working the Prom Night case."

"Apparently, he found Christ in prison," Greene said.

"Great program the mayor has there," Mooney said. "Let's pair up ex-cons, or 'ex-offenders' as he calls them, and send them out on the street so they can teach gang kids how to become better criminals."

"I don't think that's the goal of the program," Alves said. "The kids connect with these guys because they've experienced some of the same things."

"You should have seen them the other night," Greene said, "telling us not to lay a hand on them, that we had no reason to search. They're giving the kids a lesson on criminal procedure, how to tell the cops to screw—"

"You want to know what really pisses me off?" Ahearn interrupted.

Alves could see that Ahearn was angry, his hands clenched into massive grapefruit-sized fists.

"Let's hear it, big guy," Mooney said.

"We come to this meeting because we're ordered to," Ahearn started. "Fine. It's a waste of my time, but I'm told to be here, so here I am. Then we get a lecture from the super that we need to be out there stopping everything that moves. Like we're rookies and we don't know how to do our jobs. I can deal with that. She's the boss. But what the hell are those two scumbags doing at *our* intel meeting?"

Greene interrupted him. "Jackie, keep your voice down."

Alves looked around at the steady stream of bodies moving down the hall toward them, away from the Media Room and the table set up with coffee and old Danish. It was too late to stop Ahearn.

"Greenie, she invites criminals into our house and expects us to share information with them. These meetings used to be closed to everyone except the good cops, a couple of probation officers and ADAs, guys we could trust with sensitive information. It meant something to be invited here."

"Jackie's right. It's gotten to the point where she's inviting the bad guys into the room," Mark Greene said.

Maybe they were right, Alves thought. Here they were, inviting strangers into their own house.

CHAPTER 42

Luther had felt the hostility in the room. He and Zardino were pariahs. They had no reason to stay after the meeting, but they did. Maybe to make the cops feel uncomfortable, maybe to stand their ground.

The one person who'd been friendly was Conrad Darget. He'd come over before the meeting started. Told them he'd heard that he and Richie had done a great presentation at the mayor's Peace Conference. Darget was their new friend, a real politician, working the room, saying hello to everyone, shaking hands and backslapping.

"We should get going," Zardino said, pulling at the collar of a shirt that was tight for him.

Rich was right. They had made their point. Now the room was almost empty, only a few stragglers left, kissing up to the superintendent. "These meetings remind me that my people live in a police state," Luther said as they started down the long hallway, weaving through the small herds of officers. "You heard them talking about that Shot Spotter system? Homeland Security money. System's hooked up to satellite imaging and cameras that run twenty-four-seven. What do you think they're taking pictures of when shots *aren't* being fired? That money's supposed to fight terrorists, not spy on people in the city. It's Big Brother keeping an eye on the black man."

"I wanted to jump in when they were going on about Shawn Tinsley as an impact player, a shooter," Zardino said. "He was a creampuff, nothing but talk."

"Shawn never shot anyone in his life," Luther agreed, "but it's good you kept your mouth shut. We promised his boys they could talk to us confidentially. You can't break your promise."

"But they told us who committed the murder. It wasn't Shawn," Zardino said. "Tinsley's dead. His good name shouldn't die with him. You know how I feel about people being falsely accused of a crime."

"We're between a rock and a hard place. If we tell anyone that it was Michael Rogers who killed Ellis Thomas, his friend, we betray our clients' confidence. We lose our street cred. We stay quiet, a decent boy's name is ruined."

"And a killer is out there on the street. Maybe we can get out the information confidentially, tell someone familiar with the case who the shooter is. Give them the killer's name. Otherwise they'll never look at Rogers as a suspect. Never think he'd kill his friend for being a snitch."

Luther was silent for a couple minutes as they walked through the cars stuck in rush hour traffic and hopped over the jersey barriers on Tremont. "Maybe we should talk to Darget," Luther said. "He owes us a favor for not diming him out that night with the detectives. We tell him the story. Tell him we know who the killer is. But we're not giving up our source."

"We could tell Ray Figgs instead. It's his case," Zardino said.

Luther knew how Zardino felt about the prosecutor. "Decade ago, Figgs would have been our best chance, but not now." The story of a former Marine going from sharpshooter to bar stool was a sad one. Luther didn't want to see another case slip away with a detective whose heart wasn't in it. Someone had to be held responsible for the murder. But it had to be the right man. The name of an innocent boy of color ruined, blasted to nothing, immortalized as a murderer? That was wrong. Luther slipped his hand into his jacket pocket. He felt the small shape of the card the prosecutor had given him.

CHAPTER 43

Early fall night and Wollaston Beach was packed. He waited in line at the Clam Box, watching the fuzzy television over the counter showing the Red Sox and Yankees. Final home stand of the season. As his plate came up—fried clams and fries—a seat opened up by the windows. Pure luck. He could sit and eat, watch the kids rollerblading, the parade of fit young couples walking their designer dogs. Nice to be away from the stress of the job, kick back and relax, maybe get a beer at Nostalgia, a couple doors down.

The Nextel in his pocket chirped. He looked at the screen. Luther. Luther hardly ever called, except for bad news. He pushed the connect button and said, "What's going on?"

"Richie. One of ours got shot. Junior, from Humboldt."

"Stutter's little brother? Is he okay?"

"He didn't look good."

"Why would anyone shoot him? He's not in the mix." The kid was in school, not hanging on the corner.

"You're going to have to come out here, Rich. Everybody's buggin'."

"Where are you?"

"Corner of Humboldt and Ruthven."

"Be right there." Zardino hopped up and made his way to the counter. For a couple quarters he bought two toasted hot dog rolls. He could stuff in his clams, slather them with tartar sauce and eat them on the ride. Tank up for the long night ahead.

It was a quick trip. Not much traffic this late. He jumped on the Expressway and took the UMass/JFK exit. Columbia Road was like a video game, dodging pedestrians popping out from behind double-parked cars, everyone switching lanes without signaling, stopping without any warning.

When he finally turned onto Seaver, the sky ahead was lit up with the glow of police lights. Strobes, wigwags, flashbacks, all filling the night sky like the aurora borealis. He parked a block away and headed toward the maze of cars angled across the street, blocking traffic. Already the crowds of curious onlookers were forming.

He found Luther in front of the Dry and Fold Laundromat, just outside the crime scene tape.

Luther had a look. Not like they hadn't seen this kind of violence before. But when Luther's eyes met his, there was something new there, maybe a sort of desperation.

"Junior's dead," Luther told him. "I overheard one of the cops talking, trying to locate Sergeant Figgs. They found shell casings: .40's." Luther bent into him and said, "Richie, what if the weapon isn't a stash gun? What if someone's been killing these kids?"

The thought astonished him, but why would someone do that? "Maybe *we* need to talk to Figgs."

"Hasn't shown up yet."

"How'd you get here so quick?"

"I was in the neighborhood, visiting a client," Luther said. "Heard the shots fired. I couldn't have been more than a couple steps behind the shooter."

"What'd you see?"

"A smoked-out van. Driver wasn't stressing. Van was moving at a normal speed. Most likely not connected."

"Too bad the shooting wasn't on Blue," Zardino said. "What we heard about earlier at the intel meeting. Cameras would have picked up the shooter."

"I'm more concerned about Stutter. That's the reason I called you," Luther said. "He'll be looking for revenge."

"No one's seen the kid in months. We need to get to Stutter before he does something stupid." Before he retaliated, before more kids ended up in body bags.

CHAPTER 44

Visitors had to check in through security at One Schroeder Plaza before entering the building. Stepping around the metal detector, Connie nodded to the officer working security at the front entrance. A little after seven, Friday morning, so the lobby was pretty quiet except for the early birds grabbing their breakfast. Angel Alves was one of them, standing outside the cafeteria, holding a cup of coffee, talking with a lieutenant. Connie waited for them to split up. Alves looked like he hadn't slept.

"What's up, buddy?" Connie asked. "You look a little rough."

"Typical evening with Wayne Mooney will do that."

"Working with Sarge can't be good for your marriage. Everything all right with Marcy and the twins?"

"Long story," Alves said.

"I've got a meeting with Sergeant Stone in Ballistics," Connie changed the subject. "Trial prep. Gun case. Miracle of miracles, they found a fingerprint on the clip. Matches the defendant."

"Who's the defendant?" Alves was looking over Connie's shoulder, scanning the lobby.

"Nineteen-year-old kid from Dorchester. Not on anyone's radar. Got a bad record. Getting arrested with the gun made him a level three ACC. Looking at fifteen years minimum mandatory."

"Therefore, no plea deal."

"I offered him a seven to ten in Cedar Junction. Figures he'll roll the dice, try his luck with the jury."

"Any issues with the case?"

"A couple. But I got it all figured out."

"I'm sure you've already practiced your closing."

"I always know my closing before the trial starts. Fewer surprises that way. So what's going on with the Prom Night case?"

"Connie, I don't have time right now."

"Give me the CliffsNotes version."

"I'll give you a quick briefing," Alves glanced at the phone in his hand. Checking the time.

"Reports and crime scene photos."

"All I need is Mooney catching you rifling through a homicide case file. Sarge walks in while we're talking, you came to get my advice on your gun case."

They started down the hall toward the bank of elevators. "You hear about the shooting last night?" Connie asked.

"Stutter Simpson's kid brother, Junior. Took two in the hat."

"Could be a case of mistaken identity. That kid looked just like his brother."

"I couldn't tell you, Connie. That's Ray Figgs's case."

"I know. I was out there last night. You and I still have the Jesse Wilcox murder. And Stutter is our main suspect, so the murder last night could be related."

Alves stared straight ahead at the elevator lights. "Figgs has been assigned everything related to that forty. Including Wilcox. You need to talk to him."

"What the fuck, Angel." Everything he'd worked for was on the line. "This was *our* case. We had Stutter Simpson in the crosshairs. Now Figgs is going to screw everything up."

"It's not my call, Connie. It came down from the commissioner."

The elevator chimed, the doors opened, and Alves stepped in.

"You didn't even put up a fight, Angel?"

Alves shrugged his shoulders.

"You too, Angel? White college kids more important than some kids from the neighborhood?"

The elevator doors started to close. Alves put out his hand to hold them open.

"Thanks, pal, but I'll take the stairs."

CHAPTER 45

Figgs took a handful of peanuts from his pocket. He hadn't spent much time with Mrs. Simpson. She'd identified her son while he was lying on the sidewalk dying, so there was no need for her to make a formal ID. And last night wasn't the right time. But now he needed to talk with her. She'd had one whole day to get used to the idea that her son was gone. Stupid thought, that a mother would ever get used to her son being dead.

Making his way up the stairs of the duplex, Figgs checked the number and rang the bell. It took a lot of rings and a lot of time before the door swung open. Before yesterday, Junior Simpson's mother was probably an attractive woman, still on the younger side. It was a second before Figgs realized that the woman holding on to the door frame was not Junior's grandmother. Junior's mother's hair was bunched on one side of her head as though she'd slept wrong on it. Her eyes were red, and long streaks of mascara glistened on her cheeks. No tears now, she looked all cried out. That impulse, that little spark that used to drive him in the old days flared up briefly. *Maybe,* Figgs thought, *I can get a little something out of her.* "Can I come in for a minute?" he asked.

She left the door open and wandered into the living room. Figgs followed her, closing the door behind him. "What do you want, detective? I have a busy day. I have to make arrangements to bury my baby."

"I'm sorry for your loss." The words sounded lame before the woman's devastation. "I want to catch the person who shot Junior."

She reared back, as though regarding him, and laughed. "You know you're never going to catch them. No one will come forward to tell you what they saw."

"There is one person who can help. He looks a lot like Junior. He can tell me who might want to kill someone who looks like Junior."

"Stutter isn't home." Her face was closing him off. "I don't know where he is."

"Your son has warrants. There are a lot of people gunning for him. You have my number. Let him know I'm not looking to arrest him. He can meet with me anywhere he chooses, and I guarantee he walks out without the cuffs. You don't want to lose another son."

Figgs stood up and walked to the front hall. He could hear Mrs. Simpson crying as he closed the door.

CHAPTER 46

Tell us again what you saw," Alves said. He was at the ball field, Chestnut Hill Park, near Boston College. The stadium was about a quarter mile away. He was getting impatient with the witness, one of many tailgaters he and Wayne Mooney had to interview. Alves hated dealing with drunks. That was one thing he didn't miss. When he was a patrolman, a regular part of his job was dealing with drunk drivers, drunks getting into fights, drunks stumbling around their houses and injuring themselves. Most of the time they babbled, and sometimes, if you were really lucky, they'd throw up in the back of the cruiser. You could never get rid of that smell.

This one looked like he was getting ready to blow the tailgate snacks he'd been shoving down his gullet all morning. Fans milled around them, and from Alumni Stadium Alves could hear a din and the faint marching music of bands warming up.

"Take your time," Mooney said. "Try to focus. Tell us exactly what you remember."

"It was nothing. I was coming back to our spot from the stadium," the drunk waved to someone in a car passing by. "Have you ever been to the stadium? It's a nice place but they shut down the concessions too soon. Everything's so expensive. Anyway, I felt like I hadn't eaten since halftime. You ever get that feeling like you're so hungry you could throw up if you don't get something to eat?"

"What happened when you got back to the tailgate?" Alves asked.

"Like I said before, this is my favorite spot. At the top of the bleachers. You get all this extra seating, and sometimes you get entertained by a baseball game. Anyway, I'm starving so I just want to spark up the grill and get some sausages going. I love sausages. We had those Chinese ones with, like, the Ah-So sauce built right into them. Those are awesome. We had the hot Italian ones, too. I couldn't figure out which kind I wanted so I decided to grill a bunch."

Alves wanted to strangle the guy. "After you got the sausages going, you said you saw something."

"Oh, yeah. I'm sorry, officer. I saw a white van."

"What kind of van?"

"Ford. Chevy. It was American."

"Anything unusual about it? Old model, new, dents, bumper stickers, modifications?"

"An older model, in good condition. Not beat-up or rusty. Roof rack. One of those homemade jobs, built with welded pipe and a white PVC pipe attached with caps on the ends."

"Any company name on the van?"

"Just a white van. The kind you see the Irish plasterers and painters riding around Brighton in."

"How about a plate number?"

"No."

"If it was a nondescript white van, why do you remember it?"

"Because it was bouncing around."

"Did you hear any noise coming from the van?"

"No."

"Gunshots?"

"Jesus, no." His eyes widened at the suggestion.

"How close did you get?"

"Pretty close."

"How close?" Mooney asked.

"I got right up next to it. I'm no Peeping Tom. I just wanted to find out what was going on in there. See if I could hear some moans or something. That guy must have had the thing soundproofed, because it was hopping all over the place, but I couldn't hear anything. I didn't go any farther than that. I didn't try to peek in the windows or anything. You know what they say, 'if you see this van a rockin', don't come a knockin'.' I'm no Peeping Tom."

"What happened next?" Alves asked.

"The fat from the sausages made the grill flare up. I had a massive grease fire on my hands. The grill was too close to my truck, so I had to get over there and get everything under control. By the time I got it squared away, the van was gone. Too bad, because I wanted to see what they looked like, maybe give them a standing-O."

"Yeah," Alves said, "too bad. We'll be in touch." He and Mooney turned toward the next group of tailgaters.

"You get all his info?" Mooney asked.

Alves nodded. "I don't know what good it'll do us."

"We can pay him a visit at his house some time. He might remember more when he's sober."

"Maybe a good candidate for hypnosis," Alves said.

"We can take him to have his palm read while we're at it."

"I'm serious, Sarge."

"It's a waste of time, Angel. If he does remember something, we won't be able to use him at trial. Any good defense attorney will tear him apart. He'll say that the testimony was fabricated by false memories suggested by the hypnotist at the request of the police."

"Right now he isn't a witness to anything," Alves said. "He saw a white van rocking. For all we know it could have been two guys having a Greco-Roman wrestling match. If hypnosis helps him remember a plate number, maybe we'll have something. A tainted witness is better than no witness."

CHAPTER 47

Connie rang the doorbell and waited to be buzzed in. Once inside, he jogged up the stairs, two at a time, to the second floor. The door at the end of the hall was open a crack, a big striped cat paw hooked around it, trying to pull it open. Connie nudged the escaping cat back into the apartment and closed the door.

Mooney and Alves were sitting in the living room set up like a command center. A card table was stationed in the middle of the room. The walls were lined with giant colored Post-it notes.

Connie set a Box-of-Joe and half a dozen bagels from Dunkies on a ratty coffee table. "Sunday brunch is served," he said. "I appreciate you letting me in on this, Sarge."

"What's so important that it couldn't wait till tomorrow?" Alves asked, irritation in his voice. "I thought you were getting ready for a trial."

"Garden variety gun case," Connie said, easing into a folding chair. It wasn't worth getting into with Angel. Something was wrong with the detective, and Connie didn't feel like playing junior psychiatrist. "I have some ideas on the Prom Night case. Angel said you're trying to find a link between the fortunes and the victims."

"You got something that will help us?" Mooney asked.

"What were the fortunes again?"

"They're all up here on the wall," Mooney pointed. "Color-coded for each set of murders. First one, Adams and Flowers, fortune was 'STOP SEARCHING FOREVER, HAPPINESS IS RIGHT NEXT TO YOU.' With Markis and Riley he left us, 'LIFE IS AN ADVENTURE, FEAR AND WORRY ONLY SPOIL IT.' Then Picarelli and Weston, 'EVERY EXIT IS AN EN-TRANCE TO NEW HORIZONS.' "

"Now, with Steadman and Kipping," Alves said, " 'DEPART NOT FROM THE PATH WHICH FATE HAS YOU ASSIGNED.' Odd thing is the fortune looks like the ones from ten years ago."

"All came from a company called Kookie King," Mooney said. "Com-pany's still around. One of the largest suppliers in the area. Haven't changed the format over the years. The fortunes left with the original victims were printed in black ink, all capital letters. They gave a fortune and nothing else. More recently, a lot of the other companies switched to colored ink, blues and reds. They have a fortune, a lucky number and a translation of a phrase in Chinese. And they don't use all caps. The for-tunes aren't as good as the ones Kookie King uses."

"So our guy is old school, a purist, like you," Connie said. "He sticks with these cookies because they give him his true fortunes."

"Interesting." Mooney said. "Whenever Leslie and I ordered Chi-nese, before we broke into our fortune cookies she would ask if I thought this would be her one true fortune."

"And?" Alves asked.

"Let's say he has these twisted thoughts bouncing around and he's trying to give some legitimacy to the urges he's feeling," Mooney said. "Maybe he's having homicidal thoughts about the girl he rides the bus with every morning. Then he gets this fortune telling him that happiness is right next to him. Basically telling him his feelings are right."

"His one true fortune," Connie said.

"I went through every inch of Kelly Adams's life," Mooney said. "She was the first female victim. I didn't find anything."

"What if it was the boy next door that he was interested in?" Connie asked. "Did you look into Eric Flowers's life?"

"I didn't find anything." Mooney stood up and moved toward the window, looking out onto Gallivan Boulevard. Maybe he wasn't looking at anything outside, just focused on his own reflection.

"Second victims, Daria Markis and David Riley, used to go parking up on Chickatawbut Road, a known cruising spot," Alves said.

"It all fits," Connie said. "He gets that first fortune, realizes that Eric

Flowers is the one and kills him and Kelly Adams. Then one night, after he's read his *second* true fortune, he's out cruising. He runs into David and Daria parked on Chickatawbut and decides to take a risk by killing them."

"Because, 'LIFE IS AN ADVENTURE, FEAR AND WORRY ONLY SPOIL IT,' " Mooney finished.

"That all works out pretty neatly," Alves said. "But what if that first fortune wasn't meant for the victim but someone else?"

"That would mean there was no connection between the killer and the victims beyond convenience or opportunity," Mooney said. "Complicates things."

"Exactly my theory," Connie said. "The victims may be how the killer is getting out his message. To someone he's trying to impress. Someone still alive. Remember John Hinkley?"

"The guy who shot President Reagan," Alves said.

"Right. I'm at home last night thinking about Hannibal Lecter in *Silence of the Lambs*. A classic super-villain. Thomas Harris did research, creating a killer with the traits of a real serial killer. Then I started thinking about Doctor Lecter's relationship with Clarice Starling. Jody Foster in the movie."

Mooney interrupted, "John Hinkley shot Reagan to impress Jody Foster."

"Exactly."

"You've got quite a lot going on in that head of yours," Mooney said.

"So you're equating our murders with Hinkley's efforts to impress Jody Foster?" Alves asked.

"Even though his ultimate goal was to impress her, I think Hinkley was trying to gain fame by killing someone important. He committed his crime so brazenly that he couldn't help but get caught."

"But our killer is careful not to get caught," Mooney said.

"Think about it," Connie said. "He gives a fortune to someone who's dead. That doesn't make sense. But if the fortune is for someone else, a lover, an old girlfriend, then it does."

"And he doesn't spend the rest of his life in jail," Mooney concluded. He poured himself another coffee. "Not bad. Problem is no one's reading those fortunes. We held them from the media."

"I've thought about that too. Look at his first message," Connie said. " 'STOP SEARCHING FOREVER, HAPPINESS IS RIGHT NEXT TO YOU.' Say there's this woman. Sees her every day. He's afraid to tell her how he feels so he tells her through the fortune. But, key point, he doesn't know you're not going to release the message."

Alves and Mooney looked at Connie. They'd caught his drift.

"Let's say, for the sake of argument," Mooney interrupted, "that he's been in jail. Gets paroled, finds a job. She works at the same place. Or maybe they go to the same gym or she rides the same train. To you or me, that might seem like a coincidence, small world, bup-bup-bup-bup. But to him, bingo, looks like fate. The last fortune—'DEPART NOT FROM THE PATH WHICH *FATE* HAS YOU ASSIGNED.' "

"My theory? Even if he got his girl," Connie said, "he won't stop killing. He enjoys the challenge. This woman he's infatuated with gives him a good excuse."

"I like what you've come up with here," Mooney said. "Maybe I'll put you on the case instead of Angel."

Alves didn't laugh.

"Another thought. Is our mystery woman Chinese?" Connie asked. "Is there anything else of significance about Chinese culture?"

Connie watched as Alves made eye contact with Mooney. Mooney laughed. "You think fortune cookies have anything to do with real Chinese culture? There's nothing else."

There was something. Connie could tell by the way Alves had turned to Mooney for a sign. There was something they were keeping from him. He'd get it out of Alves later.

"Maybe we leak those fortunes, from an unnamed source of course, to the media," Mooney said. "Convince him we're getting sloppy or desperate."

"Too dangerous," Alves said.

Connie could see Mooney was thinking about every possibility, like a maze when you trace out your routes in your head until you find the one way that gets you to the endpoint without any dead ends.

"We have to try something, Angel," Mooney said finally.

CHAPTER 48

Sleep watched her as she pranced around her room. The attic was dark, and he stood away from the window, with his binoculars. He had such a lovely view. He could almost see the fine pores of her skin. She was getting her clothes ready for work the next day, the new work week. She had set up the ironing board and pressed several outfits, trying each of them on, always positioning herself so that he could see her changing. She knew he was watching. She had to know.

Each night she put on a show for him, acting as though she were getting ready for work. She was really just giving him a preview of the woman who, one day, would belong to him.

He held his breath as she folded the ironing board. Next she would be getting ready for bed. It was almost more than he could bear. He watched as she removed her bra and panties. She only gave him a momentary glimpse, before she pulled a long T-shirt over her head. She was such a tease. That's what he liked most about her.

He couldn't believe she was still so beautiful after all these years. His little princess. He remembered the day he'd met her, the day she moved in across the street. He fell in love with her immediately. But she was young for her age, interested in athletes, guys with cars, material things. Inevitably, she would mature and come to realize that her true love had been right there all the time.

After putting on her nightshirt she walked to the wall and flipped the light switch. He hated this part. Bedtime.

He would try to see her again tomorrow night. If he could find the time.

Now he had work to do. He walked to the opposite side of the attic, the unfinished side. He closed the door behind him before turning on the light. The brittle yellow shade was drawn on this window. It was always drawn. He bent down and pulled two old trunks from under the eaves. He unlocked them with the keys from his pocket. He was struck with the smell of mothballs as he opened them.

It was time for him to select the outfits.

He had made a guess as to the size of the tux he would need and removed it from the larger trunk. It didn't have to be a perfect fit, after all. He chose a paisley cummerbund and matching suspenders to complete the outfit. The young man would look quite dashing. He locked the trunk and slid it back under the eaves.

Then he rummaged through the other trunk and found the dress he was looking for, an ecru satin affair that would look lovely on its new model. He placed the garments on hangers to air them out, let the wrinkles fall out naturally. He turned off the light and went back down to his room.

CHAPTER 49

Judging from the line out the door of the courthouse, it was going to be a typical Monday.

Connie took out his credentials, flashed his badge, and stepped around the metal detectors. The line at the elevator bank was five people deep. No way he could wait. Connie took the stairs to the sixth floor.

He checked with the clerk. Judge wasn't in yet. He looked around the lobby for the defense attorney on the case, Sonya Jordan. Harvard professor and true believer. Almost a month ago, they'd locked horns outside the grand jury after Tracy Ward gave up the name of his shooter. It was impossible to have a discussion with her. For her, everyone was being persecuted. And all her clients were innocent. He'd first met her when she was dating his old friend Mitch Beaulieu. Much as he liked Mitch, he and Sonya had never been friends. She'd stayed in Boston after Mitch's death. Now she was on a mission to crucify the DA's office.

As the supervising attorney for the Harvard Law students in their clinical program, she led an army of budding lawyers she brainwashed into believing that prosecutors were a bunch of fascists. She kept this case for herself in superior court. Maybe *because* Connie was the prosecutor.

He spotted Sonya Jordan in the corner speaking with her client. She held up a finger asking him to wait. When she finished, she came over to him. "Mr. Darget, are you ready for trial?" She never dropped the formalities. No matter how many cases they had together, he would always be "Mr. Darget."

"Ms. Jordan," he was careful to maintain the same level of formality. "I'm as ready as I'm going to be. I just need the cops to show up with the gun." His strategy was like a pro football coach overstating injuries of key players to lull his opponents and gain an edge.

"This trial won't be an enjoyable experience. I don't care for self-righteous sheep that get their rocks off by locking up innocent people in cages. Unlike you, Mr. Darget, I protect our precious liberty and uphold the Constitution. A Constitution that serves one purpose, to protect us from an overzealous government. To protect us," she pointed her long manicured nail at his chest, "from white guys in white hats."

Connie smiled. He didn't want to let her get to him. "My job is to hold people accountable for their crimes. So let's save the histrionics for the jury, Ms. Jordan." He took a couple steps ahead and opened the courtroom door for her, bowing gallantly. Just to irritate her.

CHAPTER 50

Sleep stood outside the bar smoking a cigarette. He had smoked close to an entire pack. Even though he didn't smoke. Tonight the Sox were playing the Yankees at Fenway. Final game of the season, a make-up game for last night's rainout. Sold out, as usual. Anyone who couldn't get tickets packed into the bars, especially college kids who took advantage of any excuse to get wasted on a weeknight. Inside the bar, half the televisions were tuned in to the Sox game and the other half were on Monday Night Football.

He practiced blowing smoke rings to kill time. He wasn't very good at it. Finally, the girl stepped out of the bar. She was beautiful, even after a night of drinking. The boy, her boyfriend, was handsome, but not good-looking enough to be with her. Maybe deep down the boy knew that somehow he'd lucked into dating a goddess. Recognized that this was the only time in his life he would be with someone like her.

Sleep saw that the boy would take full advantage of her if he could. The boy put his arm around her, kissing her cheek as they stumbled down the street.

They were heading back toward her apartment. Sleep had hoped they would do that. The boy was talking loud and laughing, thinking he'd get lucky.

Not tonight. Sleep's van was parked one block ahead. Right where the boy's luck would run out.

Sleep flipped the cigarette into the sidewalk and crossed the street. He made it to the corner well ahead of the couple. Crossing back over to their side of the street, he watched as they made their way along the sidewalk. When they were a few car lengths from the van, he walked toward them. He reached them as they passed the van. He bumped into the boy. Pretending to get knocked off balance, Sleep took a pratfall onto the concrete.

Even in their drunken state, they had their manners. The boy stuck out a hand and helped him to his feet.

"Hey, I know you," the girl said, giggling. She had a stiff smile etched on her face. She was very drunk. "You're the guy that—"

"Oh, yeah," the boy said. "I remember. Are you okay, mister?" He brushed off the back of Sleep's jacket.

"You kids are out late," Sleep said. "Don't you have classes tomorrow?"

The girl giggled.

"Watching the game," the boy said. He pulled her close to him again, more to hold her up than anything. He was tugging at her, trying to get her to move away.

Sleep looked at her eyes and smiled, then turned to the boy. "Where do you live?" As if he didn't know.

"Just up Comm Ave.," the boy said.

"Why don't I give you a lift? Make sure you get there in one piece. This is my van right here."

The young Romeo took an assessing look at the girl. She could barely stand, her eyes were half closed. He knew what the boy was thinking. Get her back to her apartment before she threw up or passed out. The sooner, the better.

"Sure," he said, "we'll take a ride."

He helped the boy arrange her in the passenger's seat, strapping on her seat belt. Then he led the boy around the work van, explaining that he didn't like to use the rear and side doors. He didn't mention that they had been covered with insulation. He'd taken the bulb out of the overhead light too. He directed the boy to climb over the driver's seat and sit on an empty five-gallon paint bucket between the two seats.

The boy adjusted himself on his makeshift chair. Sleep put in his ear plugs. The girl was slumped over in her seat. Sleep closed the door, hit the automatic lock button, and turned toward the boy. He pulled the gun from his holster, and in one motion, put it to the boy's chest and pulled the trigger. Sleep was ready for the recoil this time. The boy flew back onto the large canvas set up in back. The canvas covered a plastic tarp. An effective way to minimize the mess.

The shot woke the girl from her stupor. She looked around, stunned by the blast of the gunshot. She looked at the gun in his hand and turned to look at the boy's body sprawled in the back of the van. It was a few seconds before she could put all the pieces together. When it all fit, she screamed. No one could hear her. The soundproofing muffled the shot, so it would certainly stifle her cries of fear.

He casually removed the earplugs. He wanted to enjoy her death with all of his senses.

She reached for the door handle, fumbled around, clawing for it, but it wasn't there. It had been removed a long time ago.

He felt her stiffen when he undid her seat belt, slid it gently off her shoulder, and wrapped his fingers around her throat. He had her from behind, which was a good thing. It made it more difficult for her to scratch at his face. She struggled to get away from him, but he held a firm grip. He didn't want her to hurt herself in the struggle. The last thing he wanted was to damage her perfect face.

He pulled her close, away from the door, away from any hard surfaces, protecting her. He dragged her into the back of the van, her arms and legs flailing.

Then he squeezed.

CHAPTER 51

Connie made his way toward Peter's Hill and stopped at the yellow crime scene tape. He stood on Bussey Street at the base of the hill near a dozen police cars. The message had come across the alpha pager twenty minutes earlier. Two bodies, one male and one female, discovered by a runner in the Arnold Arboretum. This was an upscale neighborhood. All the old houses were being bought up and renovated by a new generation. More gentrified by the day.

He had been on his way to meet Greene and Ahearn at the station, but when he got the page, his plans for the evening changed. He didn't have much going with them anyway. Not since Shawn Tinsley's death. With a shooter like Tinsley out of the picture, things would quiet down in District 2.

Connie kept an eye out for Alves. He'd already called the DA's office and spoken with the chief of homicide. He wanted them to know that there was no need to page the Homicide Response ADA. Connie would handle things at the scene and give updates.

Connie skirted the perimeter of the crime scene, taking in as much as he could, which was very little. He was familiar with the area. When he was a teenager, Peter's Hill was a popular place for parties. The gentle rise of tree-covered ground provided a spectacular view of downtown Boston at night. And it offered plenty of hideaways if a couple wanted to slip away for some privacy. From where he stood, the police seemed focused on one of those spots, well off the paved path that looped around the hill.

He saw Alves and a familiar figure lumbering from a thicket. Wayne Mooney. He was carrying a stack of small, numbered orange cones that he was using to mark evidence. Working slowly around the scene, Alves gestured to the criminalists and directed the photographer.

Connie could provide valuable information about Peter's Hill. He could point out the different entrances to the park and the best place to conceal a vehicle if someone was trying to drop something off unnoticed. The killer had done that with two bodies. If the investigators looked in the right spots, they might find tire treads or shoe imprints in the dirt paths near one of the entrances.

Angel Alves acknowledged Connie with a nod. That was all he needed. Alves was balking a little at letting him into this case, but Mooney had liked his ideas on the fortunes. One of the two would let him know when he could have access to the crime scene. Then he could dig deeper into what this killer was about. When things started to fit together, he could point Alves and Mooney in the right direction.

CHAPTER 52

Sleep waited in the line of cars on Walter Street in Roslindale. He thought he could see the glare of unnatural light coming from Peter's Hill. The police roadblock closed off Bussey Street, and when he got that far, probably Mendum Street too. All the direct public accesses to the Arboretum were blocked. The commotion indicated that the police had found his perfect couple.

It made him sad. The lovers would get to repose only a short time more.

With these two, he could see that he was getting better at his art. The girl was beautiful and didn't need much makeup, even after meeting Brother Death. The dress Sleep had chosen for her slipped on, a perfect fit. The boy was the boy. Just like at weddings and proms, you could put a call into central casting and get a handsome groom or a date in a white shirt and black tux. But the boy was a necessary part of the tableau. Sleep was getting better with hair too. Momma had left a generous supply of beauty products. All in all, a very successful venture.

There was a time, long ago, when he didn't understand his purpose. Before he'd discovered all those books about mythology in the library. Before he'd met his brother Death. A time when he lived for his Little Things. Dressing them, buying new outfits for them at yard sales. Browsing through stores, pretending he was selecting a gift for an imaginary sister.

It was exactly at that time that his father caught on.

Then his Little Things started demanding even more.

He could remember every detail of that day. The two of them, Sleep and his father, were alone at the bakery. They'd been working since one in the morning. It was three when his father, the black hairs of his arms dusted in flour, his round face greasy from frying oil, said, "When are you gonna get a girlfriend? Act like other kids your age? When I get home, I'm gonna go up to that attic and get those dolls. I'm gonna bring 'em here and hang them in the window with a sign that says 'These are my half-a-fag son's toys.' Week after that, we'll hang Cinderella's pissy wet bedsheet in the window."

Something like a dozen plane engines roaring filled Sleep's head. His old man was relentless. He watched girls on the street and nudged Sleep to watch too. If a love scene came on the TV screen, he jacked up the volume. Once they had been waiting for Momma in Filene's and his old man had shoved him into a rack of bras.

Sleep could see himself reaching for the rolling pin. He could see himself waiting for his old man to show the back of his head. He could see himself raise the pin, feel the heft of the wood. Before he could stop himself, he remembered trying to say something like "oh no," he could see himself hammering until his father was quiet at last.

When the police came, he told them he had come in late that morning and found his father on the floor, the register open and empty.

He didn't tell the police about his father nattering at him, humiliating him, pushing him. And he didn't tell them about the queen of the gods and the dwelling of Sleep and his Brother Death. He bet none of the cops had ever read *The Tales of Troy*.

Sleep was startled by the loud noise. The driver in the car behind him was leaning on his horn. Traffic was moving. Sleep adjusted his sunglasses and pulled his Bruins cap down tighter on his head. He drove toward the patrolman directing traffic. He waved to the officer as he passed close to Peter's Hill, taking one last look.

CHAPTER 53

Connie followed Alves up Peter's Hill. He'd stood in the cold, watching Mooney setting up cones while a photographer snapped pictures, for close to two hours before getting inside the yellow tape.

"Aren't you in the middle of a trial?" Alves asked.

Alves was treating him like a punk DA, making him wait, greeting him with a sarcastic question first thing. "Trial's over," Connie said. "A simple gun case, remember? Jury came back in ten minutes with a guilty. Angel, I'm out here because this case is important to me."

Alves didn't say anything as he led Connie around a thicket of bushes, toward the glow of the klieg lights. The hill was lit up like a night game at Fenway. Connie stopped when he saw the girl. She was lovely, even in death. She reminded him of Andi, his ex-girlfriend, but without the long red hair. The victim was a brunette, like the others. "Have they been moved?" Connie asked.

"Not yet. We've marked off everything that might have evidentiary value. Sarge had the ID unit take about a thousand pictures. Mooney wanted me to give you a walk-though before the ME takes the bodies. Eunice Curran and her crew are standing by to collect everything else."

"Their poses are different from the last time," Connie said. "These two are having a picnic."

"Yeah. A post-prom snack. He has them set up to make you think, next thing, the dress comes off."

"You're wrong," Connie said. "Look at the scene. It's more like a romantic dinner. She's wearing a dress that will never come off. The killer doesn't want it to. He wants them in this position, at this moment in time, happy, before the relationship is consummated. Before everything goes to shit. He wants them to live happily ever after, like in fairy tales."

Alves's face betrayed a range of emotions, pain among them. Connie had heard the rumors that Marcy Alves wasn't sleeping in the big bed anymore. "You got all that from looking at this setup?" Alves seemed impressed, then doubtful. "Creative, but it doesn't fit. Remember, he's re-creating prom night."

"Who gave him the name Prom Night Killer? The media? The police? He's never called himself that." Connie closed his eyes and imagined himself at the first crime scene. "The first victims were coming from their prom, but our killer didn't know that. Male was in a tux. Female was in a fancy white dress. To him they could have looked like newlyweds going for a stroll in the park. Picture those miniature plastic figures, those wedding cake toppers. He's dressing the victims up as though they've just been married. That's why all the women are wearing white instead of the carnival of colors you'd normally see in prom dresses."

Connie opened his eyes again to find that Alves was staring at him. He had to know that Connie could be right. Connie did not avoid his stare. "What have you been holding back from me, Angel?"

"What are you talking about?" Alves asked.

"There's something else. Something related to Chinese culture. I saw the look you gave Mooney the other day at his place. You let him answer for you."

"I can't tell you, Connie. Mooney will flip. He's kept this thing under wraps for ten years. Hardly anybody knows about it. It's one of the reasons we're convinced he's not a copycat."

"I haven't held anything back from you, Angel. I can't help you if I don't know all the facts."

Alves seemed to think over his options for a couple seconds. "If I show you, it goes nowhere. You can't tell Mooney. If you come up with anything based on what I show you, you come to me. Then I'll relay it to Mooney as my idea. Got it?"

"I'm not looking for credit."

Alves walked over to the girl and lifted the hair off the back of her neck.

Under the bright lights, stamped with black ink, Connie saw the familiar Yin-Yang symbol. The Tai-ji. It was upside down. The killer didn't know anything about Chinese culture. But he wanted the police to *think* he did.

Alves lowered her hair and stepped away from her. "Mooney's coming."

CHAPTER 54

Mooney stood aside as the photographer took pictures of the tire tread in the mud on the corner of South and Bussey.

"I think we can get a decent mold," Eunice Curran said.

"Good. I'll see you back on the hill." He turned and followed the asphalt path, partly hidden in shadow, toward the opening ahead. The area looked so different at night. He remembered coming here on one of his first dates with Leslie. A warm spring day. It was Lilac Day, and Leslie thought it would be nice to go for a walk and have some bread and cheese outdoors near the little brook that ran through the woods.

Like his two unidentified victims on the hill.

That was a long time ago. Before he'd seen so much death. He and Leslie had stopped at the lilacs as they made their way through the maze of paths that wound through the trees. Peter's Hill and the rest of the Arboretum were maintained by Harvard University, she'd explained to him. The best kept park in the city, she'd said. The most beautiful jewel in the . . .

Mooney stopped. He was alone, not quite at the path at the base of the hill where most of the other units were gathering. One by one, and in order, he ticked off the murder sites. The Fens. The Riverway. Olmsted Park. Franklin Park. And now Peter's Hill, the Arnold Arboretum. It made perfect sense.

He picked up his pace. At the base of the hill, he stepped off the path and cut across the grass toward the scene the killer had left for them. He spotted Alves walking Connie through it.

When Mooney caught up with them, Alves said, "Connie doesn't think the murders have anything to do with prom night. Thinks he dressed them up as newlyweds for their picnic in the park."

"Interesting. 'Cause I don't think this has anything to do with a picnic in the park." Mooney waved his hand at the victims. "It's more like a picnic on the Emerald Necklace."

"I don't get it," Alves said.

"He's not familiar with Boston's history," he said to Connie. "This minute, we're standing on Peter's Hill, which is a part of the Arnold Arboretum. Which is—"

"One of the jewels in Olmsted's Emerald Necklace," Connie interrupted.

Mooney nodded, then turned to Alves. "You've never heard of Frederick Law Olmsted, have you?"

Connie began, "Olmsted designed half of Central Park in New York City. Then he did the system of parks in Boston that runs from the Common to Franklin Park. Each one is a 'jewel' in what he called the Emerald Necklace. What kind of Bostonian are you?"

"I'm from Jamaica Plain," Alves said.

"Most of the Necklace is in J.P.," Mooney continued. "The Arborway, the Arboretum, Jamaica Pond, Franklin Park—"

"Got it. I'll study up on my history of the Boston Parks tomorrow. How does this tie in?" Alves asked Mooney.

"The Boston Common and the Public Garden are the first two jewels in the necklace. Then you have the Commonwealth Mall, the grassy area that runs down the middle of Comm Ave. That leads right into the Back Bay Fens where Kelly Adams and Eric Flowers were found. Then you have the Riverway, which leads into Olmsted Park and the Jamaica Pond."

"So the killer's taking us on a tour of the Emerald Necklace," Connie said. "But why?"

"Don't know yet. Maybe Adams's necklace gave him the idea to take us on a tour of his Emerald Necklace. Maybe he works for the Parks Department, a laborer, a supervisor." Mooney paused. "Or a park ranger. Someone with a badge who might be able to gain your trust."

Mooney studied the two men in front of him on the dark hill. One of them was a student of Boston's history, the other was not. The killer was someone with knowledge beyond knowing that kids from Dorchester hated kids from Southie, and that kids from Southie hated kids from Charlestown. The killer was someone who understood Boston. Here, all along, they'd been thinking that the killer was giving them clues—the Tai-ji stamps and the fortunes. That was crap. The real clues were much more subtle. The killer was challenging them on a level he didn't usually find in criminals.

CHAPTER 55

Connie had seen something at Peter's Hill that he hadn't mentioned to Alves. He was irritated that Alves had kept the Tai-ji from him. Alves had never held back anything before. Maybe Alves was following Mooney's orders to keep the symbol a secret. Maybe Alves didn't trust him. For whatever reason, things had changed.

But Connie had the details now. He stretched out on the couch in his basement. The one place he could really focus. Here he could block out distractions and think, and now he was running possible scenarios through his head.

The Tai-ji symbol might be the key to everything. It represented the Yin and the Yang, symbols of the opposite forces of nature, in balance, continually changing. But what did the symbol mean to the killer? Was it an obsession, however misguided, with Chinese culture and philosophy? Or was he trying to give them a false lead? Either way, it would reveal something about the killer.

Interesting thought. What if it was just by chance that the first female victim had a Tai-ji tattooed on the back of her neck? Now, maybe, he was copying the symbol to make each murder look the same.

He believed that the first murders were the most important. The murders of Adams and Flowers were unorganized, spontaneous, unplanned. Something provoked the killer to strike. Stressors. A lost job, a fight with a girlfriend, sure, but more likely something like a surge of electricity scouring through the circuitry of the body till there was no choice but to act.

Connie needed to bring himself back to that time, to visualize things as they were ten years earlier. The murders had all occurred in the summer months, when Connie was home from college in Arizona, between his junior and senior years.

Connie remembered where *he* was and what *he* was doing that summer, but he needed to put himself back into the climate in the city. He couldn't just *think* back on the time, he had to relive it. Then he could turn his focus on the murders and put himself in the place of the killer.

That was something that Alves and Mooney didn't understand. They were good at processing crime scenes and pursuing leads doggedly, but they had no idea how to think like a killer.

Connie was good at that.

CHAPTER 56

Sleep was a careful driver, not too fast and certainly not too slow. Just a couple of miles over the speed limit so as not to draw attention to himself. He didn't want anyone to notice him, especially the police. His headlights, taillights and signals were all working properly. He checked them each time before he went out.

He would have liked to have gotten closer to the investigation on Peter's Hill, but he knew where to draw the line. Push too hard and people start asking questions. He had come close enough to get a taste of the investigation, to smell the scent of the grass on a cool autumn evening, to imagine himself back on that hill with the young lovers. They must have been marvelous under those brilliant lights.

He was sure no one had noticed him, tangled in the stalled traffic. And if they did bother to take a look, that's where his little disguise came in handy.

Now he needed to get back to work, check on his next subjects. He knew their hangouts. It was amazing how many couples were out there every night. He was sure their parents didn't know what they were up to, drinking and partying. Or maybe their parents didn't care.

The not caring, the indifference, that's what made it so easy for Sleep and his brother Death to enter their lives.

CHAPTER 57

It had been years since Connie had set foot in the microfiche room at the main branch of the Boston Public Library in Copley Square. He had spent so many summer afternoons in this room, staring into the screens, doing research for his honors thesis in history. Even after recent renovations to the building, the room still had the dusty feel of an old library, a true depository of information. That was what Connie loved about it.

Instead of taking a rare sick day, Connie could have stayed in his office and Googled key terms related to the Prom Night Killer. There were plenty of articles online about the killer and his crimes. But sitting at a computer wouldn't take him back to the time of the original murders. Reading the newspaper articles, seeing the ads and announcements from the time would remind him of everything that was going on, from the Boston sports teams to the local political landscape. He could read about which department stores were having sales, what movies were playing in theaters, and, most of all, how the public was reacting to the killings.

Connie planned to read every issue of the *Globe* and the *Herald* from that summer. That was how he worked, slow, methodical, and thorough. Each line he read brought him back in time. The heat came early that year, before the murders began. One of the hottest summers on record. He thought back to the Tai-ji, the Yin and the Yang, opposite forces at balance in nature. The hot and the cold. Was the killer trying to send a message about the heat that summer, that things were out of balance, that the hot was too hot, that it lasted well into fall? That wouldn't explain why he'd stopped.

As he was going through the papers, he came across a short article on page three of the Metro Region section, just below the fold. ONE DEAD IN ROXBURY SHOOTING, the small headline proclaimed. *In a bold daylight shooting, notorious gang member Marcus Little was shot and killed on Columbia Road. Although the shooting occurred on a busy section of the street, no witnesses have stepped forward. The victim's younger brother, Darius "D-Lite" Little was arrested after a brief altercation with police. When questioned by reporters, the officer who ordered the arrest, Homicide Sergeant Wayne Mooney, refused comment.*

Connie could see why Darius Little—Luther—hated Wayne Mooney. Their first meeting ended with Luther getting arrested at his brother's murder scene. The family was vocal about their mistrust of the department and Mooney, telling the newspapers that he should take himself off the case. He had arrested an innocent grieving boy, they claimed. They suggested that he would have worked harder to catch Marcus's killer if Marcus had been white. Mooney stayed on the case, but he never caught Marcus's killer.

Within weeks, Adams and Flowers turned up dead. Two white high school seniors murdered. With all the pressure to catch the Prom Night Killer, Marcus Little's murder must have slipped down on the priority list. Connie wondered if Mooney did put enough effort into solving Marcus's murder. How could he, when Mooney was in the paper nearly every day trying to catch his first serial killer, trying to make a name for himself?

Connie was not distracted by the high-pitched squeal of the microfiche machines fast-forwarding and rewinding around him. He savored the sounds of this place. They were comforting, reassuring. Other researchers had come here hunting for information, learning about their history, reading old newspapers from as far back as the early 1800s. He had to trust that his thoroughness would lead him to more discoveries. More links in the case.

Interesting story in early September 1998. It was an article about a mob wannabe named Richard Zardino getting fingered on a gangland murder. A federal informant had testified before a grand jury that Zardino shot and killed a man in retaliation for an earlier murder.

Zardino was taken into custody and didn't breathe fresh air outside the prison walls for eight years.

The summer of '98 had been interesting for a lot of people. Luther going crazy after his brother's unsolved murder, Zardino taking a hit on a murder he didn't commit, a city in fear of a violent killer, and Wayne Mooney at the center of it all.

Connie rewound the microfiche and pushed away from the machine and let his eyes adjust to the light in the room. After a few minutes he got up and returned his stack of microfiche reels to the librarian.

He hadn't realized how long he was tucked away in the room. The late afternoon sun cast a long shadow of the library toward the Trinity Church. He had spent the entire day squinting into the gray screen. Not even a lunch break. It was worth it, though. He had learned a lot about that summer, and so much had come back to him. He walked toward the church, the sun at his back, a cool afternoon breeze in his face. He would walk down Boylston and then cut over to Comm Ave. and make his way to the Public Garden and the Common. He loved that walk. He needed to relax a bit.

He called his investigators on the cell. He needed them to get some information for him. Now his head was right. Tomorrow he would get his hands dirty. He was looking forward to it.

CHAPTER 58

Alves held the receiver to his ear. He wasn't certain if he should make the call. But Marcy was standing firm. She wasn't coming back with the twins till the killer was caught. And if he didn't mention it to Mooney, the Sarge didn't need to know about the call. Why close off any avenue that might lead to something?

As he listened to the dial tone, he thought about his day—interviewing students about the last time they'd seen their friends Nathan Tucker and Karen Pine alive. They were students, sophomores at Boston University, found on Peter's Hill. All he'd uncovered after a day of interviews was that they'd been out with friends at a bar on Monday night. Used fake IDs to get in. Nathan's friends said he was hoping to go back to her place after they left the bar, but they never made it.

He should be out on the street doing something, but right now he didn't know what that something was. Alves dialed the number.

A woman with a pleasant voice answered, "FBI. How may I direct your call?"

"Special Agent John Bland, please."

Alves had met Bland and his partner when they were called in on a case three years ago. But Mooney had seen that their working relationship ended in bad feelings. Mooney had "fired" them, accusing them of undercutting his investigation. Luckily Alves had saved Bland's card. He was pretty sure Bland was the taller of the two, the one who did most of the talking.

"Detective Alves, nice to hear from you." He recognized Bland's voice. "How are things?"

"Not bad." Alves lied. "You told me three years ago if I ever needed you to give a call."

"The Prom Night Killer is back."

"I was wondering if you could look over the case files. Tell me what we might be looking at here."

"Do you want me to come up to Boston?"

Alves could only imagine Mooney walking in on the agent reading the files.

"Or you can send me copies of the reports, photos, everything from the crime lab and the ME."

"Sounds good." Alves couldn't help but think what a good guy Bland was. He put aside all the bullshit and focused on what was important. "I really appreciate you helping me with this, especially since we haven't been overly hospitable to you."

"I understand the position you're in, detective. I don't blame you for any of this. Any time we can help catch a murderer, we're glad to help."

"I'll FedEx that stuff to you today."

"Detective Alves? About that Blood Bath case. That one still bothers me," Bland said. "I'm not convinced Beaulieu was your killer."

The accusation was a sucker punch. Robyn Stokes, one of the victims, was a childhood friend. Another was a colleague in the DA's office. A wave of nausea washed over Alves. Bland's instinct hit on something he had been asking himself since the day Mitch Beaulieu jumped from that courthouse balcony, taking the truth with him. Something didn't sit right with the way the case ended.

"We had solid evidence against him," Alves said, trying to convince himself. "We never got a confession. But the answers he gave us during our interview were evasive. They showed his consciousness of guilt. Beaulieu also had the opportunity and means to kill each of the victims. Then he killed one of his co-workers, Nick Costa, maybe when he got too close to the truth. And Agent Bland, the killings stopped when he died."

"I remember reading about the evidence at the time. It was all circumstantial," Bland continued the argument.

"Sometimes circumstantial evidence is the best kind," Alves said.

"Circumstances can't be mistaken, and they certainly don't lie. We had his shoe print outside a victim's house, we had his hairs at the scene of the last murder, we found his brand of condom near the same house." Alves was aware of how he sounded—like he was arguing a losing cause.

Bland said, "If I recall, the finishing touch was the room in his house where he had built a shrine to his father. Video of that room was leaked to the media."

"That wasn't our fault. That came straight from the mayor. It was a bizarre scene."

"I'm sure it was. But it's not what I would have expected to find in the killer's home. It sounds like a memorial put together by a lonely, depressed young man who missed his father. A father who had also committed suicide, if I remember right. I think Mitch Beaulieu was more likely to have suicidal ideation, rather than homicidal. When the pressure gets to a guy like that he directs his frustration internally, on himself. He wouldn't have an external lashing out at others."

"So you don't think he was the killer?" Alves asked.

"I'm not saying that. I'm not sure. I like to question everything. And what you found in his apartment wasn't what I had expected." Bland was silent for a couple of seconds. "Were there any other suspects at the time?"

"Everyone in the courthouse was a suspect."

"So anyone who worked there would have had the same means and opportunity that Beaulieu had?"

"We had physical evidence that pointed to him."

"Could any of that evidence have been planted?"

Alves was starting to see what had infuriated Mooney. What was Bland suggesting? That any of the items could have been placed there by someone else who had access to Mitch and his stuff? And they were too stupid to know the difference?

Bland continued, "Don't you find it odd that this guy was so careful not to leave any evidence at the crime scenes? There was no indication that he was doing anything sexual with his victims. Yet as the police are converging on the courthouse, trying to find out who may have had access the jurors, the killer suddenly decides to make a post mortem sexual assault on his final victim, leaving hairs and a condom at the scene that point directly to Mitch Beaulieu."

"The condom was found outside the apartment in a sewer," Alves said with resignation.

"Of course it was. It wouldn't be a very good frame-up if someone had left it on the bed with a name tag. The condom was hidden, but in a place that the police were likely to find it."

"Why would anyone think we'd find a condom in a sewer?"

"Because Wayne Mooney was the lead investigator. Remember, I've looked at your case files. I've seen Mooney's work. He processes a crime scene as thoroughly as anyone I've ever seen. And he understands the importance of making his crime scene as large as possible. Spares no expense on the yellow tape. Anyone who knows Mooney would have known the condom would be discovered."

"What about the shoe print?" Alves felt like he was manning a sinking ship. "That was recovered at a crime scene several months and several victims *before* we focused on Beaulieu."

"Think about it. If someone was planning on framing Beaulieu, they didn't decide to do it the day before you interrogated him. The real killer had probably been planning it for months, possibly from the beginning. He may have known how it was all going to end before he even started killing."

Another blow. More like a kick than a punch. If he subscribed to Bland's theory, someone—most likely someone Alves knew personally—was responsible, not only for the Blood Bath murders, but for setting up and, in effect, causing Mitch Beaulieu's suicide. "That doesn't explain why the killing stopped after Beaulieu was dead."

"It's not unusual for a killer to stop for a variety of reasons," Bland said, "especially an organized killer. If the end game was to kill as many people as he could before police caught his scapegoat, then he had accomplished his goal. He couldn't then go out and kill more people in the same way. Not without bringing the attention to himself. That doesn't mean he's not still killing. Remember, no bodies were ever recovered. We have no idea why he took the bodies or what he did with them. For all we know, he could be doing the same thing, only without leaving a bathtub full of blood for the police to find."

It was a stunning idea. That the Blood Bath killer could still be out there. The dark and threatening shadow of a terrible idea crossed his mind. Could the Blood Bath Killer also be the Prom Night Killer?

"I'll FedEx that stuff right away," Alves said.

CHAPTER 59

The Healey Library at UMass Boston maintained all the student yearbooks from its first graduating class in 1969. Connie discovered that Richard Zardino had never graduated. But the yearbooks were full of the photos of the students around him who did. Connie wasn't sure what he was looking for. Maybe for a good-looking dark-haired girl. Maybe a name or a face he recognized from Alves's files. Anything tying Zardino to Kelly Adams. Hours of searching, and there was nothing. Maybe he'd wasted a day off coming here this morning.

Connie took the catwalk to the Registrar's Office in the new Campus Center, flashed his prosecutor's badge, and worked his way through the phalanx of state workers guarding the Registrar. A skeleton of a man with tobacco-stained fingers came out from behind a bank of computers.

Connie flashed his credentials again and introduced himself. "I'm conducting a grand jury investigation into a serious matter. I'll need to see a complete list of students registered to take classes at the time a certain student was enrolled here. We're looking back ten years," Connie said.

The Registrar gave a cough that seemed to allow him to speak. "I would need to see a subpoena before I could turn over those kinds of records."

"I understand. I'll have my secretary fax one over right now. If you don't mind, I'll wait for the records." Connie took out his cell phone and hit #1 on his speed dial.

Within minutes the Registrar was holding a subpoena under the heading of a John Doe investigation.

"Records just for that one year, 1997–'98," Connie reminded him.

"Probably take more than an hour. There's a coffee kiosk on the lower level," he told Connie as he turned away.

In less than two hours, Connie was back at the library. The printouts listed the names and addresses of every student in attendance that year. Connie sorted through the sheets of names, looking for anything that might be significant.

Connie's cell rang. He didn't recognize the number but he caught it on the second ring. A couple of students stared at him for interrupting their studies, but he was glad to have picked up. It was Luther on the line. He waited while Connie made his way out of the library.

"Mr. Darget," Luther said, "Rich Zardino and I would like to meet with you."

"What about?"

"We need to see you in person. We have information on a homicide. It came from some kids we work with. You need to consider this an anonymous tip."

"When do you want to meet?"

"As soon as you're available."

"One hour. At the Victoria Diner." Connie looked down at the printouts. He flipped to the end of the alphabet.

Richard Zardino.

Residence: 2252 Paris Street

East Boston

Rich Zardino's address had not changed in more than ten years.

CHAPTER 60

Ray Figgs parked across from Grady's Barber Shop on Columbus Avenue. The antique barber's pole was turning and the "OPEN" sign was in the window. Beyond that, there didn't seem to be any sign that Grady's was open for business. Figgs checked his reflection in a car window. Good enough for a meeting with Stutter Simpson.

The little bell on the door jingled when Figgs stepped inside. A short, chubby man with a mustache and beard appeared from a door at the back of the shop. Grady. He waved Figgs in and waited for him to step into the back room. He closed the door behind Figgs.

Stutter Simpson sat on the edge of a cot in the small office. There was a duffel bag serving as a pillow at one end of the bed. Stutter had a moth-eaten wool blanket draped around his shoulders. A barbershop hideout. Simpson had been hiding out from the police and his enemies. Figgs had never seen Stutter in the flesh, only in booking photos. The boy looked as though he'd lost twenty pounds since his last drug arrest a year ago. The irony of the situation did not escape Figgs. Simpson's hair was in serious need of a trim and he hadn't shaved in a week. Probably the last time he showered, too.

Figgs sat on a little stool across from Stutter's bed. Let the kid get uncomfortable with the silence, he told himself. Let him make the first move.

"W-w-what chou want with me?" Stutter asked.

No mystery how he got his nickname. The impairment probably accelerated with an injection of nerves. And he was plenty nervous right now. Figgs took his time answering. "I want to talk with you about your brother Junior. I need you to tell me who would have shot him."

"N-nobody."

"Let's try this one. Who wants to kill *you*?"

"Everybody."

"Narrow that down for me."

"I can't trust no one. My dogs don't want n-n-nothing to do with me. Think I'm a marked man. Jesse Wilcox's boys are gunning for me."

"You have anything to do with Jesse's death, Stutter?" Figgs asked.

"No, I s-swear."

"Why haven't you cooperated with the police in the investigation?"

"Can't trust Five-O neither. I'm not talking about getting busted. I'm talking about getting p-popped."

"By Five-O?"

Stutter Simpson nodded. "Some funny shit going on. Only reason I'm meeting you is my moms said you's okay. You one of us. Says you've got a good rep for helping people. I can't hide out here much longer. Grady's stressing. Thinks he's gonna get straightened if I chill here much longer. Look at me, man. I'm living in the back room of a barber shop. Can't even get a haircut."

"What do you know about Junior's death?"

"Heard a van rolled up on him. The kind with the sliding doors on both sides. Smoked out windows. Junior walk right up to it. Someone he knew. Trusted. Then . . . pop, pop, pop. No chance to jet."

"You have any idea who was in that van?"

Stutter Simpson nodded. "I told him not to trust no one on the street. So it had to be someone who wasn't street. That's all I know."

"You're not going to do anything stupid, right?"

"Can't say what I m-might do. I find who killed Junior, likely, I'll smoke him."

"Your mother's already lost one son."

"She lost both her sons. Look around, detective. This ain't no way to

live. I'm doing this for her. Least she'll know her boys went down fighting. Not a couple of bitches. That's all, and that's it."

The kid was scared enough to be telling the truth, Figgs thought. And
if what he said *was* the truth, then Junior Simpson was killed by someone
with a badge, or someone like a church worker, a teacher, a parole or probation officer. Someone comfortable in the neighborhood. Someone he
trusted.

CHAPTER 61

It was starting to fit into place. It had to be Zardino. It made perfect sense. Connie had been on the computer since he got back from his meeting at the Vic with Luther and Zardino.

The information the two Street Saviors gave him was interesting. Their sources told them that Shawn Tinsley never touched a gun in his life. If that was true, Tracy Ward had lied up the grand jury so he could get a cigarette. Now Tinsley was dead and the shooter—the same one that killed his own friend Ellis Thomas because he thought he'd snitched—was still out there. Connie told Luther and Zardino he'd speak with Figgs and they'd figure out what to do about Michael Rogers, the real shooter.

But that could wait. Connie was focused on the Prom Night Killer, and he'd read every article ever written about Zardino's arrest and wrongful conviction.

Mooney and Alves had it all wrong. They were focusing on recently released, known sex offenders that went to jail around the time the killings stopped. Their next step would be to look at all recent parolees, no matter what their crime. That was too broad a net to cast.

Did they ever think to look at someone who got out of jail, not because he was paroled, but because he had been exonerated? Rich Zardino fit perfectly. When the first murders were committed, Zardino was a kid with no record. The murders stopped when he was taken into custody. Eight years later, he was kicked loose, exonerated. Then the victims started turning up dead again. But not for two years. What happened during those two years?

Connie's study of serial killers had taught him the way they think, the way they act, how stressors trigger their acts. Connie sat back down at his computer and Googled the name Zardino. It didn't take long to find the mother's obituary.

Rose Zardino. Dead of heart failure. May 7, 2008.

Not six months later, before Columbus Day, 2008, Courtney and Josh, then Nathan and Karen were all dead.

CHAPTER 62

The conversation with Bland had gotten Alves thinking. He remembered what Mooney had said when they were close to catching the Blood Bath Killer. *Everyone's a suspect.*

Alves walked into Mooney's office. "How'd it go with the hypnotist?" he asked before he took a seat.

"Waste of time. It took awhile to get him under. Couldn't remember anything else about the van," Mooney said. "I had the BRIC cross-reference our list of sex offenders with the RMV. See if any of them owns a white van. Checked their known relatives. Killer could have borrowed the van. Reached out to the Sex Offender Registry Board too. Got about a dozen level three sex offenders who live in the areas where the vics were last seen. All of them tracked on GPS bracelets. No one anywhere near their exclusion zones, which include parks and playgrounds."

"You have their addresses?"

"Right here." Mooney tapped the top folder on his desk. "How'd it go with you?" he asked.

"Still looking into Karen Pine. Checked every roster at BU, every professor, tutor and teaching assistant from every class she ever took. Nothing. I'm going to run all their BOPs," Alves said. "I've got the list of recent DOC releases. If you want, I can focus on parolees with links to the area around your Emerald Necklace."

"I spent some time trying to figure out who would be interested in Boston's Emerald Necklace. Called a few people. The Superintendent of the Parks Department for one. He gave us Rangers, tour guides, Duck Tour drivers, even the kids who pedal tourists around on the Swan Boats. Then I tried a professor of American Urban History over at UMass Boston. No hits for students writing theses on the Necklace in the last couple years, although I did learn quite a bit about the Great Molasses Flood of 1919. A lot of the workers at the Parks Department have records. You want to start with them or the sex offenders?" Mooney stood up and reached for the jacket hanging on the back of his chair.

Alves had had enough of his quiet house. Late-night cups of coffee alone. No line for the bathroom. He wanted Marcy and the twins back home where they belonged. "Let's flip a coin. Can I buy you a coffee?" he asked, knowing Mooney never refused anything free.

CHAPTER 63

The early morning sun shone through the windows of the catwalk at UMass Boston. Connie watched the students changing classes. They moved in slow groups, texting and talking on their cell phones.

He'd come prepared with subpoenas for four professors. Zardino's math teacher was dead, and his psychology and economics professors had nothing to add, as the classes were held in lecture halls with hundreds of students.

One old-timer left to talk to.

He took the elevator to the sixth floor and checked the office schedules on the wall outside the main office. He located the office he was looking for and took a seat at a small round table designed for students to meet with their tutors. On the table was a stack of school newspapers, the *Mass Media*. He thumbed through the pages full of safety tips: *avoid being alone in the deserted spots like the library's upper floors,* and *always walk to isolated parking spots with a friend.* The school was implementing a Safe Escort program that would operate nights and Saturdays. It was his habit to read everything—from the front page to the sports reports.

He was almost finished when he saw the quarter-page announcement for an upcoming lecture.

Brown Bag Lecture Series

*Learn how unjust our criminal justice system is. Meet Rich Zardino, a man who
spent eight years in prison for a crime he didn't commit. Hear, in his own words,
about his nightmare. His is a story told with power and emotion. Don't miss it.*

Cookies and beverages provided by the Anarchists Club

Sponsored by the Philosophy Club

It seemed Richard Zardino was everywhere.

When she finally showed up, herbal tea in hand, Zardino's silver-
haired English professor held Connie up for what seemed like an hour
while she dug through old mimeographed files and dusty student essays.
But it was worth the time. Richard Zardino, student in English 101, section 18, had written an essay about a myth. "Sleep, and Death, his
brother, dwelt in the lower world. Dreams too ascended from there to
men. They passed through two gates, one of horn through which true
dreams went, one of ivory for false dreams." The professor had given him
an F, with the notation: "Source is Edith Hamilton. Always properly cite
your sources." The plagiarized essay was presented to the Dean of Students, who promptly ruled that Richard Zardino receive an F for a class
grade.

Within a month, Kelly Adams and Eric Flowers were dead.

CHAPTER 64

No one would be in the office yet, not on a Saturday morning . . . except for one person.

It was a little after seven A.M. when Connie stepped into the assignment office where the closed case files were archived. Jason Reece had worked in the office for close to twenty years. He had started in the assignment office out of college, and he took his job seriously. He was the first one in every day, including Saturdays, making sure he kept the information in his database active.

Every time he went near Jason's office, Connie stopped in to say hello and chat. A rabid Bruins fan, Jason was always willing to talk about the good old days when the NHL let the Black and Gold inflict a lot more black and blue. His ultimate fantasy would be an early '70s home game at the old Garden—not an unobstructed seat in the house—with the Philadelphia Flyers, the Broad Street Bullies, in town to take on the Big Bad Bruins. Every hockey fan in Boston knew they would never witness that style of hockey again.

"Hey, Jay," Connie called out. But Jason wasn't at his desk. He was in, though. Otherwise the door would have been locked. Not so much to protect the files that were stored there, but the Bruins memorabilia on the walls. They were covered with autographed photos and sticks and pucks. There was a 1972 pennant signed by Derek Sanderson, Bobby Orr and Pie McKenzie and a framed, autographed Cam Neely jersey.

"What's up, Connie?" Jason popped out of the back room where the case files were stored. "You're here early."

"I'm trying to draft an opposition to a motion for a new trial that's due next week. Could you pull a file for me? It has some good motions and oppositions that I can use as samples."

"Case name, buddy?"

"It's an old one, but the motions were just heard within the last few years. I'm hoping you haven't sent it off to the state archives. Defendant's name is Richard Zardino."

"I remember that one. He got a new trial."

Connie nodded. "The DA eventually had us assent to the motion. Then we dismissed the case. But the motions that were filed early on were good. Mind if I take a look through the file? I'll get it back to you Monday morning, first thing."

"No hurry. Keep it as long as you want. Let me see if I still have it."

"Jason," Connie called. "Nine days, thirteen hours, and fifteen minutes."

"You're the man, Connie," Jason called back. "Can't wait for that first puck to drop."

CHAPTER 65

Alves lay in bed listening to the comforting sound of the shower running. The twins would wake up any minute. Then everyone would rush around getting ready for church, just like it used to be, before the killings started again. And after church, there was the big dinner at Marcy's mother's house, where Marcy and the twins were bunking out. They were back for the weekend—so Marcy could catch up on the laundry and her paperwork for school. Give him a taste of all he was missing.

Even with all the pleasant distractions, Alves couldn't keep his mind off work. After his conversation with John Bland, he understood that it was at least a possibility that Mitch Beaulieu was not the Blood Bath Killer. That meant that someone else was. Because his old friend from the neighborhood, Robyn Stokes, was one of that killer's victims, he couldn't talk to Marcy about his doubts. Robyn had been one of Marcy's best friends growing up, and Marcy was already nerved up enough about the Prom Night killings, never mind rehashing cases they all considered closed.

The last person he could talk to was Wayne Mooney. Mooney hated the feds. His last face-to-face meeting with John Bland and his partner had ended in a dustup of epic proportions. He'd basically thrown the feds off the case and gotten himself launched to Evidence Management. Besides, the Blood Bath case was closed. Solved. Why open up all the grief for the victims' families and friends? For the Department? Still . . .

It bothered Alves not to tell Marcy. Despite their recent problems, they had a strong marriage. They trusted each other and kept no secrets. He couldn't think of any other way to put it. They knew each other at the core.

The shower stopped and he could hear Marcy singing "Winter Wonderland." Down the hall, he could hear the twins giggling. Slowly, things would return to normal. It would be great to sit in the stuffy church, go through the paces—up-down-kneel-stand. Great to offer a silent prayer that his family seemed to be coming through the horror of the past few weeks. His wife was humming, his children were outside the bedroom door, arguing over which one of them got to turn the doorknob. In that peaceful moment of thankfulness, a thought came to him.

How do you find out who a man really is?

Simple enough.

You go talk to the woman.

CHAPTER 66

Wayne Mooney knew he was ambitious, trying to make the run from the Common to Franklin Park, taking the scenic route along the Emerald Necklace. It had to be five miles, maybe closer to seven or eight. A gorgeous Sunday afternoon in late September might not have been the best time for him to make the journey. People were everywhere, with kids in strollers, on bikes, riding Razors, and those sneakers with the wheels. It was a freaking obstacle course.

The killer wouldn't be setting up his couples now. He would wait until dark, during the quiet time, somewhere between midnight and four in the morning. Any earlier, he could run into people coming home from a night out. Any later and he'd likely be spotted by some early bird runner, a newspaper delivery man. Mooney needed to talk to the Commissioner about borrowing some bodies from the Strike Force, setting them up at strategic locations around the Necklace. But which locations?

The killer had started out at the Fens. He'd skipped the Common, the Public Garden and Commonwealth Mall. Why? Too wide open, heavily populated with the homeless, runaways, and the elderly. Then he goes from the Fens to the Riverway. Next stop Olmsted Park, where Mooney was right now, where the MDC skating rink used to be.

Then he stops killing for ten years. Logically, he should pick up where he left off. Jamaica Pond should be next. Sure, there are houses around the perimeter, but there are still secluded spots that would create beautiful backdrops. But he skips the Pond and starts working from the other end of the Necklace. Why? Why go to Franklin Park then the Arboretum? Why start working back in the opposite direction?

As Mooney jogged down the hill toward the Jamaica Pond, he saw the boathouse, some of the sailboats already tipped over in neat lines, in preparation for winter. He saw the groomed walking paths, the woods surrounding the pond, the thick shadows cast on the little spans of neat grass. This had to be the next spot. Besides the risky spots near the Common, Jamaica Pond was the one Jewel missing in the killer's Necklace. This was where the killer would come next.

CHAPTER 67

Michael Rogers felt something warm and sticky on the ground under him. His legs were useless and it hurt to use his arms. His insides were messed up pretty good, otherwise he wouldn't be tasting blood in his mouth, coughing it up from his lungs.

His legs had gone numb the second he heard the shot. If he had only seen the van coming down Walnut. He'd gone behind that thorn bush to take a leak. When he stepped back under the street light, the van was parked not ten feet away. The sliding side door was already open. Funny thing, he hadn't heard it slide. And the interior lights weren't lit. Right away he knew something was wrong, but he hadn't had time to run. No time to reach for his toast. It had happened so fast.

The first shot tore into his gut. He felt the burning in his back and belly, but nothing else. Once he hit the ground, he was useless.

The dude that got out of the van had a dark hoodie drawn tight around his face, black gloves and jeans. Maybe dude was one of Tracy Ward's crew, maybe one of Ellis Thomas's cousins. Payback. But he couldn't make out anything familiar about him. Not even his walk.

Michael Rogers wanted to see his face. He tried to tell the shooter, but the words wouldn't come out. Only choking and more blood. He tried to gather enough saliva in his mouth to spit, but he couldn't. He wasn't afraid to take chrome to the dome. But he wanted to see who the shooter was first.

Dude stood over him for what seemed like the longest time before he took the heater out of his waist and aimed it down at his head. Then Dude opened up his hoodie enough so the street light lit half his face.

Michael Rogers nodded.

At least he had an answer.

CHAPTER 68

Figgs spotted something. A small shiny object threw back the light of his flashlight. He pulled on a pair of latex gloves and knelt in the mulch groundcover of the playground. Michael Rogers was lying ten feet away in this quiet corner of Mothers' Peace Park. Ironic. What mother would be at peace knowing her kids were playing here? At night, this kiddie playground was the most dangerous area of the park. Surrounded by tall shrubs and isolated from neighbors by an old church on one side and a school across the street, it offered the perfect seclusion necessary for drug dealing.

Aside from the first responders who found the body, no one had been in or out of the playground. Figgs had ordered everyone to stand by while he made a cursory walk-through. He reached forward and picked up the object. A shell casing: .40 caliber. He placed it back down where he had found it. His knee popped as he stood up: another sign of aging.

Figgs made his way toward the patrol supervisor from District B-2. He motioned toward the broken street lights. "We need the lighting crew out here. Ballistics, too. Sergeant Stone, if you can get him."

Michael Rogers lay on the mulch, eyes staring skyward, a dark bullet hole in his forehead. The blood pooling beneath him was thick and glistening. Another mother had lost another son. Another mother's life would come to nothing but grief here in what was supposed to be a place of healing.

CHAPTER 69

It was almost noon on Monday before Connie entered the main office of East Boston High, flashed his badge, and asked to speak with the headmaster.

The weekend had been productive. He'd spent time in his basement going through the two archive boxes that made up *Commonwealth v. Richard Zardino.* Police reports, grand jury minutes, trial transcripts, motions for new trial. Everything.

Zardino had been set up good. The prosecution had a single witness who testified that Zardino had murdered a local thug. The witness had a bad record, and that came out at trial. What didn't come out was that he was an FBI informant who caught a break for trafficking guns and drugs. The witness had to have been looking at thirty years, on a good day. To give him a break on a serious case, the feds needed something big in return. Information that helped solve a murder was good. But testifying for the prosecution at a murder trial was winning the Triple Crown.

When the information became public, a judge allowed Zardino's motion for a new trial. The DA decided not to prosecute the case and Zardino was free. Since he'd been exonerated, his name would not appear on a list of parolees from the DOC.

That's why Mooney and Alves had overlooked Zardino as a suspect.

He'd returned the files to Jason Reece early enough, but it had been

almost ten o'clock before he reached his contact at the School Department. The power of another grand jury subpoena, and he had records
showing Zardino's school assignments from elementary through high
school. And he'd confirmed that the first two victims hadn't attended the
Boston Public Schools.

On the drive through the Ted, Connie had thought how there was a
lot of information in old yearbooks, most of it useless, until you needed
a youthful detail on a person that could only be found in those deposito-
ries of nostalgia.

The headmaster was a small, tidy woman wearing the kind of dark
suit a politician might wear. Connie flashed his badge and she was on the
phone, requesting a copy of the yearbook from Zardino's graduation
year, 1997, the year before the murders began.

"Could you tell me again why you need this yearbook, Mr. Darget?"
she asked while they waited. She was so slight she seemed to float when
she moved.

"I'm sorry, ma'am. A grand jury investigation is a secret proceeding.
To protect the innocent more than anything else. Suppose I tell you I'm
looking for information on a Jane or John Doe and my investigation ultimately turns up nothing," Connie wanted to soften her up, win her
over to his side. "You would still know that we investigated that person
and it might damage his or her reputation."

Her assistant appeared with the book, and the headmaster held it
close to her chest like armor. She didn't offer it to Connie. "I understand,
Mr. Darget. But I would have to make some calls first." She still held the
book close. "I'm the one getting sued if a student's privacy is violated."

Connie reached into his breast pocket and pulled out a piece of paper.
"What I have here is a grand jury subpoena with your name on it, ma'am.
It would require you to appear and bring whatever records I request."
Connie watched the look of concern deepen on her clear face. No
makeup, just a hint of shine on her thin lips. Nobody liked going to court
to testify. It was an inherent fear in people.

"I don't think that's—"

"Why don't you let me look at the book today, here, on premises. If I
find what I'm looking for, you're all set. No need to testify. If, on the
other hand, you feel uncomfortable with that, I can see you up the grand
jury tomorrow at One Pemberton Square, downtown."

"That won't be necessary, Mr. Darget." She handed him the book.
"Let me find you someplace where you can look through this in private."

"I may need to make some photocopies if I find anything useful."

"Of course. Anything you need."

Ten minutes later Connie was sitting in an empty teachers' lounge going through the book. He didn't want to miss anything.

There wasn't much to miss. Zardino wasn't the most popular guy. No pictures of him except for his yearbook portrait. Age had carved some measure of distinction into the puffy adolescent face. His features were more defined now, his eyes no longer downcast in teenage angst. The Richard Zardino Connie knew had made the best of his prison years, his face a map of his hard-earned successes. His eye, droopy in the old studio photo, now looked more like a trophy from a prison brawl.

But the text below his photo was what Connie had been looking for.

> Nickname: Richie
> Activities: Stage crew, Photography Club
> Ambition: To marry the girl of my dreams
> Favorite Quote: *The arms of night restrain both men and immortals.*

Connie heard the bell, followed by the sounds of kids shuffling from one class to the next, of shrill screams and laughter, the slamming of locker doors.

That quote. The other kids had things like *Life is what you make it* and *To be half the man my father is*. Zardino went for something from a classics class. At East Boston High? And that girl of his dreams. Was she real or imaginary?

CHAPTER 70

Alves waited outside the classroom in Austin Hall until her law students had filtered out. Sonya Jordan stood at the front of the room packing her bag.

"Can I help you?" she asked without looking up.

"I'd like to talk with you about Mitch Beaulieu," he said.

As she looked up, he saw a flash of recognition in her eyes. Then she went back to arranging her notebooks and textbook in her bag.

"I only need a few minutes of your time," he persisted.

"I asked for a few minutes of *your* time three years ago. I tried to tell you about Mitch, to explain that he wasn't capable of doing the things you believed he had done. I wanted to convince you that he was a good man, his only mistake was trusting whoever it was that set him up. You didn't want to listen then. You, Detective Alves, treated me like some dumb bitch girlfriend in denial of her boyfriend's criminal behavior."

The anger in her voice stunned him into near silence. "I'm sorry," was all he could manage.

"Sorry doesn't cut it, Detective. You and your boss were so hell-bent on closing your case, putting it into the solved column, that you didn't want to hear the truth. You had your man. All the better, a black man. Mitch Beaulieu was dead, and his suicide was as good as a confession. Now you come in here and think I'm going to speak with you?"

Sonya Jordan had the reputation as a fierce defender of her clients and as a brilliant but difficult lawyer. Alves had to get through to her. "I lost someone, too. One of the victims, Robyn Stokes. My wife Marcy and I grew up with her."

Sonya Jordan looked away for a moment. "Marisela Alves is your wife?"

Alves nodded. "How do you know Marcy?"

"I represented Richard Zardino in his appeals. He and I make the rounds of the area colleges and law schools, letting students know about the injustices inherent in our criminal justice system. I speak with her classes at UMass Boston every semester. I didn't know she was married to a cop."

Alves smarted at the pejorative word. *Cop.* "Opposites attract." Alves smiled.

Sonya Jordan didn't. "What do you want from me?"

Alves knew what he had to say. And he knew that once he said the words out loud, they could never be taken back. No matter what the collateral damage. "I have to ask you to keep this conversation confidential, Ms. Jordan. At least for now. I think I might have been wrong about Mitch."

PART THREE

· · · · · · · · ·

Death ain't nuthin

but a heartbeat away

—COOLIO, "Gangsta's Paradise"

CHAPTER 71

It was not overly efficient, but it was the best Connie could manage with his work schedule. A couple weeks ago, after he'd wrestled Zardino's yearbook away from the prim little headmaster, he'd splurged and gone to Santarpio's for pizza and a side of hot Italian sausage and peppers for lunch. While he was sitting there in one of the vintage 1950s booths in the dim shop that offered the best pizza in Boston, the idea struck. How close he was to Richard Zardino's residence. He could easily park somewhere near the house and look for something. He wasn't sure what, but he was pretty sure he'd know it when he saw it. Riding around with Greene and Ahearn and hanging around with Mooney and Alves had prepared him for the drag of a stakeout—not the take-a-bite-of-your-sandwich-and-there-comes-your-target-right-on-cue of television show stakeouts.

Since that day, any time Connie finished up early in court, he told his secretary that he had a meeting or that he was taking a long lunch. Minus the thirty-minutes-total drive time to Eastie and back, that gave him almost an hour and a half to watch Zardino's house.

He used his early mornings and free evenings to sit behind the heavily tinted windows of the office ride. He was more than worried about his diet. Short on time, he was eating at every takeout place on the other side of the Mystic River—Spinelli's, The Italian Kitchen, Katz's Bagels in

Chelsea. But his healthy diet would have to take the hit. Mooney and Alves had spent the last couple weeks chasing down leads and getting nowhere.

It was early in the morning, over a plain bagel and a quart of skim milk, that he saw her. Small, dark-haired. She was coming out of the bungalow directly across from Zardino's old colonial, turning to be sure the door behind her was locked. She adjusted the strap of her pocketbook and tossed her hair back over her shoulder. The early light touched her face. Small, heart-shaped. A potential dream girl.

By the time she reached the sidewalk, she had her keys in her hand. She opened the door of a pale gold Honda Civic. Connie jotted down the plate number, and glancing over his shoulder as he pulled out of his spot to follow her, he noted the street number next to the mailbox.

He almost lost her in Maverick Square and at the toll booths at the Sumner Tunnel, but fortunately she was a conservative driver. It was a tough merge onto Storrow Drive, but he kept focused on the gold Honda.

She pulled into a small, private lot on Newbury Street. Connie pulled over into a loading zone and watched as the young woman crossed the street. She used her keys and entered *Natalie's*. Once he got out onto the street, he could see the shop window was filled with women's clothing and accessories. He rapped on the glass door and waited.

He watched as the young woman stepped out from a rear office, waving her hands and pointing to the store hours stenciled on the door. She was wearing a sleeveless black dress cut just above the knee.

Connie held his badge up to the glass. "I need to speak with you," he called in.

She stepped back into her office and emerged a moment later with a big sweater. Like a woman coming out of the ocean, wrapping herself in a towel to walk in front of a man, this young woman was modest, cautious. The black dress was for the benefit of the female shoppers, to show them how good they could look if they bought something from the shop. For talking to a strange man, the bulky sweater was good.

She came to the door but didn't open it. "Can I see your ID again?" she said, holding her sweater closed protectively with one hand.

It was good to see that she was careful. He reached into his left breast pocket and showed her his badge again, then flipped it open to show his credentials.

"Why does the DA's office want to speak with me, Mr. . . . Darget, is it?"

"If you would just let me in, ma'am, I won't take more than a few minutes of your time. I just need to ask you a few questions."

"I'm kind of busy right now." She looked more frightened than irritated.

"If you'd like, we can talk up at the grand jury." Connie removed a subpoena from the same breast pocket. "I was just trying to save you some trouble."

She unlocked the door and let him in. He followed her into the back office and closed the door behind her.

CHAPTER 72

What the hell was *he* doing here, that prosecutor, Darget, showing up at Natalie's boutique before business hours?

Sleep watched as she came to the door. Under the ratty sweater, she was wearing her A-line shift, dark as night. One of his favorites. Darget had flashed his badge and she opened the door.

Darget was not on a shopping excursion. He didn't wander into a shop on Newbury Street by coincidence. He was here on business. But it made no sense. How could Darget have found her? And, if he knew about her, what else did he know?

Sleep tried not to panic. If Darget knew about everything, he wouldn't need to speak with her. So maybe he was on a fishing expedition. But how could he have known what pond to fish?

And he was by himself. He was a prosecutor, not a cop. He had to be conducting his own, unofficial investigation. Otherwise, he would have a detective with him. Sleep looked down at the newspaper folded on his lap. The smaller of the headlines read PHANTOM GUN LINKED TO SIX GANG MURDERS. He had read the article earlier. Sergeant Detective Ray Figgs was asking for the public's help with the rash of shootings tied to one "community" gun—a .40 caliber that was apparently being passed around from one shooter to the next.

The main headline above the fold read COPYCAT KILLER? The authorities were trying to provoke him, get him to say or to do something to prove he was the killer. Tickle his ego. Force him into a mistake. The article was accompanied by a photo of Wayne Mooney. The same detective who had been on the killer's trail for ten years. The attempt to start a dialogue with the "Prom Night Killer" was amateurish. Transparent.

The only way Sleep would communicate with the police was with more bodies.

So if the police were pursuing this copycat angle to get the killer to talk, what the hell was Darget doing on Newbury Street talking to Natalie?

Conrad Darget, the ambitious prosecutor, was on his own.

And after Darget finished speaking with Natalie, he'd know too much.

CHAPTER 73

The back room was tiny, little more than a walk-in closet. There had to be another room, maybe in the basement, where they stocked their inventory. Natalie Fresco, as the young shop owner had introduced herself, sat behind a small metal desk with a computer monitor and little else on it. Connie took a seat across from her.

"How can I help you, Mr. Darget?"

"I'd like to speak with you about someone, one of your neighbors. Rich Zardino."

"What about him?"

Despite the fancy setting on Newbury Street, her dark good looks and the sweater still wrapped tightly around her, Connie could sense a toughness in her, a streetwise sense. Somehow a kid from the neighborhood had managed to start a business on tony Newbury. "How long have you known him?"

"Since we were kids. We moved in across the street from his family the summer before Richie and I started high school."

"How much do you know about him?"

"What do you mean? He's a neighbor. People in the neighborhood say hi to each other. He's a quiet guy. Lost both his parents. Lives alone in the family house."

"Sounds like a normal guy."

She studied his face. Assessing him. Their situation. "As normal as you could be, considering all he's been through."

"What's not normal about him?"

She must have decided that what she knew wasn't worth hiding from him. "When we were younger, he used to follow me everywhere." She was quiet for a moment, maybe thinking about how she was talking to an authority. She quickly added, "He never did anything to hurt me, you know. He was just always . . . there."

"When was this?"

"A long time ago. It didn't start that way. When we first met we were pretty close friends. You might even say we went out with each other. But at that age, all that meant was we used to hang around and talk and hold hands. Then I told him that I just wanted to be friends. I told him that my parents didn't like me dating him."

"Was he okay with that?"

"He seemed all right at first." She thought for a second. "But looking back on it, he probably figured he could work his way back to being my boyfriend. You know, hang around long enough and you notice that you're in love with your best friend."

"Did he ever figure out that you didn't want to date him?"

"I don't know. It was hard to get away from him. He lived across the street, you know. I didn't mind him being there at first, but it got to be a drag. It was hard to date other boys with him following us around."

"How long did that last?"

"Until I went away to college. Then it got worse. In the spring of our senior year at Eastie High, his dad died. He was supposedly murdered during a botched robbery. But everyone knew it was a mob hit. Word on the street was his dad owed the wrong people money and couldn't or wouldn't pay. They killed him to send a message. Rich flipped out. He was running around saying that he was going to get revenge. There was talk that he was going to get himself killed."

Death of a parent. No, worse: *murder* of a parent. That had to be a major stressor in Zardino's life.

"I figured I'd go away and he'd get over me. The summer after my freshman year, I was living in the South End. I started working here as a salesperson. I thought being out of the old neighborhood would make a difference. But things got creepy. He got a job across the street." She pointed toward the front of the store.

Connie did a quick calculation. The store across the street was a block away from the Sheraton—where Kelly Adams and Eric Flowers were last seen alive coming from their prom. From the hotel, you could walk down Boylston, cut across Mass Ave., past Little Stevie's Pizza, and you're in the Fens. Where Adams and Flowers were found.

"He was looking in the window at me, following me at lunchtime. . . . I was scared, fed up. I went over and called him out in front of his boss. Told him to leave me alone. I think he got fired because of it."

Major stressors number two and three, Connie thought. Dream girl and job gone.

"My mother told me he'd been taking classes at UMass Boston. I was happy for him. Then she called that September and told me he'd been charged with murder. He was tried, convicted, and gone from the neighborhood."

"Have you seen him since he got out of jail?"

"Now and then. He seems to have gotten over me. When he first got out, I was living in the South End. I had an apartment with some friends. Then my dad passed away and I moved back in with my mother, to help her out. She's getting older. So, as fate would have it, I'm back living in the neighborhood."

Fate had brought them back together. Connie couldn't help thinking of the fortune, DEPART NOT FROM THE PATH WHICH FATE HAS YOU ASSIGNED. "So you were both back home taking care of your mothers?"

"Until his mother passed away over the summer. I felt bad for him. She was all he had. She was the only one who visited him in jail, who believed he was innocent. She was his whole life."

Another stressor, at the same time fate brought his true love back to him. "How did he handle losing her?"

"He seemed to take it okay. He has some odd ideas about the gods and fate. He believes that everything in nature is in a constant flow. In death there is life. He talked about this symbol, like two polliwogs, one black, one white. Yin and Yang?"

CHAPTER 74

Sleep found a better parking spot on Newbury, down the street from *Natalie's*. He wasn't sure what car Darget was driving, he'd only seen him walking up the street, away from the Common. Had Darget even driven? But it was worth a shot. He would wait for him to come out of the shop, and if Darget walked in his direction, that would be a sign.

Darget had been in the store for quite a while. Not good, but there was no need to panic. If Darget came in his direction, he would get out of the van and make his move. He knew Darget would be leery of him, so he would have to act quickly. Catch him off guard. Hope no one was walking by. Because that's all it would take: one thing not going right. He didn't like doing things like this, not working out every detail beforehand, working on a crowded street in daylight. He had to get Darget close enough to the van and then pull out the gun. Again, without witnesses. Get him into the back of the van. But once the van door closed with its soundproof walls, Conrad Darget would no longer be a threat.

Darget stepped out of the door. He stood on the sidewalk and surveyed the street in both directions.

Sleep pulled his Bruins cap down over his face and stepped out of the van. He moved to the back and opened the doors, pretending to adjust his tools inside. He could see Darget through the windshield as he turned in the van's direction. Sleep lifted two five-gallon buckets, one filled with joint compound and the other with his tools. Arranging them on the ground, he waited as Darget made his way down the sidewalk.

One car length away.

Sleep walked around the van doors and picked up the buckets. He put his head down and walked in Darget's direction. He could see Darget's feet. He picked up his pace.

"Yo, Sleepy!" someone shouted from behind him. "How ya doin,' brother?"

At the corner, waving, was some bum from the old neighborhood. Some loser in gold neck chains and white sneakers. Vinnie or Tony Something, maybe?

Darget stepped aside, and Sleep bumped around him, his tools jangling as he tried to keep his face down.

Sleep turned and looked up beyond the brim of his cap, trying to see just enough. But all he could see was Vinnie or Tony heading for him at a brisk clip, smiling, his hand out, ready to shake. And Conrad Darget, turning on his heels, smiling a little, walking away.

CHAPTER 75

I'm kind of busy right now," Alves said.

Alves hadn't heard from Connie in a while. And after his meeting with Sonya Jordan, Alves was hesitant about calling him. He had always trusted Connie, valued their friendship. But he needed to treat everyone—friends included—as a suspect. He'd spent a lot of time thinking about who might have known Mitch well enough to set him up. And Connie was at the top of that list. The first person he and Mooney had interviewed that day at the courthouse was Conrad Darget.

"Angel," Connie's voice brought him back. "I know who the Prom Night Killer is."

"Let's hear it."

"Don't sound so excited."

"I've got Mooney crawling up my ass, riding me twenty-four-seven to catch this nut. My wife and kids are living with my mother-in-law. I'm eating SpaghettiOs out of a can. Now I've got you moonlighting as a detective. Who's the killer, Connie?"

"Richard Zardino."

God. One of the mayor's precious Street Saviors. Alves thought back to his conversation with John Bland. *If you decide to frame somebody, you don't decide that day.* Alves's mind filled with images of Mitch Beaulieu—a poor guy with the unfortunate luck of befriending a killer. Would they now find obvious evidence leading them in Zardino's direction?

"Did you hear me? It's Rich Zardino."

Alves kept his voice level. "You want to pin eight more murders on Zardino? He's one of the mayor's Street Saviors. Poster child for the wrongly convicted. You want me to lose my job, Connie?"

"You're not *pinning* anything on him."

"You and Greene and Ahearn had a run-in with him. Is that when you got this idea to look into him as a suspect?"

"You think I'm saying this because Jackie Ahearn had an argument with him?"

"Isn't it? What made you look at him?"

"I saw him drive by the scene that night on Peter's Hill."

A wave of anger washed over Alves. "And you forgot to tell me this until now."

Silence on the other end of the line.

"If it makes you feel better, we'll look into him," Alves said.

"I've already looked into him. I've built a rock solid case against him. He knows I'm onto him. He tried to come after me this morning on Newbury Street."

"Connie, you've got to back off and leave the homicide investigations to the homicide detectives. Otherwise Mooney's going to talk to the DA about you."

"Screw you, Angel. I hand you a killer and you patronize me. When he kills again . . ." Before he finished his thought, Connie cut off the call and the line went quiet.

CHAPTER 76

Connie held onto the seats in front of him as Greene slammed to a stop. Greene could never ease up on the gas and glide to a stop. It was all jerky movements with him. Stop, go, stop, go. But Connie had other problems on his mind. He couldn't get the conversation with Alves out of his head. How could Alves think he was setting up Richard Zardino? All he had to do was look at the evidence.

To their left was a car already stopped at the light. A hoopty—a dull silver older model Toyota Tercel. The driver tried to look straight ahead, both hands on the wheel. He sat rigidly, obviously avoiding looking over at them. He had to know they were police. It didn't matter that Greene and Ahearn rode in an unmarked cruiser; it was obvious who they were. Especially when Connie was with them. Three white guys in polo shirts riding around in a beat-up Crown Vic. It didn't take a rocket scientist to figure it out.

"Greenie," Connie said, "I can't be sure from this angle, but isn't that Stutter Simpson?" Their main suspect in the Jesse Wilcox shooting. Connie felt a rush. He had been looking to talk with Stutter since Wilcox turned up dead. No one had seen him in a couple months. Word was that he'd left the state. Simpson had plenty of enemies, but none bigger than Wilcox. A couple years earlier, Simpson had been shot. Connie knew that Wilcox was the shooter, but Simpson wouldn't give him up. Said he could handle his own business. It was a matter of time before they killed each other.

Greene kept his head straight.

Ahearn turned slowly, using Greene as a blocker. "You could be right."

Greene tilted his head to get a sidelong look. "Looks like him. Hard to tell with the 'fro. Last time I saw him he had corn rows."

When the light changed, Greene waited for the car to move, staying a few lengths back as they drove down Dudley Street.

"Bravo eight-o-two. Can I get a check on a silver Toyota Tercel, Mass reg seven-two-zero Delta-Michael-Zebra," Ahearn said into the radio.

Greene was going to follow the car until the driver made a mistake. The car was going exactly thirty-five miles an hour, the speed limit. Nobody drove the speed limit except senior citizens and people who knew they were being followed. The driver was riding the brakes. He had to be nervous. It was easy to commit a chapter 90 moving violation.

The radio crackled. "Bravo eight-o-two. That Tercel comes back to Shirley Simpson on Humboldt."

The car came to a complete stop for a red light at Blue Hill Ave., then the driver turned right.

"I got him, no turn signal." Greene activated his lights and siren, but the car didn't stop. It moved at a steady thirty-five till they came to the light at Quincy Street, where they both stopped behind a line of cars. Greene pulled in tight, trying to box him in. "Jackie, let's go get this clown."

As the detectives stepped out of the cruiser, Stutter made his move. He gunned it and crossed the double yellows, fishtailing around the line of traffic. Then, as the light turned green, he banged a right around the other cars.

The detectives scrambled back into the car. Stutter had a big lead. Connie slammed back in the seat as Greene put his foot to the floor.

"You still see him, Jackie?" Greene asked.

"I've got him. He's still on Quincy, but we'd better pick it up."

Connie was pinned back in his seat. He was going to have whiplash by the end of the ride. A glimpse of the speedometer and he could see they were doing close to eighty. Ahearn radioed their position calmly, as if they were in a slow speed pursuit. "Bravo eight-o-two. We're following that Tercel. Westbound on Quincy toward Warren. Could we get a couple of marked units to head him off?" If the duty supervisor knew they were driving through neighborhoods at eighty miles an hour, he would call off the chase.

"We can't let him get away," Connie said. "He's a ghost."

"Take it easy back there," Greene said. "I'll get him. He's driving a Tercel." If Greene was pissed that he let the guy make that move at the light, he wasn't showing it.

Greene was gaining ground as they came up on Warren Street. The car flew into the busy intersection and almost made it through unscathed. But he clipped the curb trying to avoid another car. After that, the car slowed down. He had some kind of damage. Halfway down Townsend, he bailed out of the car.

Connie got a better look at him as he ran across the street and into a yard. It was Stutter Simpson, and he was about to get caught. Mark Greene wasn't just a crazy driver. He was one of the fastest guys in the department. Stutter didn't have a chance.

"Connie, you stay here and wait for backup," Greene shouted as he sprang from the car.

Ahearn followed behind him, shouting into his radio. They were in pursuit of a possible murder suspect.

Connie got out of the car and walked toward the Tercel. The motor was running, the driver's door gaping open. The lights from Boston Latin Academy flooded the street, casting the small car in a dull silver haze. He pulled on a pair of latex gloves, took out his Mag, and leaned into the car to check the backseat and under the front seats. He switched off the ignition.

Then he heard the shot.

There would be plenty of backup on scene in a matter of seconds.

CHAPTER 77

Figgs was finishing up his walk on the treadmill at Headquarters when he saw the screen on his BlackBerry lighting up. He had turned off the ringer when he started his workout. It felt good to be up early, exercising. Full of energy. It had been a long time. The sun hadn't even been up for an hour and Figgs was ready. He picked up the phone and checked the screen. He could tell from the 8-7-2 that it was someone from the DA's office. Not sure who.

"Ray Figgs, Homicide."

"Sergeant Figgs. This is Conrad Darget. Angel Alves told me you've been assigned the Jesse Wilcox homicide."

Figgs said nothing. He didn't like prosecutors getting involved in his investigations. He would work the case, solve it if possible, *then* hand it over to the prosecutor. For now it was his case, not Conrad Darget's.

"Our main suspect has always been Stutter Simpson," Darget said. "We ran into him last night. Tried to take off on us but Mark Greene caught him."

Figgs stiffened. Punk ADA. "Why didn't you call me last night?"

"No reason to bother you. He lawyered up pretty quick," Darget said.

"I'm the one that should have been questioning him. He should have been lawyering up with me."

Darget either didn't care about or didn't notice the anger in his voice.

"We found a gun in his car. Under the driver's seat. A .40 cal. Glock, obliterated serial number. I'm wondering if it's the stash gun that's getting passed around. Same gun used to kill Jesse Wilcox."

Figgs didn't respond and the prosecutor continued. "I'm on my way in to see Sergeant Stone. Hoping he can give us a quick match this morning. Help me get Stutter held on a high bail. Stone's the best," the prosecutor rambled on. "Had a case with him before he made sergeant. Taught me all about the IBIS system and how it's changed the way they match ballistics. In the old days they only made matches if a detective had a hunch about a gun and had ballistics check it out. Now they enter everything into the system and it gives them possible matches."

"I know all that." The prosecutor was wasting his time. "Now you're not only a detective, you're a ballistics expert."

Darget ignored him. "The flaws in the database, Detective Figgs, are that it only tracks guns recovered since '91 and can only track crime guns, otherwise the system would overload. So this gun was either lawfully purchased or it was a crime gun recovered before '91, maybe entered into evidence in a trial, stored away in some clerk's office in case of appeals. Somehow the gun ends up in the wrong person's hands."

"You've got it all figured out, Mr. Darget." Figgs was tired of hotshots riding on the backs of others to get promoted. "You trying to make a name for yourself?"

"Excuse me? I'm trying to solve shootings. Take bad guys off the street."

The prosecutor was sounding defensive. "Why don't you leave the case solving to the detectives, Mr. Darget. Save your heroics for the courtroom. Either that, or take the police exam, get through the academy, and work your way up through the ranks like the rest of us."

"I'm sorry." Darget sounded angry now. "Did I hurt your feelings by solving your case?"

"You didn't solve anything, son. If you were smart enough to see it, you'd realize that even if it *is* the .40 we've been looking for, it doesn't mean Stutter Simpson shot anyone. I know Simpson. I've spoken to him about this case."

"When?"

"That doesn't concern you."

"Everything about this case concerns me."

"Let's just say I spoke with Simpson, and I'm comfortable in saying I don't think he had anything to do with Wilcox's death."

"Maybe you know him too well. Maybe you're too close to him, Detective. Maybe you need to take yourself off the case."

"Who the f—"

"Listen, Sarge. I'm going to see Stone this morning. I'm not concerned about the other shootings. But if he tells me we have a match to the Jesse Wilcox homicide, I'm setting up a meeting with my supervisors to get their approval to indict Simpson for murder. If you've got an issue with that, then that's your problem." The line went dead.

That was the end of his workout. Quick shower and Figgs could get to Stone's office down the hall before the prosecutor found a parking spot out on Tremont Street.

CHAPTER 78

Alves carefully angled the sedan toward the man standing in the belly of the ferry. It was the middle of the week, off-season, otherwise there would have been no room for the car. Once the staff knew he was travel-ing on official police business, they'd waved him on. He gave a few of the crew his business card. Told them to give him a call if they ever needed anything in the city. That usually meant taking care of an arrest for dis-orderly at Fenway or the Garden. No big deal.

Alves parked next to a Coke truck, a reminder that all supplies had to be ferried over, especially refreshing beverages. The steel steps led him from the freight deck to the main passenger cabin. It was a sunny day, warm for early October. He made his way outside. He looked out at the Woods Hole Oceanographic Institute. He continued around the perimeter of the ferry, taking in the picturesque harbor, the Elizabeth Islands to the southwest and Martha's Vineyard to the southeast.

The Vineyard was his destination. Alves had had to lie to Mooney about where he was. He'd said that Marcy's mom was having medical is-sues, that he had to help with a doctor's appointment. He'd promised to be back by early afternoon and that he'd stay as late as Mooney wanted. Alves couldn't tell him that he was having doubts about Mitch Beaulieu being a killer, that he was doing a little investigation on the side to clear up a few things.

As he leaned on the rail, he thought about his conversation with Sonya Jordan. Now he understood why she was considered one of the top defense lawyers in Boston. She had reiterated many of the points made by FBI Agent Bland, but hammered them home with her personal knowledge of Mitch Beaulieu.

"I've seen Mitch's so-called secret room," she had said, her eyes blazing with intensity. "It wasn't a secret to me. He probably didn't want anyone teasing him about it. That's why I was so angry when I learned that his friends from the office made it sound like he had this secret room. Some shrine to the murder victims."

"You have to admit it looked suspicious," Alves had said.

"Suspicious of what? A man who lost his father to suicide, the only person in his life." Exactly what Bland had said. "He was all alone in this world. That room was the only place he could go to feel like he was with his dad. He wasn't homicidal, Detective. He wanted to be with his father. And I was too self-absorbed to see that he'd do anything to be reunited with him. I shouldn't have left the way I did." Alves could see the guilt she felt in her eyes.

He'd spent the rest of his time with her listening to stories about Mitch. The raw emotion that she showed had worked to convince Alves that it was at least worth digging a little deeper into Mitch's suicide and the accusations against him.

The ship's whistle blew. It was loud, nearly causing him to jump. He turned and shot a look up at the pilothouse. He couldn't see anything through the glare on the glass, but he assumed they were laughing at the folks who had been surprised by the shrill blast.

He felt the chill in the air as soon as the ferry began moving forward. But it was a good feeling, better than being trapped inside with chatty tourists. He had his badge and his gun on his belt—guaranteed conversation pieces. If he went inside, someone was sure to corner him and irritate him with bad policeman stories. It was windy. He walked to the bow of the ship, where he stood alone at the rail, looking out toward Gay Head, a deep wall of cliffs, almost like the island had been cut away from the mainland.

Alves had always loved the ocean. He imagined himself on a tiny ship sailing across Vineyard Sound. They were traveling the exact course he had mapped out in his head. Off in the distance he could see Vineyard Haven as it grew. It was nice to get away from the investigation, if only for a few hours. But then he wasn't really getting away. He was walking himself back into another investigation, one that had caused him pain, an investigation that he thought was behind him.

He breathed in the air, salty and clean. It was different from the summer smells, the crowds of people. He closed his eyes, took some deep breaths. His muscles started to loosen, the tension in his neck easing.

He was startled by the whistle. This time he might have jumped. He wasn't sure, because he had almost fallen asleep. He didn't turn toward the pilothouse. His focus was on the buildings in town as the ferry moved into the harbor.

Soon he would be talking with the one person who really knew Conrad Darget. The one person who might have some insight into his mind and his private thoughts. Today he might get some answers.

That's what scared him more than anything.

CHAPTER 79

Figgs stepped into Grady's Barber Shop. There was one customer, sitting and chatting with Grady.

"Time to go, Pops," Figgs said, holding the door open.

The customer got up, put his Kangol on his head, and left. No questions asked.

Figgs locked the door behind him, put up the closed sign and pulled the shade down over the door window. "Let's talk, Grady."

"'Bout what?"

"Stutter got locked up last night. I just had a nice sit down with him. Told me how everything went down. I'm going to ask you some of the same questions. You lie to me even once, Grady, and I'll have the state licensing board come in here and shut you down permanently." Figgs knew it was an idle threat. There were only a couple of inspectors in the whole state. And even if they did shut him down, Grady would be back in business in a day or so, cutting hair in the boiler room of his apartment building. By appointment only.

The old man looked down at the floor, covered with clots of hair, despite the fact that actual haircuts seemed to be a rare occurrence in the shop.

Figgs's phone vibrated on his hip. He looked at the screen: Reggie

Stone. He held up a finger to Grady. "One second. Hi, Reg. What have you got?"

"Ray, I test fired the .40. It's definitely the gun we've been looking for. I've matched it to the casings and projectiles from about half the cases so far."

"Prints?"

"Nothing. I took the gun apart before fuming it. No ridge detail on anything, the receiver, the slide, the barrel, not even the magazine or the ammunition."

"Wiped clean?"

"Seems that way."

"That's what I expected. Thanks, Reg." Figgs hung up and turned his attention back to the barber. "Why did you let Stutter Simpson stay here?"

"His mom is an old friend. Told me her son was in trouble, afraid to be seen anywheres. I let him crash till things cooled down."

"You ever see him walking around with a big gun, .40 caliber?"

"I told him he could stay here, no guns. I don't want no drama coming down on me. Told me with his record if he got popped with a heater, he'd be going federally."

"Where'd he go last night?"

"Said he was going over to see his mom, then to visit his grandmother in the hospital. She's been having panic attacks since Junior got killed. Said he wanted to let her see he was okay."

"Did he take a gun with him?"

"Like I said, I ain't seen no guns."

The old man was old school all the way. No lying to the authorities. Grady was telling the same story Stutter Simpson had. Figgs pulled the ring on the shade and let it snap, unlocked the door, and stepped into the bright October sun.

CHAPTER 80

The Dukes County Courthouse was situated next to the Old Whaling Church and across the street from the so-called Amity Town Hall of *Jaws* fame. One of the older buildings in Edgartown, built in the early 1800s, the courthouse was brick with two white pillars and four granite steps. It was not hectic like South Bay. Angel Alves sensed a laid-back attitude in everyone from the lawyers and the cops to the defendants.

A short distance from the courthouse was the wharf and, not more than five hundred feet of water away, Chappaquiddick Island. He and Marcy had gone over once when they were dating. They took their bicycle over on the raft, barely big enough to carry a few cars and some passengers with bikes. They rode to the Chappaquiddick Dike Bridge. Looking over the side of the bridge, Alves saw that the water below was little more than a glorified stream.

It was after eight thirty when Alves made his way up the stairs of the courthouse. He flashed his badge to the blue shirts manning the tight space adapted to accommodate the metal detector, and they waved him through. The District Attorney's office was on the second floor. The tiny single room, which he'd heard used to be the foyer of the ladies' room in grander times, now served as Andi Norton's office.

She was on the telephone. She shot him a smile. "Someone just came into my office," she said. "I have to go. Talk to you later."

She hung up the phone and stood to greet Alves with a hug. "It's nice to see you, Angel."

"What a great courthouse," Alves said. "Easy commute, old building, stress-free environment. I could get to like this place. And I start my day with a hug from a gorgeous redhead."

"Not everyone gets the hug. Just the cute Homicide detectives from Boston. Otherwise, my husband would get jealous. That was Will on the phone. Have a seat."

"He's smart, keeping an eye on you," Alves winked.

"So what are you doing here on the Island?" she asked. She pointed to his gun and badge. "It doesn't look like you're down here on vacation. You looking for a witness?"

"You could say that."

"If you had called ahead, I could have had someone from the P.D. or the Sheriff's Department help you find him."

"I know where the witness is."

"I bet I know him if he's involved with a murder."

"I came here to see you, Andi."

The young woman seemed to shrink back in her chair. "What about?"

"I need your word you won't tell anyone we spoke. Not even that jealous husband of yours."

"I don't know if I can do that. Am I in any trouble?"

"No. I promise. I just need information. And I don't want anyone to find out I was here. Not Wayne Mooney. Not Connie."

"Why would I talk to Connie?"

"I thought maybe you might still be friends."

"We're not. Not my choice, although I hate to admit it."

"I know this is awkward, and I'm sorry. I need to ask you about him."

She instantly went from good-buddy Andi to lawyer full of piss and vinegar, as his mother used to say. "What's going on? Angel, is Connie in trouble?"

"Andi, you know I can't talk about an investigation. I need to ask you some questions and I need your honest answers."

She picked up on his formality and the seriousness of his tone. She knew enough about interviewing witnesses. She nodded.

"What happened between you two?"

"I can honestly say I don't know. I thought things were going well. I knew from the beginning that he wasn't interested in me for just one thing, if you know what I mean."

Interesting, considering that she was quite a good-looking woman.

"Connie took an interest in my career. I wouldn't be the lawyer I am without his help. He gave me my first trial, taught me how to work up a case and prep for trial. He was an amazing teacher. And a real gentleman. He never tried to do more than kiss me. He was affectionate, but he never forced the issue. Because of Rachel."

He wanted to ask about her young daughter. Tell Andi how he wished he and Marcy and the twins could come over on the ferry, spend the day with Andi and Will on South Beach, drive over to Oak Bluffs and let the kids ride the old carousel and reach for that one brass ring.

"By the way, Rachel's doing great. She loves the ocean, walking on the beach, collecting shells. Moving here was the best thing I could have done for both of us."

He nodded, but it still seemed odd to him. Why didn't their relationship, which ran its course over a period of almost a year, never move beyond the affectionate peck stage? "If everything was going so well, why'd you break up?"

She thought for a second. "I don't know. Maybe it was the stress after Nick's disappearance and Mitch's suicide. At first, we helped each other out. It was hard to come to work without Nick and Mitch. Connie was almost in denial, trying to convince himself that Mitch couldn't have been a killer. Then he started getting a little religious on me, talking about how he knew Mitch's victims were in a better place."

Alves had never known Connie to be religious. "How was he with Rachel?"

"Great. He tried not to act like a father toward her." Angel must have had a look, because she quickly added, "That's a good thing. The worst is a guy who tries to insinuate himself into a child's life to get to the mother. Every single mother has dated plenty of those guys."

That made sense. "When did things start to fall apart?"

"After law school, I focused my attention on studying for the bar exam. Connie and I talked on the phone, but only saw each other once a week, on the weekend. My plan was to wait until after the exam and then maybe. . . ." She looked at him, almost shyly, and he was walloped by *her*— her looks, yes, but beyond that, her intensity. "Angel, I did love him. I didn't want to make him wait too long."

"You're doing great, Andi. You've got to tell me anything you think might help me understand him. So you never . . ."

"No. I hope I'm not telling you more than you want to hear."

"You know yourself, sometimes it's the smallest detail that makes everything fall into place."

She smiled. "Don't worry, Angel, it doesn't get any more graphic than that. After I took the bar exam, I started interning in the DA's office again. Everything was good between Connie and me. I tried to get him to go away on a romantic weekend—a bed-and-breakfast in New Hampshire—one of those couples deals with the champagne and spa treatment. He kept finding excuses. Then I tried to get him alone for a romantic dinner at my condo—Rachel tucked away at my parents. He showed up. But he was expecting me *and* Rachel. When it dawned on him that we were alone, that I had ulterior motives, he kind of freaked out."

Alves recognized that spark of alertness he felt every time an interview veered unexpectedly into pay dirt. "What did he do?"

"He said I shouldn't have misled him. He said that once we have intercourse, it shifts the power of a relationship, upsets the balance. He said he was only thinking of Rachel, making it sound like I was a bad mother. He left my apartment and never came back. After that, we were never alone, not even at work. When the summer ended, I had to make money. I couldn't intern anymore. I had sent out résumés to other prosecutors' offices around the state. I was lucky to end up in Falmouth District Court. My parents own a house in Falmouth, so I stayed there. When the job opened up on the Island, Rachel and I moved out here."

"It's a nice life. Are you happy?"

"I am. Will is a wonderful guy. He's a great father to Rachel."

"That's all that matters."

"Angel, I've never figured Connie out. I don't think he's gay, and I'm not buying that line about him thinking of Rachel. If that were the case, he never would have walked out of her life that night. That's what bothers me most. I'm a grown woman, and I've had my dealings with worthless men. But he can go to hell if he thinks I'm going to let him hurt my daughter."

"Have you ever been over his house?" Alves asked.

"That's another thing he was weird about. I dated him for a year and I never set foot in that house. He always had excuses, that he was plastering or painting, that the house was a mess, that he didn't want me to see it until it was done."

Angel could see that rehashing her relationship with Connie was upsetting her. "Things don't make a lot of sense right now, Andi. Soon as I know anything for sure, I'll tell you what I can. Thanks for seeing me. If I think of anything else, can I call you?"

"Sure." She smiled, a little worn and weary after their conversation. "And I know, you and I never had this conversation."

"You're a doll, Andi." He stood and hugged her. "Give Rachel a kiss from me."

CHAPTER 81

Earlier, Sleep had made the mistake of not following Darget from his home in Hyde Park. Instead, Sleep had been watching the DA's office in Government Center from across the street on one of the benches in front of the JFK Building.

He played a game while he was waiting. First he'd find a number—say, the number of pigeons that waddled past him in five minutes. With that number, he'd count the males—old and young—who walked by his bench. When he hit the right number, that one was his brother for the day.

Sleep was good at the game. He'd been playing it since he was a kid, sitting by himself at the attic window, watching the passersby on the sidewalk below. First he imagined a name—Gussy, Tony, Billy—and then a life for his new brother. Sometimes it was going to school—and a good one, like Boston University or Harvard even. Sometimes it was a great job and co-workers, a family waiting for him back on their family's street. Little nieces and nephews Sleep could play with and babysit for.

He liked the game. It always calmed him down, made his mind stop jumping ahead to questions and back to bad times. And when the game didn't work for him, he always had Brother Death. His almost-twin, separated when their father had to be ferried across the River Styx to the underworld. Sleep couldn't go with his father. He'd never make it back to the living. But Brother Death, he could wade back across the river if he wanted to.

Now Sleep was tired with the game. There had been no sign of Darget.

Yesterday, Newbury Street had been a debacle. Sleep didn't know if Darget had recognized him on the street or not. If he did, that meant that Sleep wouldn't be able to get close enough. In fact, he couldn't use the van anymore. Darget had seen it and would recognize it immediately. So he had rented a minivan. An electric blue monstrosity with tinted windows and sliding doors on each side, the kind that the gang kids in the city used for their missions. What he needed to do now was a quick drive-by. Catch Darget off guard and it would be done. Make it look like a gang hit.

A little after nine o'clock, Darget finally showed up. Late, for him, and he didn't look happy. Something was definitely wrong. The fact that Darget had talked to Natalie meant that Darget was on to him. After leaving Natalie's store, the next logical move for Darget would have been to tell his detective friends what Natalie had said about him. If the detectives knew anything, Sleep would already be in custody. But they hadn't come for him. Not yet. Which meant that Darget hadn't told them anything. Yet. But why not?

CHAPTER 82

Figgs turned onto Townsend Street and pulled over, left the motor running. The ID Unit had put a rush on the photos taken of the scene and the gun in Stutter Simpson's mother's car. They were ready by the time he finished talking with Grady at the barber shop. He placed the photos on his lap, resting them against the steering wheel as he examined each one. Big question: Where had Stutter's car stopped? In one photo, he saw a hydrant, and behind that, the trunk of a tree. Figgs found the hydrant easily and pulled up to that spot.

Something was nagging at him. It was too convenient, that gun found under Stutter Simpson's butt. A gun that Simpson had supposedly used months earlier. A gun that had been passed around from one street gang to the next, all over the city. Why would it end up back in Simpson's possession? Simpson had to know the gun had a body on it. So why would he keep it with him? Especially when he knew the police were looking for him.

Figgs stepped out of the car, surveying the neighborhood. Which houses had the best vantage point to observe the stop, the foot pursuit, the arrest, the recovery of the gun? The houses on Hazelwood Street. Figgs knocked on a few doors, the houses closest to Townsend, but mostly nobody answered. Those that did hadn't seen anything. He made his way across a small parking lot to the next group of houses when he thought of something. There was someone he could talk to who lived in the neighborhood. Sort of. Figgs just hoped the man was "home."

He walked across Townsend Street toward the Boston Latin Academy, one of Boston's exam schools. When Figgs was a kid, it was called the Girls' Latin and it was housed in Dorchester, not Roxbury. He turned right, heading toward Humboldt, then made his way through an empty park on a worn footpath that cut diagonally across the brown grass. He spotted the shopping cart, piled high with cans, at the other end of the park, near Humboldt.

"Hey, Figgsy," the man called out as he got closer.

The man was lying underneath a tree at the edge of the park, bundled in layers of coats, despite the unseasonably warm weather. His face was aged with drug and alcohol abuse.

"Hey there, Leo. How you been?" Figgs said.

"Doin' okay. What's a big Homicide detective doin' out here in the hood? Slummin'?"

"I'm looking into something. Leo. You didn't happen to be out here last night?"

"Might've been."

"You see a dude with a 'fro get pinched by a couple of cowboys?"

"More 'n a couple."

"What'd you see?"

"Heard them buzzing up the street. Toyota smashes into the curb and the kid bails. Big guy and little guy chase him down. Heard one cap. Figured the brother was toast. Then they bring him back."

"You heard gunshots?" Figgs turned back toward the street.

"One shot."

That wiseass prosecutor forgot to mention anything about shots being fired. There was no mention of it in the 1.1 either. That's because Simpson didn't shoot at Greene and Ahearn—they shot at him. And missed. They wouldn't mention anything about a police officer discharging his firearm in the official police report, a public record. Figgs would have to pull the form 26s to find out everything that had happened out here last night.

Figgs looked back toward Townsend Street. He remembered the telephone poles at the end of the street. He hit the speed dial on his Black-Berry. "Inchie, you at the House? Take a walk down to Operations for me. Tell them to pull all the footage the Shot Spotter might have picked up on the officer discharge last night near the corner of Warren and

Townsend. I'll be there soon." Figgs clipped the phone back on his belt and turned his attention back to Leo. "You said there were more than a couple of cowboys. How many were there?"

"Three. Third d-boy takes his time getting out of the backseat. Leans into the Toyota. Pokes around. Shuts it down. Then the cavalry shows up and I went about my business. I know when I'm not welcome."

"Thanks, Leo. You've been a big help."

"Don't mention it. Listen, Figgsy. You think you could . . . For old times' sake." Leo held his hand out to Figgs.

"Sure," Figgs said. He took a twenty out of his pocket and handed it to his old friend. For old times' sake.

CHAPTER 83

The ferry ride back to Woods Hole was cold, long, and lonesome. But it provided the isolation Alves needed before he hit the land and the reality of what he had to do next. Alves's feelings of loyalty toward Connie were pretty dinged up. The reinvestigation, the reopening of the case, all of it had to be just another case.

The things Andi Norton had told him created a picture of a man he didn't recognize, a man he never knew. It had been right there in front of him all along. In many ways, Conrad Darget fit Mooney's profile of the killer. He fit Special Agent John Bland's profile. But could Connie, a friend, a top prosecutor, be a killer? Could he frame a friend and stand by while that friend committed suicide? More than that, could he have whispered something to Mitch that encouraged him to jump from that court balcony? Connie would have known that Mitch's final act would show consciousness of guilt.

Maybe he and Mooney *had* been too quick wrapping up the case after Mitch's death.

All the victims were linked to the South Bay District Courthouse. All of them were linked to Darget's juries. That's why he and Mooney had interviewed Connie first. But, he remembered, that interview had been cut short, interrupted by the phone call from Eunice Curran. With the analysis of the hairs and condom recovered at the final crime scene. The "evidence" that led them to Mitch Beaulieu.

But evidence can be planted.

And what about Nick Costa's disappearance? The two had a contentious relationship at best. Had Connie's co-worker gotten too close, seen something Connie didn't want him to see? Nick Costa's body had never been found. None of the Blood Bath Killer's victims' bodies had ever been recovered. None of those souls ever laid to rest.

After his talk with Andi Norton, he had a good idea where those bodies were.

It's not inconceivable that a killer would change his MO. It's not likely, but it happens, especially with killers of high intelligence. Killers close to the investigation. Alves remembered a conversation he'd had with Connie about serial killers. Alves was telling him about one of his criminology classes, how one of three things happens to killers: they either repent, continue killing, or kill themselves.

Connie had argued, and Alves remembered his words, his intensity, that a killer can transform himself into something else. If a killer is locked into one MO, it has to end at some point. A smart detective will figure his pattern out. Organized. Unorganized. Both patterns that control most killers, but a smart killer? He can change. He has to. Because what's important is not the *how*, but the *why*.

The shore, the city of Boston itself—all of it seemed like another world. If Conrad Darget was the Blood Bath Killer, was it possible that he killed those couples ten years ago, as the Prom Night Killer? The murders *had* stopped around the time he went away to school in Arizona. Seven years later Darget shifted his MO and murdered as the Blood Bath Killer. He learned that by providing a suspect—Mitch Beaulieu—the case was closed, allowing him to shift his MO back again.

Now, as the Prom Night Killer, before the police close in, he reverts to what's worked in the past. Make Richard Zardino, a Street Savior, a man who had served time in prison, the goat.

CHAPTER 84

Figgs stepped off the elevator on the fourth floor of One Schroeder Plaza. He didn't make his way up here very often. Didn't usually have a need to see anyone in the command staff, or in operations.

Today was an exception. He had read through the 26s. Greene and Ahearn had written consistent, almost identical, reports. They'd spotted Stutter driving a car on Blue, followed him at speeds that weren't excessive, which was different from what Stutter had told him, chased Stutter on foot after he cracked up the Tercel, and caught him just after Ahearn's "accidental" firearm discharge.

Figgs wanted to ask the detectives some questions, but it was too late for that. The Commissioner's Firearm Discharge Team had arrived on scene within minutes of the shot being fired. They took the detectives' guns and did a quick briefing before the union rep showed up with the union lawyer. Greene and Ahearn were immediately taken to the hospital to be treated for stress-related injuries, standard operating procedure in the aftermath of a police shooting. Now Figgs couldn't speak with them without the lawyer being present.

There was only one lawyer he wanted to speak with right now. Darget hadn't written a report. He wasn't a member of the department, but he had given a statement to the patrol supervisor on scene. His story was consistent with the two detectives, only he didn't get involved in the foot pursuit. He laid back at the crash site until backup units arrived. Never saw what happened when the detectives followed Stutter through the yards. Only heard the shot and saw the detectives come out with the suspect unharmed and in custody a few seconds later. Darget would be worth talking to. When the time was right.

Figgs stepped through the double doors into Operations. He walked up the short set of stairs into the room where the Shot Spotter techs monitored the system. No sign of Inchie. Figgs angled his way around some tables with computer monitors and printers, toward the one human in the room, the tech with his eyes fixed on the three massive computer monitors—widescreen TVs, really—in front of him. "Sergeant Figgs, Homicide. Detective O'Neill talk to you about the shots fired last night at Quincy and Warren?"

"Officer discharge," the tech said, not looking away from the screens. "Didn't pick much up. They were in the backyards when the shot went off."

"That's okay. I want to see what was happening in the street. How's this thing work?" Figgs asked, looking at the LCDs.

"The Shot Spotter picks up the shot and an alarm sounds within four to seven seconds." The tech had obviously given this speech a few dozen times. "The system immediately pulls up a grid map, an aerial image of the surrounding streets, the whole neighborhood. Then it uses the sound sensors to triangulate and pinpoint the location of the shot. The closest cameras will zoom in on that location. I'll show you."

Figgs watched as he pulled up the aerial image of the familiar neighborhood he had visited that morning. Then the tech switched to the video footage. The camera shot a wide angle. It focused on the yards on the left side of the street, across the street from where Leo was resting, across the street from Stutter's cracked up car.

But there was the car on the far right of the screen. And Conrad Darget walking up to the car, doing something with his hands, looking into the car, leaning in on the driver's side. Exactly where the gun was located. Funny, Darget forgot to mention all that to the PS when he gave his statement. Must have slipped his mind.

CHAPTER 35

Luther sat on the steps of the old Victorian watching the sun set over Highland Park. The Crispus Attucks Youth Center was buzzing, a group of boys playing hoops in the driveway—skins versus the shirts, even in this cool weather—with a few girls cheering them on. Inside the Center, boys and girls were using the computers to do research for school papers or getting tutored by older kids.

Luther checked his watch. Richard Zardino should have been here by now. They had planned to go out tonight and meet with some of the potential clients they had been mentoring on the street, the ones who refused to come to the Youth Center. Luther and Zardino had to meet these kids on their own turf if they were going to get through to them. This was the part of the job that Luther loved, working with the kids everyone else had given up on.

This would be the second time Zardino had blown him off in the last week. What was wrong? Rich was acting different, preoccupied, and when Luther tried to talk to him, he was distant. When they did meet the kids, Zardino wasn't listening to what they had to say, and listening was the only way to gain their trust.

Luther saw a set of headlights turn the corner onto St. James from Warren and climb the hill. He stood and walked to the edge of the curb. This had to be Zardino.

But it wasn't.

It was a late model, dust-covered Ford Five Hundred. When it pulled next to the curb, he could see that it had blue lights in the grill and strobes mounted on the dash. *Jump Out Boys.* Detectives.

Ray Figgs eased himself out of the driver's seat. He didn't look like the same Ray Figgs he'd seen when George Wheeler's body had been discovered or on the night Junior Simpson was shot and killed. He looked more like the Ray Figgs who used to chase Luther and his boys around when they were younger, runnin' and gunnin,' before Luther found his calling. More color to his face, more meat on his bones.

"Good evening, Darius," Figgs said, extending his hand. "Or is it D-Lite? It's been a long time."

"It's Luther."

"We need to talk, Luther."

"I tried to talk to you the night Junior got straightened. Said you were too busy. Now you want to talk."

"Lot of violence in the city, lately."

"Always has been." Luther pointed to the hand-carved and painted sign hanging above the door of the Youth Center. "Crispus Attucks met a violent death. Took two in the chest. March 5th, 1770. Boston Massacre. Right outside the Old State House. Brothers have been dying violent deaths in the city ever since."

"I'm not talking back in the day. I'm talking about violence caused by a specific gun. The .40 caliber being passed around. Talked about it at the meeting a few weeks ago. Same meeting you and your partner were hiding out in the back of the room."

"Maybe you should talk to one of the cowboys you got working at the Youth Violence Strike Force."

"You know more about what's going on out in the streets than they do. What I want to know is how could one gun get passed around from one gang to the next, causing the deaths of Jesse Wilcox, George Wheeler, and Michael Rogers?"

Luther hesitated a moment before he answered the detective. "You forgot Junior Simpson. He got killed with a Four-o."

"Different .40, confirmed by ballistics."

"Word on the street is it was the same gun."

"Word on the street is wrong. The gun that killed Wilcox, Wheeler and Rogers ended up under the front seat of Stutter Simpson's car. How could that have happened?"

"It couldn't have. Doesn't make sense." Luther glanced over at the driveway. He didn't want the kids to see him standing there, talking to the detective, but it was better than talking to him in his car. "They were from different crews, not beefing with each other. Yet they end up shot by the same gun? Then the gun 'conveniently' ends up in the hands of the man who supposedly committed the Wilcox murder? All neat and clean for you."

"What do you know about Stutter?" Figgs asked.

The man seemed genuine. Like he was looking for answers, not just a boy to hang a rap on. "For one thing, he's old school. He'd use a revolver, not a semi. No casings, no evidence. Why would a seasoned kid like Stutter Simpson have a gun he knew had a body on it? Detective, he'd get rid of that gun, maybe cut it in pieces, spread it around the city. Not ride around like a fool sittin' on top of a gun."

When Ray Figgs shook his hand, Luther saw something new in the detective's eyes. He'd seen the look before, in kids who wanted to get out of the life. Kids who really wanted to change. It was the look of determination.

CHAPTER 86

The living room was dark. Connie opened a crack in the drapes and checked out the street. The fluorescent blue minivan parked at the corner didn't belong. It had been parked there at odd times over the last couple of days. It had to be Zardino.

It was irritating to have Zardino following him. It interfered with his schedule. He couldn't go for his run. A run would create an opportunity for Zardino to catch him alone on a quiet, dark street. He could handle Zardino, no problem, in a hand-to-hand situation. But Zardino liked to use a gun.

Connie couldn't give him any openings. Just one more day was all he needed. Then their roles would be reversed, the would-be-hunter becoming the hunted. Connie had done his homework, fine-tuned his moves. Everything was in place. Zardino would be back where he belonged.

Connie walked through the dark house, making his way to the basement stairs. He needed to go to his work area, sit in the dark, think things through a final time. The banister was cool and smooth under his hand. He could see the headlights of passing cars making swimming disks of light, moving across the room and ceiling. He thought he heard a car door slam.

Then the doorbell chimed.

CHAPTER 87

Alves moved to the side of the door after ringing the bell. This wasn't a social call, although he wanted Connie to think it was. He rang the bell a second time. He kept his left hand behind his back. Maybe Connie was out.

Another minute and the door opened. Connie was dressed in shorts and a T-shirt.

"Going for a run?" Alves asked.

"Not now."

Alves swung his left hand out from behind his back, revealing a six-pack of Miller High Life, and extended it toward Connie. "Peace offering."

"You didn't need to do that," Connie said.

"I felt bad about yesterday. I shouldn't have blown you off. It's the stress getting to me. And you know how Mooney is."

"Not a big deal. I shouldn't involve myself in your investigations. Just thought I could help with this one."

Alves took a step toward Connie and raised the beer a little higher. "You going to invite me in or are we going to talk through a screen door all night."

Connie hesitated, maybe a second too long, then said, "Sure, come on in. I was down the basement stretching. Lucky I heard the doorbell."

Connie turned on the living room lamp and they sat on the couch. The room had furniture and simple curtains but no framed pictures on the walls or knickknacks scattered around. It took a woman to decorate a house, make it look like a home. He tried not to think about his own house, decorated but empty without Marcy and the twins. Alves left the beer on the coffee table.

"I don't think I've ever been in here," Alves said. "The place looks great."

"Thanks."

"You do all this work yourself?"

"Everything. Plaster, paint, woodwork, floors."

"Nice job. How about the grand tour?"

Connie smiled. "I can do that, but then you'd know all my intimate secrets, and I'd have to kill you."

The comment, usually meant as a joke, unsettled Alves. Maybe he should have told Mooney he was coming here. "I already know your secrets," Alves said, trying to maintain a ribbing tone. "You eat giant bowls of oatmeal for breakfast among other disgusting culinary treats."

"That's nothing," Connie laughed. "Wait till you see what I have in the basement."

Instinctively, Alves patted the Glock on his hip. They headed down the hall toward the bedrooms. Everything neat and tidy. There were three bedrooms, only one of them had a bed and bureau. One of them was set up as a computer room and the other one looked like a small study, a quiet reading area with a comfortable, worn upholstered chair.

"You know, Marcy and I have been thinking of buying a ranch like this, but she's concerned they don't have enough storage space."

"I haven't had any trouble," Connie said, "but I don't have a wife and two kids. The attic's a small crawl space. I don't use it much, but I'm sure you could do something with it if you needed the space." Connie pulled a piece of window rope in the hallway and a set of stairs folded down. "Check it out for yourself."

Alves climbed the rough pine stairs carefully. Halfway up he realized he was in a pretty vulnerable position—his back to Connie. The single bulb on a pull chain lit the space, but there was nothing under the pitched roof but fiberglass insulation, a couple of small boxes and lots of dust.

Connie called from below, "I hate going up there. It feels like you're in a coffin, doesn't it?"

Was Connie joking or messing with his head? Connie had to know he wasn't there as a peace offering. But he was being so open about his house, showing Alves everything. And everything seemed so normal. Of course, there was still the basement. Alves started backward down the stairs. Looking between his legs and the rough pine stairs, he tried to locate Connie. He took the last couple steps in tandem.

The hall seemed dim after the glow of the bright bulb in the attic. The house was quiet. As he was moving instinctively into a back-to-the-wall position, he felt the sudden jerk of one arm being pinned behind him in an awkward position, his head twisted to the side. The pain in his shoulders and back was searing. Alves was immobilized.

He tried to pull away, tried not to panic. Just as suddenly the pressure eased and he was free.

Connie laughed. "Scared the crap out of you, didn't I?"

"You got me with that one," Alves said.

"Chin and Chicken. My favorite wrestling hold. Won a lot of matches that way."

"I'm sure you did." Alves rubbed his jaw, and shook his arms, trying to get the blood flowing.

After checking out Connie's power lifting gym in the attached garage, they started down to the basement.

"Nice setup," Alves said. Connie had the room arranged with a couch and a couple of recliners facing a big screen plasma TV. In the back corner was a bar with a large antique refrigerator. "How come you've never had me over here for a ballgame?"

"I just finished it up a few months ago. Been too busy to think about having anyone over."

"What's in the little safe?"

"Personal papers, my guns."

"Anything interesting?"

Connie hesitated, giving him a little smile. Then he knelt down and worked the combination. "I've got a .38, a .357, and my little two-shot derringer." He swung the door open, took out his .38, and handed it to Alves. It was a five shot S&W snubby. Just like his own, a Chief Special. Connie had even replaced the wooden grips with Pachmayr grips just as he had. "I taught you well," Alves said, admiring the revolver.

"I used to keep a .40 SIG Sauer upstairs in the closet. But it got stolen. That's why I got the safe."

"Did you file a stolen gun report?"

"I did. District detectives came out and dusted for prints. Nothing. They figured probably some neighborhood junkie."

Alves handed the gun back to Connie and moved through the basement, checking out the fridge, the recliners. He walked toward a room behind the television. There wasn't much light back there, but he could see that it was a laundry room—a massive enamel table along one wall, opposite a water heater and furnace. The table was covered with piles of dirty laundry and bottles of detergent. Marcy would have loved a big table like that for folding.

Maybe he was wrong about everything. He let his imagination get the better of him. If Connie was a master criminal, a mass murderer, Alves would have found some evidence in the house. So far, nothing. And Connie was more than willing to let him look around. There was only one other door, back by the bar. Alves had initially assumed it was the room with the furnace and water heater. But they were in the laundry room.

"What's in there?" he asked.

"Personal stuff."

Alves couldn't help but think of his talk with Sonya Jordan. How Mitch Beaulieu had a room set up like a shrine for his dead father. Alves paused. It was worth a shot. "Kind of like the personal stuff Mitch Beaulieu kept in a locked room."

Connie's face tensed. "That's not funny, Angel."

"Sorry. That didn't come out right,"

"If I show you, I really will have to kill you," Connie said.

The air between them seemed clearer, colder. "Show me anyway. I'll take the risk."

Connie took a key from above the doorframe and moved over to unlock the door. He stood aside for Alves. The light was off as Alves took a few steps into the room. First thing, Alves checked with his foot to be sure there was no plastic over the carpet. Was he walking himself into a trap? Did Connie still have the snubby in his hand?

Behind him, Connie switched on the light and stepped up close.

There was no mistaking what the room was. Alves took in every detail. Still he couldn't believe what he was seeing.

You could know a man for years and still never really know him.

CHAPTER 88

Mooney hung up the phone. Where the hell was Angel? He got up from his desk and walked the length of the Homicide Unit, looking in every cubicle. He knew Alves wasn't there, but he checked anyway. Back behind his desk, he tried calling his BlackBerry again. Straight into voicemail on the first ring. Again. He didn't bother to leave a message.

He threw on his jacket and took the keys off the desk. The two of them were going to sit on Jamaica Pond tonight. All night if they had to. They had hoped to catch the killer on his reconnaissance mission, prepping his next dump site. Now he would do it with or without Alves.

Alves had been useless all day, spending the morning at some bogus doctor's appointment and now disappearing for half the night. Not showing up for their stakeout. Not answering his cell.

Mooney had a coach in high school who used to say, "The only excuse good enough to miss football practice is when there's been a death in your family." Coach would hesitate just a beat, then add, "Your own."

Alves had better be dead and getting stuffed for his own funeral. Mooney knew that Alves going AWOL probably had something to do with his wife and kids. It was always the same story, Alves letting some family drama get in the way of being a topnotch Homicide detective.

But then, that didn't make sense either. If there'd been some family trauma drama, Alves would have called in, left a message for him. Even if he got distracted. Alves was reliable that way. Calling in *too much,* if anything. As Wayne Mooney took the flight of stairs to the first floor, the slightest hint of doubt and worry began to nag at him.

CHAPTER 89

Not a word to anyone," Connie warned Alves.

Alves was dumbfounded. Even with all the crazy thoughts he'd been having lately, his imagination hadn't come anywhere near the real thing. "Is this what I think it is?"

Connie nodded.

"You built a courtroom in your basement? It's the jury session at the South Bay courthouse. You've got the bench, the witness stand, and the jury box. But why?" When Connie didn't answer him, he asked again, "Why would you build a courtroom in your basement?"

"To practice for my trials," Connie explained, as though he were telling why he stretched before a workout. "How do you think I got so good at what I do? I used to practice in the living room or in front of a mirror. But it wasn't the same. I wanted it to be as realistic as possible. So this is what I came up with."

Angel was walking around the courtroom, running his hand along the rail in front of the jury box. Every detail was so realistic he could have been standing in an actual courtroom.

"It helps me visualize where the judge and the witnesses will be. I can pretend I'm practicing my openings and closings in front of a jury."

"So you practice down here for all your trials?" Alves was trying to sound as normal as he could manage.

"Not quite as religiously as I used to. It depends on the case. If it's a garden variety gun case, I can just wing it, but if it's a serious shooting or a robbery I like to get down here and practice the whole trial."

"This is a bit strange, you have to admit," Alves said, thinking it was far worse than strange.

Connie didn't respond and moved to usher Alves out of the room. "And that, Detective Alves, completes your warrantless search . . . I mean that completes the grand tour. Why don't we go back up and drink that beer?"

Figgs finished the last of his club soda. He sat at the bar munching on the ice cubes, a dish of salted peanuts untouched in front of him.

The Red Sox were hanging in the League Championship Series, but he was too distracted to follow every pitch. Some nights he'd missed the game entirely. He finally had the gun he'd been looking for. No one else would end up dead because of it. But he didn't have the answers he'd hoped for. He'd imagined someone getting arrested with the gun, getting a statement out of him, finding out where he'd gotten it, who had it before him, following the trail, connecting the dots, getting a complete history of where that gun had been and who had used it.

Instead, he had Stutter Simpson flipping out that the gun had been found in his mother's car with him driving it. He denied ever seeing that gun. Said he'd never even touched a 4-0 in his life.

Sure, Stutter was a criminal, had been his whole life. His younger brother Junior had been a good kid, but Stutter was always into something, dealing drugs, stealing cars, robbing people. He had a four-page juvenile record. By the time he graduated to adult court, he'd established himself as a shooter.

So why should Figgs trust him now? Maybe because he was so scared when they'd first met in the barbershop. Maybe because someone with that much experience with the criminal justice system wouldn't be stupid enough to drive around with a murder weapon in his car. Maybe because Figgs's gut told him Simpson seemed to be telling the truth. This morning in the lockup at District 2, Simpson said he didn't know anything about the gun. And Figgs was starting to believe him.

Then how did the .40 get there? Greene and Ahearn had the reputation of getting aggressive, maybe crossing the line now and then. But planting a gun? And not just any gun, a crime gun, hot, a murder weapon.

His witness, Leo, from his vantage point near the parking lot, saw another man step out of Greene and Ahearn's car. Saw him look into Simpson's running vehicle. Saw him turn off the engine. Figgs himself had gone to Operations and watched the Shot Spotter footage of a man walk up to that car and lean in.

That man was Conrad Darget. He seemed to have a hard-on for Stutter. But would he cross the line out on the street? It would take a lot of nerve to walk up and drop a gun, knowing that every patrol and unmarked car in the district would be on scene in seconds.

The crowd in the bar yelled, and Figgs glanced up at the screen. The Cardiac Kids, as his father used to call the Sox, were making a late inning comeback.

There were a couple questions he still couldn't answer. If Conrad Darget did plant the gun in Simpson's car, where did Darget get the gun? And why set up Stutter Simpson?

In the noise of the bar, Figgs tried out the last piece of logic. What kind of man would not only plant the evidence, but prosecute the patsy he'd set up? Answer? A very sick man.

CHAPTER 91

Alves stepped out of Connie's house into the cool evening air. He had a slight buzz going from the two beers. Fatherhood had turned him into a lightweight, he thought. Connie had killed off the rest of the six-pack and wasn't showing a thing.

Alves stumbled a little on a crack in the walkway, his mind racing. How could there be nothing in the house linking Connie to the murders? He had shown up unannounced and Connie had taken him through the place from the attic to the basement. He didn't seem to be hiding anything, except for his basement courtroom. Alves didn't know what to make of that room. It was bizarre to have gone through the effort to build something like that in a basement, but lots of people did strange things. One of his neighbors built a Dale Earnhardt racecar bed for his son, actual size #3. The courtroom didn't make Connie a killer.

Connie had explained how being in that room was his way of practicing. People didn't think it was crazy when professional baseball players had batting cages in their houses, so why was it odd for a professional trial lawyer to have a courtroom in his basement? Especially someone like Connie, who preached the importance of trial preparation.

Still, to build an exact replica of a courtroom...And it was all there—from the American flag, the state flag of Massachusetts, the seal of the Commonwealth, right down to the eight seats for the jurors and alternates.

A little crazy, yes. But nothing he'd seen that night made Connie a killer.

CHAPTER 92

What had Detective Angel Alves been doing in Conrad Darget's house all that time? Drinking the alcoholic beverages Alves had hidden behind his back? What could they have been talking about? If they had discussed Sleep's involvement in the murders, then the detective wouldn't have come stumbling out of the house the way he had. He would have been walking with a sense of purpose, with a mission. And certainly Sergeant Wayne Mooney would have joined them in their victory celebration.

It appeared more as though Detective Alves had just come over to drink and socialize. But that didn't make sense either. Which got him thinking. Maybe Darget really didn't know anything. Maybe it was just a coincidence that he was at *Natalie's* on Newbury Street. Had the store been robbed recently? Was Darget there on official business unrelated to the murders? That had to be it. Nothing else made sense.

He watched as Alves started his car and drove off. Sleep had to leave too. His Little Things had been in their trunks too long.

He could come back in the morning, early. He could follow Darget, see what he was up to.

He had eaten dinner earlier, but now he was suddenly in the mood for Chinese. He'd pick up a dinner plate at his favorite place, the Pearl Pagoda on Mass Ave. He'd learned that if he put in too large an order, he got too many fortune cookies. Then how could he figure out which one was the *real* one? Small order, one cookie, and he could save it for a bit, savor the fortune tucked inside. Delight for a while in the anticipation. And when he finally cracked open that brittle yellow cookie, he'd know for sure what to do about Conrad Darget.

CHAPTER 93

Figgs leaned back against the sculpture in front of the DA's office. He didn't know what it was supposed to be, but it looked like a giant tooth, a huge white molar maybe. He'd figured Conrad Darget to be an early bird, but it was almost eight o'clock and there'd been no sign of him yet.

He'd wait another half hour then head over to the firing range. See if he could still hit the ten ring from twenty-five yards with the two-inch Smith. It was more satisfying with the old targets, silhouettes of bad guys, instead of the giant, politically correct milk bottles they used today. He just needed to concentrate, get back to the basics. Steady hand, look through the rear sight—front sight sharp like the fin of a shark, target blurry.

The door to the DA's office opened and Darget stepped out.

"How'd you get in there without me seeing you?" Figgs asked. "I've been out here close to an hour."

"I was in here before you hit the snooze button."

"You got a minute?"

"Can we walk and talk? I'm heading over to superior court. I've got some witnesses coming in to the grand jury this morning, and I've got to do some prep first."

Figgs walked with Darget as they crossed Sudbury and Cambridge

Streets toward Center Plaza. "Let me get to the point. I went out to Townsend Street and knocked on some doors. I've got a witness says you leaned into Stutter Simpson's car."

"Who's your witness?"

"Let's just leave it that I have a witness who saw you lean into the car. Is my witness lying?"

"No, your witness isn't lying."

"Why did you go into that car?"

"To turn it off," Darget said. "Stutter crashed the car and took off running. He left the car in gear, up against the curb. Greene and Ahearn went after him. I walked up, threw it into park, and shut it off."

"Did you put on rubber gloves?"

"Of course. Latex. I always carry a pair when I'm on a ride-along. I was careful not to leave prints or contaminate the car in any way. I knew we'd be dusting, especially with a murder suspect like Simpson."

The prosecutor had an answer for everything. "That's all for now. I'll see you later." Figgs turned and started toward his car, then stopped. "Darget, one more thing." He waited for the prosecutor to turn and face him. "Why didn't you tell any of this to the PS on scene who took your statement?"

"I didn't think it was important. The car was in gear. I put on a pair of gloves and turned off the engine before someone got hurt." His gaze was steady, no blinking, no glancing away.

Darget was good. It didn't matter if there was a witness who saw him messing around that car. Darget claimed he had to turn off the engine. And that he *had* to use the gloves to do it. Neat. Clean. And neither the witness nor the Shot Spotter said anything different.

CHAPTER 94

It was chilly for an early fall evening. Connie sat on a bench by the Boston Harbor, looking out at Marina Bay, outside the new UMass Boston Student Center. He was there a good half hour before the start of the lecture, situated in a good position for watching cars as they arrived and parked in the North Lot.

Ten minutes before his lecture was scheduled to start, Zardino pulled up. Connie watched him park in the lot, climb the stairs to the bus drop-off and enter the building. Connie took his time crossing the perimeter road and driveway. Zardino would be speaking in the large function room on the third floor of the Student Center. Connie waited a few minutes before heading for the stairs. He didn't need to hear Zardino speak. He knew his shtick.

What was more interesting was the audience. He found a spot outside the door that gave him a view into the lecture hall. From his vantage point, he scanned the crowd, a surprising mix, older students, professor types in baggy cotton clothes, younger students, bored already and sneaking looks at their text messages. And up on stage, sitting next to Zardino, was Sonya Jordan.

At the podium was Marcy Alves, giving introductory remarks. Connie had forgotten that she taught here. Marcy was introducing, "My esteemed colleague and good friend, the best lawyer anyone could have—Sonya Jordan." The crowd clapped. "And let's also welcome back to our campus a remarkable man who has endured and· prevailed— Richard Zardino."

The crowd erupted in applause as Zardino stepped up to the podium. Connie scanned the crowd. At the back, nearly concealed by a group of students who looked ready to bolt the second the lecture was over, backpacks on their laps, jackets still on, was Zardino's sidekick, Luther. He was the only one in the room not clapping for the guest of honor. Why wasn't Luther front and center, showing support for his buddy during his big presentation?

Connie surveilled the crowd. Tight little groups of classes sitting together, couples holding hands, students taking advantage of the warm lecture hall to catch up on some sleep. Nothing out of the ordinary.

Then he saw her. Second row, staring up at the stage, transfixed by Zardino. And right next to her, a boy mesmerized by *her* every move. She was not the prettiest girl in the room, but there was something about her that held his attention. Her intensity maybe. Her curiosity. He wasn't sure if she measured up to Zardino's standards, but she was dark-haired, small, pretty. She would do.

Connie remembered girls like her from college, girls who would sit up front and make a beeline for the professor the second class had ended. Connie knew she would do that tonight. She would be the first one up to the podium. She would have a personal question, lean in close as Zardino answered her, listen intently to every word. Just the idea that she was talking, standing so close to a semi-celebrity would have her in a near-frenzy. Her boyfriend hoped to carry that excitement over to his private after-party in his car or his apartment.

The boyfriend would work out nicely because he was kind of scrawny. When you had something so special planned for a couple, you didn't need to be dealing with a big hero.

CHAPTER 95

Luther slumped back in his seat and crossed his arms over his chest. Why was Richard freezing him out, not telling him what was going on, disappearing on him, not answering his phone? Richard hadn't been honest about what he was doing tonight. He was letting the kids down. For a lot of them, Richard was the first white dude they had trusted.

A look at the crowd and he understood what was going on. Hadn't Richard stated it clearly enough a couple months ago? These speaking gigs were a way for him to meet young women. A way to pump up his social life after prison. A way to make himself look like a rock star in front of a bunch of suburban white kids longing to make a difference in the world.

Luther felt the familiar fire of anger flare up in his stomach—and it would burn, he knew, till he took some kind of action. All the good Luther had tried to do. Working with the kids. Hanging at night on street corners. The endless meetings at the Crispus Attucks House with folks who didn't really understand his kids, didn't really care beyond their empty words and their sappy smiles—all of it lasting just long enough to take out their checkbooks. Then, consciences appeased, they could go back to their apple-polished suburbs thinking they'd made a difference.

Richard Zardino was no different.

That wasn't quite true. Richard Zardino was worse. Back in the day, Luther would have put a cap in his ass.

Luther had seen enough. He excused himself, wove his way out of the pack of students half-listening to Zardino's hard luck story, and slipped out the door.

At least out in the corridor he could breathe some fresh air.

CHAPTER 96

Connie had watched as Zardino's sidekick hit the door.

Up front, his little girl was on cue and perfect. She got to Zardino first. Then she did so much more than he'd expected from her. She'd hung on to Zardino, monopolizing him for at least ten minutes as a line formed behind her. She wrote something on a piece of paper torn from her notebook and handed it to him. A phone number? An address, maybe? Quite a system Zardino had. An idealistic kid inviting him into her life. What she didn't know was that it was an invitation to get killed, along with her unsuspecting boyfriend. Connie played out what would happen next in his head.

Zardino followed the young couple as they made their way out of the hall and down the stairs. The girl gushing. Talking loud, giggling, drunk on her brush with celebrity, notoriety. A wounded man, jailed unjustly, telling his sad story. Perfect girl-bait.

Once outside, the couple walked hand-in-hand past the shuttle bus, motor running and door open, toward the North Lot.

Excellent.

Weaving through the crowd of students, he kept his distance. They must have arrived late and had to park in one of the temporary lots at the edge of campus. The van was parked there. It was late, no one else walking in their direction. Zardino jogged ahead to catch up with them. He needed to steer them toward the van—that was the key. Then he could use the weapon.

"Excuse me," he said, "I was wondering if you could help me out." They were so inno-

cent. And he'd just delivered that powerful talk. Shown them how he was a good man, giving back to society in spite of what society had done to him. He could tell them anything and they would walk themselves right into the trap, the horny boyfriend along for the ride. "I'm sorry, but my battery died. I was wondering if you have time to give me a jump."

"I don't have jumper cables." The boy didn't like sharing his girl's affections.

"That's okay. I've got them. It'll just take a minute."

"We have to help him," the girl said, high on the emotions of the night. She looked across the lot. There was no one in sight. "We can't just leave him out here with a car that won't start."

She was a sweet kid. He could keep her like that. Forever.

He walked with them toward their car, then pointed out where he was parked. "I'll meet you over by my van," he told them, careful not to crowd their space by walking them all the way to their car. He heard the motor start up, saw the lights splash into the darkness and then the boy pulled up close to the front of the van. They both got out.

Good.

They walked toward him. Not giggly kids anymore, but purposeful young adults, the weight of their do-gooding giving them a certain dignity. He felt the heft of the gun in his jacket pocket. The lot was still empty, the only light the twin disks from the car's headlights.

"Let me get those cables," he said, swinging the back door to the van open.

"Hi, Connie."

He looked over to see Marcy Alves. She looked tired.

"I'm surprised to see you here," she said. "You don't have enough meetings during the day to keep you busy?"

"How are the kids doing? Angel told me about what happened at Franklin Park."

"Then he probably told you we're staying at my mother's place. We feel safer there."

"Don't give up on him, Marcy. Angel's a good man." Connie looked around. The room was almost empty. At the front of the room, still standing at the podium was Richard Zardino. And beside him, a half dozen stragglers talking and gesturing.

There was a lot more he could say to Marcy, but he had to stay focused. He put his hand on her shoulder. Together they turned and walked toward the podium. Connie wanted to let Zardino know he was in the audience. Watching him. Give him a little tickle. "Zardino puts on a great show, doesn't he?"

"It's more than a show, Connie," Marcy said. "A man like Zardino reminds us all what can happen when someone is unjustly prosecuted."

"True enough. That's why I always make sure I have the right man."

CHAPTER 97

Alves had spent most of the day looking into Connie's background. He had to keep it from Mooney for now, but not much longer. He'd checked the registry's database and verified that Connie was thirty years old. If he *was* the Blood Bath Killer, it didn't make sense that he would have started killing for the first time at the age of twenty-seven. Even if he had, there certainly would have been indicators leading up to those murders. But he had checked Connie's BOP and ran a Triple I. No criminal record, not even as a juvenile. No sealed records.

But the Prom Night killings had started in '98. Connie would have been twenty years old. A quick call to the registrar at the University of Arizona, and Alves learned that Connie would have been on summer break when the first three couples were murdered. If Connie *had* come home for the summer, he could have committed those murders and gone back to school. He would never have been suspected of anything.

Alves then made a call to the Tucson Police Department. If Connie had started killing during his college years, he might have done it out of state. Alves reached a clerk in the Homicide Unit and asked if they had any unsolved murders at or near the school in the mid-to-late '90s.

That's when he was passed off to a detective.

"Clairimundo Sanchez, Homicide, how can I help you?" the man shouted into Alves's ear.

"Detective, my name is Angel Alves. I'm working an active series of homicides up here in Boston."

"I got that message. You wanted to know if we had any unsolved cases from about ten, twelve years back. What kind of murders you dealing with, Detective Alves?"

"We've got young couples, college students. The males are shot close range, in the chest, and the females are strangled. Bare hands."

"We had some unusual unsolveds dating back. The Dumpster Killer left armless torsos in dumpsters all over Tucson. Let me think. We had a string of bodies found in arroyos. Prostitutes. Migrant workers. Nothing with college students. Wait a minute. We had a college girl, turned up strangled in the U of A library one night. Studying. Library staff found her when they were closing up for the night. No boy, though. Just the girl."

"Ever make an arrest?"

"No."

"Any suspects?"

"We had one person of interest. It wasn't my case, though. I don't know much about the investigation."

"Detective Sanchez, anything you can give me would help."

"What I remember, he was another student. One of the few people in the library at the time of the murder. We didn't like his attitude. Real smug. The man you want to talk to is Detective Mike Decandia. He figured this kid killed her and then stayed in the library studying to give himself an alibi. Why would a guilty man stay in the library after killing an absolute stranger? Pretty good reasoning. Came in and spoke with Mike, but we got nothing out of him."

"Do you remember his name? The victim's name?"

"Can't say I do."

"Is Decandia around?"

"Vacation. He'll be back in a week."

"Can you give him a message to call me when he gets back?"

"Sure thing."

Alves hung up the phone. He looked at the clock on his computer screen. It was almost nine. He'd been at this most of the day. The red light on his office phone was lit. There was a single message on his phone. He punched in his code and heard Mooney's voice.

"Angel, Connie stopped in. He's got a solid lead. We're heading over to East Boston. Paris Street. Richie Zardino's house."

Mooney negotiated the Expressway traffic, exiting off the ramp to the tunnel. "I don't understand. Why didn't I know about this sooner?" Mooney asked. "You talk with Angel just about every day, and you didn't tell him about Zardino?"

Mooney shot a look at his passenger. Connie was facing straight ahead. The tunnel lights created flickering shadows across his face. "I did tell him," Connie said, his voice edged in anger. "He wouldn't listen. And tonight I figured out that Zardino's picking his victims from the audience. He's using his celebrity as a wrongly convicted man to work these college kids, to gain their trust."

"You've confirmed that?" Mooney asked.

"Earlier I checked with BU and BC. Both schools had Zardino in for his lecture."

"Did any of the vics go to those lectures?"

"I haven't confirmed that yet, but each of the female victims bears a striking resemblance to a woman Zardino grew up with. Her name is Natalie Fresco."

"And?" Mooney said.

"She claims he used to be her stalker. She was so spooked by him ten years ago that she got him fired from his job. Around the time of the first murders."

"Where was he working?" Mooney asked.

"A store across the street from her shop. Newbury Street."

"Right near the Fens," Mooney said. "He had opportunity."

"I had the manager at the store check their old records. Zardino used to help set up window displays. Lugged around props, helped move the mannequins."

"So he dressed up dolls? I wonder if he likes dressing people?" Mooney asked.

"I know a lot of this is circumstantial, but there's more. The day I went to interview Natalie at her store, guess who was parked out front in a white van?" The prosecutor was quiet for a beat. For effect. "Sarge, I saw him in the same van, stuck in traffic on Walter Street the night Tucker and Pine were found on Peter's Hill. Both times he had a Bruin's cap pulled down over his head. It's enough to bring him in for questioning. And it's enough for a search warrant."

"I think I need to have a talk with Mr. Zardino," Mooney said. "Maybe freeze the house and get that search warrant."

"Look for the white van in his garage. Older model, mint condition, registered in his mother's name. Used to be his dad's," Connie said. "Probably sat in the garage all those years until he needed it again."

"Does Zardino know you saw him tonight at UMass?"

Connie nodded. "After the speech, I went up and said hello. It made me nervous, seeing him so close to Marcy Alves. I walked Marcy to her car, then I tried to call Angel, but he didn't pick up. So I drove over to talk to you. I don't think Zardino knows I suspect him of anything."

"We can't take that chance." Mooney flipped on his wigwags and strobes, accelerating through the tunnel. He struggled to control his anger. What the hell had Alves been thinking? Connie had come up with some of the best leads in the investigation. This was not the time for some bullshit pissing contest. He had eight dead kids on his hands. He'd deal with Alves later. Now he needed to get to Zardino's house before he took off or tried to destroy any potential evidence.

Or worse, before Zardino went out in his van, trolling for his next victims.

CHAPTER 99

Connie watched as the roof of 2252 Paris Street crashed down onto the attic below, sending up a plume of flames and smoke darker than the sky. Richard Zardino's old colonial was fully engulfed. Fanned by the steady wind off Boston Harbor, the fire was burning almost blue hot. Once an object as dry as the timber skeleton of an old house began to burn hot, there was no putting out the flames. The only thing the Boston Fire Department could do was control the fire and try to save the other houses by wetting down neighboring roofs.

He and Mooney stood across the street as the old house and the garage with its white van full of trace evidence burned with roaring heat. He could feel his face and hands tingling with it, his lungs filling with the sooty warm air.

The fire reminded him of the times he helped his grandfather with his annual smudge fire to get rid of brush and trash on the farm. But as his grandmother predicted, the conservative little smudge fire always bloomed into a massive bonfire.

But those fires weren't as fascinating as the incinerator the old man had designed using an old oil tank with an attached blower. You could burn anything in that thing. You could feed even a good-sized log in and it would disintegrate as you pushed. Fire could burn evidence clean. He knew it and Richard Zardino did too.

Connie felt a hand on his shoulder. "What a tragedy," Angel Alves said. "Is he in there?"

"That's the fifty-thousand-dollar question," Connie said, turning to Alves. He hadn't noticed the crowd that had gathered along the street, just beyond the barriers set up by the police department.

"Thanks to you, we're not going to know until they put out this damn fire," Mooney said, his face flushed with heat and anger. "I wanted to talk to Zardino. I wanted the evidence to wrap up this case. Now we don't have either. We don't know if he's dead or alive. All because someone bruised your ego."

"That's not it, Sarge—"

"Later," Mooney cut him off. "I don't know where your head has been the last few days. At least Connie gives a shit about catching this guy."

Connie didn't want to put himself between the two partners. He turned away from Alves. Looking past Mooney, he saw that every house on the street was lit up, people gathering to gossip the way they always did when something bad happened to one of their neighbors. This was the event of the century for most of these people. Young kids in pajamas riding their bikes back and forth across the street. An elderly woman in a bathrobe at the end of the block, holding on to her walker, complete with tennis ball gliders. For an old lady, this would be like a front row seat on the fifty yard line at the Super Bowl.

Interesting. Out of the corner of his eye Connie noticed that there were no lights on in the Fresco house. Natalie might still be at work or out for a movie, but it was getting late. And where was the elderly Mrs. Fresco? He turned to Mooney. "Sarge?" he said.

"Yeah?"

"Don't turn around. Keep looking at me. I just thought of something."

CHAPTER 188

When his Little Things got too demanding, Sleep put them in the trunk in the attic and latched it. He could still hear them banging around, but it was always a little quieter. Now they wouldn't be bothering him anymore. He couldn't think about them, all twisted flesh-colored plastic, their hair burned away, their beautiful clothes nothing but ash. He had to focus on what was important.

He had brought his wire, and he'd found a roll of duct tape in the pantry. He tried to explain to Natalie and her mother that if they waited in the closet until the police and firemen were done across the street, then the three of them could sit at the kitchen table and have a cup of tea. The one thing he'd taken with him from the house was Momma's wedding album. He'd show them the gorgeous photos of Momma in her satin wedding gown. They'd work their way through the pages—Momma standing with her bouquet, his father in his natty suit. The attendants, smiling and young. And the last few pages, meant for the inscribed well-wishes of their wedding guests, on those final yellowed and smooth pages were the photos he'd taken of his couples, capturing forever their most joyous time.

But even with the tape and wire, he could hear someone kicking the locked closet door. Fortunately the ruckus outside was enough to drown out the noise. He'd check on them in a minute, but now he had to get back to the front room, pull back the curtain and see what was going on.

By the time he got back to his position in the living room, Momma's house looked like a skeleton of wood, the orange flames garish and scary, dancing wildly in the burst windows. In all the confusion, it took a minute but he finally saw something significant. Standing on the sidewalk a few houses down from Natalie's house were Darget, Mooney, and Alves.

He watched as the prosecutor and the sergeant got into one car. Alves into his own. Then Sleep watched as the two cars slowly wound through the maze of emergency vehicles and moved away down the street.

CHAPTER 101

Connie's adrenaline was pumping. This wasn't like a ride-along, or a foot pursuit of a suspect, or even an execution of a search warrant in a drug house. For the first time he had used his skills to identify a killer. He knew Zardino had to be inside Natalie Fresco's house, probably with Natalie and her mother. The question was, were any of them still alive?

"You sure this is the house?" Mooney asked.

"I've seen Natalie come out the front door. And I ran her license. Her mother is incapacitated, took a bad fall a while back, but she stays up pretty late every night. Probably watching the eleven o'clock news, followed by Leno. I've been out here a few times. I've never seen the lights out this early."

"Connie, you stay back," Mooney said. "I don't want a situation here. He's got two potential hostages. If Angel and I can do this quick enough, no one will get hurt."

"Sarge," Connie said, "I'm carrying."

"All the more reason you're staying here." Mooney handed Connie his radio. "If anything goes wrong, you hear shots fired, call for backup. But don't try to be a hero. Stay outside."

Connie watched as the two detectives got low and made their way onto the small back porch, positioning themselves on either side of the door. Alves had his Glock in his right hand. Mooney was carrying the

Blackhawk Battle Ram he'd taken out of the trunk. Once they were in position, Alves moved deliberately, looking in the glass panel of the door, at the same time trying the doorknob. He turned to Mooney, shaking his head. As expected, the door was locked.

From his position, Connie couldn't see any movement in the house. After a few minutes Mooney made his move. This was when he was the most vulnerable. He tried to keep his body to the side of the door as he leaned back to swing the Ram hard into the doorjamb. Connie saw a shadow move across a casement window near the back door as Mooney prepared to launch the full weight of his body into the head of the Ram. Connie wanted to warn Mooney, but he couldn't make any noise, not until Mooney broke the silence with his assault on the door.

Connie heard the loud bang and the sound of splintering wood as the first blow split the doorframe.

"Movement inside, Sarge," Connie shouted.

Mooney followed through with the second blow, and the door flew open. Dropping the Ram, he removed the Glock from its holster and led the way into the house.

Connie was already holding his .38 as he moved on to the porch. Then he heard the shots echoing inside, multiple rounds in rapid succession, almost like one continuous shot.

Zardino's machine gun.

CHAPTER 102

Sleep didn't see anything outside, but he thought he heard a noise.

It always started like this. A faint sound that grew louder until he had to put his hands over his ears. He couldn't think when his Little Things made such a racket. They had to be quiet or the detectives would find them. But they would never listen. That's how his father had found them in the attic together. "Shut up," he hissed. Momma did not like that language, but this was an emergency. Where was the sound coming from?

The closet.

He looked out the window. No sign of the detectives. He put his gun down on the lamp table. He wouldn't need it. At the hall closet he rested his head against the cool, painted wood for just a second. Just to gather his thoughts, as Momma used to say. Then he pulled the door open.

He took his flashlight out of his pocket and switched it on. It wasn't his Little Things. Just lovely Natalie and her interfering mother. The old biddy was always in the way. She and Natalie's old man were the ones that had turned Natalie against Sleep. But he needed her now. She would be the one to give Natalie away at the wedding, to give him her hand in marriage. The old woman was pushed back in the corner, Natalie in front of her, protecting her.

Natalie tried to speak, but with the duct tape he couldn't understand her. She kept using her feet to push herself back into her mother, as if she were trying to drive the old lady back through the back wall of the closet.

Sleep put his index finger to his lips. "Shhh. You must be quiet."

She kept distorting her face, trying to speak.

"You want to say something?" he asked.

She nodded her head.

"Promise to keep your voice down? No screaming?"

She nodded again.

Sleep leaned forward to remove the tape, pointing his flashlight in her face. Poor thing. He watched as she struggled to catch her breath, her face covered with sweat, her silky black hair matted to her forehead. He carefully peeled a corner of the tape, then quickly pulled it from her face. "What is it you want, dear?"

"Please don't hurt my mother," she gasped. "She didn't do anything. It's me you want. I'll do anything. But she's an old woman. She's having trouble breathing in here. She needs her medication. It's in a small bottle on the nightstand next to her bed."

Sleep heard another noise. He put the tape back over Natalie's mouth. He put his finger up to his mouth and closed the closet door. He listened carefully.

The back door. Someone was jiggling the doorknob.

He moved into the kitchen, standing away from the window, in the darkness. Still, he saw nothing. Then Sergeant Mooney appeared in the shadows outside the window. He was holding something in his hand. A log. Sleep moved across the kitchen. The gun was in the front room. He was in the hallway when he heard the first blow to the door. He reached the gun just as the door came flying open and Mooney burst into the kitchen and made his way to the front of the house.

Sleep wheeled around and took one shot. He couldn't get close the way he usually did. He aimed for the center of mass. Mooney went down and dropped his gun. Sleep made a move for Mooney's gun just as someone pounced on him. Whoever it was tried to pull Sleep's hands behind his back and cuff him.

It had to be Angel Alves. But he had made the mistake of underestimating Sleep's power. Alves was not a street fighter. He had never been to prison, never had to use his fighting skills to survive every day.

Sleep sprang to his feet with Alves's weight on his back. He repeatedly drove the detective into the wall until he felt his grip slacken and slip away. The detective slumped to the floor. Sleep saw a gun in the middle of the floor. He wasn't sure whose it was, but it didn't matter.

As he made a move for the gun, he felt a bone-crushing blow to his ribs. He heard a crack as a sharp pain ran up his side, his breath leaving him. He tried a few feeble swings, but the room around them, the prosecutor holding the log, all of it was going gray.

CHAPTER 103

How's Mooney doing?" Connie asked.

"He got dinged up pretty good," Alves said. "Zardino's gun fired four rounds, caught Mooney with three of them. Luckily none hit any bone. Those small rounds do the most damage bouncing around," Alves said.

"I plan to go to the hospital tomorrow," Connie said.

"He's not going anywhere for a couple weeks. Leslie's been there regularly, keeping him company."

"My victim witness advocate told me that Natalie's mother had some chest pains for a day or so, but she's doing okay. She's out of the hospital and back in the house on Paris with Natalie."

Connie watched as Alves ate his baked macaroni and cheese, the house specialty at Silvertone, a small upscale restaurant on Bromfield Street. Connie had ordered two plates of steamed mussels. Low in fat and high in cholesterol. Meeting for dinner had been Alves's idea.

"How's the case against Zardino?" Connie asked.

"Solid. He made incriminating statements to Natalie and her mother. We've got the wire he used to bind the two women. Matches the wire used on all the vics. We have the twenty-two-caliber Beretta. Ballistics is a match. And best of all, we have photos of the dead college students pasted into an album. We're reopening the investigation into his father's death, too." Alves tore a bit of bread and sopped up some mussel broth from Connie's bowl.

"What about his sidekick Luther? He have any involvement in this thing?"

"Negative. In fact, Luther was able to corroborate that Zardino had the opportunity to commit the murders. Their program is funded by a grant, and Luther kept detailed logs of the time they spent working the streets at night. Zardino's hours got pretty spotty over the last few months. When I talked with Luther at Crispus Attucks House he was beyond pissed that Zardino would betray 'his kids' trust' this way."

"I bet he's glad we caught Zardino," Connie said. "Imagine working that closely with a serial killer. Especially when Luther could have become a suspect in the murders. People are always willing to believe the black guy did it."

"He's not happy about anything. Still thinks the police care more about white college students getting killed than we do about poor black kids. Like his brother."

"You think that case will ever get solved?" Connie asked.

Alves shook his head. "How's your case against Stutter Simpson? Ray Figgs treating you okay? I ran into him last week. Looks like Figgsy went to Bridgewater for a spin dry. Word is he hasn't had a drink in weeks. Working out at the gym again. Seems on top of things."

"The grand jury has everything they need to indict, the murder weapon, motive—Stutter and Jesse Wilcox were shooting back and forth at each other for months before Jesse turned up dead. My problem is Figgs. He's busting my chops, complaining we should do more investigation before we indict."

"Probably just wants a solid case," Alves said. "So it doesn't go south on you at trial."

"Stutter Simpson is a murderer. I'm going to indict and convict him for killing Jesse Wilcox."

They ordered coffee. It was nice to be comfortable with Angel again—talking about their cases like old friends. He didn't like it when Alves was guarded around him, keeping things from him. Things were getting back to normal.

CHAPTER 104

Alves held the door to Silvertone open for Connie, who was still making his way up the stairs. The cold air smacked Alves in the face, waking him up, helping him shake off the effects of the heavy meal and the warm restaurant. "That was the best mac and cheese ever," Alves said. "Now I need a nap."

"You really are an old man," Connie said as he buttoned his coat. "You're not going to fall asleep behind the wheel are you? I knew I should have driven."

"How can you call me an old man? You're the one who drives a minivan. A single man with no kids tooting around like a soccer mom. That's sad." Alves could feel himself straining for the playfulness that used to be a natural part of their relationship. "I can't be seen riding around the city in that thing with you."

"It's not just a minivan, it's the 'snitch mobile,' " Connie laughed. "My investigators use it to pick up witnesses and victims. And, as we say in the Gang Unit, today's victim is tomorrow's defendant. They're all afraid of being labeled snitches. So we had the windows smoked out. It's so dark, it's an illegal tint. I have trouble driving the thing at night."

"And you've got lights, siren, and a police radio installed. But no matter how you dress it up, it's still a minivan."

"It's better than this shit box Ford you're driving around in," Connie slapped the roof of the car. "You're on homicide and they don't give you the honor of a ride like a Crown Vic or a real police car."

"Shut up and get in," Alves laughed. He had to keep the mood light. At some point he needed to get some information from Connie. He didn't want to confront him yet. He just wanted to talk about the Blood Bath case. Bring up some of the things that were still bothering him.

"You want to come back to my house for a beer?" Connie asked.

"I've got a better idea. I have a six pack in the trunk. Let's go to White Stadium and have a few."

"Angel, you may not have noticed, but it's almost November and it's freaking cold."

"Don't be a crybaby. It's a great place to drink. Back when I was a ju-venile delinquent, me and my boys used to hop the fence and get trashed in there. Then we'd end up playing tackle football in the dark. What a blast. That's where I played my games in high school."

"Me, too, but I'm not jumping any fences to go have a beer and relive my high school glory."

"No fence jumping. I used to work the detail for the mayor's Friday Night Game of the Week. I've still got the key to the gate."

"I don't even have a drinking glove."

Alves reached into the back seat and pulled out two ratty looking gloves. "We each have a drinking glove. Now you have no excuses."

"I'll go for a beer or two, but no football tonight." Connie laughed.

CHAPTER 105

Connie held the six-pack in his gloved hand while Alves unlocked the gate. This was an interesting development, coming out to the stadium where they'd both played high school football games. With a fresh coat of paint in the stands and well kept turf, the stadium looked better than it had in years.

As they made their way to the bleachers, Connie imagined the smell of fresh cut grass on a field with neatly painted lines. He felt a rush of adrenaline. It was the same feeling he got every time the "Star Spangled Banner" played before a game or a wrestling meet. Most people never paid attention to the lyrics. Sure, they might mouth the words as the anthem was played, but they didn't actually think about what the words meant. For Connie, the words meant a great deal.

He would go into a zone while the song played. Everything else around him disappeared. He would imagine himself watching the sun come up over Baltimore Harbor the morning after the Battle of Fort McHenry, the American flag undaunted, standing out like a beacon. No matter how it was bombarded it kept waving in the wind. The flag itself was like an absolute truth that could withstand any attack.

That was how Connie thought of himself, especially before a wrestling match. Connie was an Absolute Truth that could not be defeated. He had never been defeated. Not in high school. And not in college.

Tonight, out on the cold ball field, a hint of doubt edged into his mind. Angel Alves might be *acting* as though things between them were back to normal. Acting a bit too normal, working him, trying to win back his trust. But why? There had to be more to it. Maybe Alves was working a hunch. Before that hunch developed into a theory and then an indictment, Connie needed to find out what Alves was up to.

It was time for some ultimate truth to reveal itself.

CHAPTER 106

Alves's butt was numb. He stood up. "These metal benches are brutal. Thank God I never had to sit and watch a game here. It's like watching a Pat's game at the old Foxboro Stadium. Or as Sarge says, Shaefer Stadium."

Connie took a swig of his beer. "What are we doing up here anyway? Let's go down on the field."

"The moonlight is brighter up here. And there's no place to sit down there."

"I saw some benches down by the locker room entrance. C'mon," Connie said.

Alves was surprised that the ground was hard, but not frozen. It must have warmed during the day. By morning, the blades of grass would be frozen crystals, snapping under your feet when you walked. But right now it was a perfect football surface. Walking out to the middle of the field felt right.

"Remember how much fun it was to be in high school," Alves said. "Coming out here and playing games in front of a big crowd. The cheer-leaders, the band, the whole atmosphere. How many times did I stand on this field, anxious to return a kick, each time, certain that I would run it all the way for a touchdown? At that moment, nothing else mattered in the world. Everyone in the stands was watching the ball, waiting for the kick. Then, as the ball rotated through the air, end over end, everyone watched to see what I was going to do with it. I was a pretty good ballplayer, so I always gave them a show. I wasn't the biggest guy on the field, but I had great feet. There was always some big goon or a speedster who thought he was going to come down and drill me as I caught the ball, but I always made them miss. The first guy never got me."

"If you'd played a few years later, I would have been one of those goons," Connie said, lunging at Alves.

Alves juked to the left and then back and Connie grasped at air.

"I'm still too quick for you, even as an old man," Alves said.

The two men laughed and started to walk back toward the bleachers. Alves looked up into the sky. "Connie, can I ask you something?"

"Sure, pal."

"How did you know Rich Zardino was the killer?"

"I tried to think like the killer. It's something I learned from you and Mooney and from FBI profilers. If you think like the killer, you can catch the killer."

"But how did that lead you to Zardino? I can see if you came up with some characteristics that made him a possible suspect. But that's not what happened."

"I looked past the obvious. Everyone was looking at known sex offenders who had done time. But I got to thinking, what if this guy had never been caught for a sex crime. What if he had just been out of state? What if he had done time for something else? What if he had done time for a crime he hadn't committed? Bingo. This guy's flying under everyone's radar because he's some kind of martyr, a victim of organized crime and corrupt cops. What a great story. No one else took the time to dig any deeper."

"So that's what got you thinking it was him. But how did you *know* it was him?"

"Like I said, I made myself think like the killer. I became the killer." Connie grabbed the back of Alves's neck with both hands.

Alves was startled. He shrugged Connie off and turned to face him.

Connie laughed. "Not literally, but I tried to put myself in his head, to determine the who, what, where, when, why and how of it. How was he selecting his victims? That was the biggest question that needed to be answered. Then the mayor had his annual Peace Conference. I saw a news clip. Zardino and Luther talking about their involvement with the criminal system. I tried to learn more about Zardino and Luther after

2 IN THE HAT   285

that. I found out that Zardino was doing his lecture at all the area colleges. That's when it started to fall into place. I started putting the pieces
of the puzzle into Zardino's life and they all fit."

"Okay, Connie. That explains the Prom Night killings. But I got a
question." Alves knew that once he started this line of questioning, he'd
have to push until he had all the answers. "I spoke with Sonya Jordan and
Andi Norton. I need to ask you about Mitch Beaulieu."

"What about?"

"Nothing big. Just a couple of things I want to clear up."

"Angel, let's go sit down. It's windy out here." Connie led him toward
the row of benches against the concrete wall at the base of the stands.
They walked out of the moonlight and into the shadow of the stadium.
"I'm going to tell you the whole truth about Mitch, but you realize I'll
have to kill you afterward, right?" Connie laughed.

Alves let out an awkward chuckle, then felt Connie's hands on his
neck again. Connie slipped his left arm around Alves's arm and pulled it
back. Alves struggled to get loose. Connie reached under his chin with
his other hand and pulled his head back to the right. The Chin and
Chicken. Alves could feel Connie tighten his grip and start to crank with
both hands. He tried to elbow Connie with his right arm, but he
couldn't put any force behind it. Connie lifted him in the air.

Alves was immobilized.

CHAPTER 187

Alves tried to move and a pain shot up from his shoulder into his neck. His head was throbbing. The cold metal bench he was lying on didn't help. He opened his eyes and a gun was pointed at his head: his own Glock. Alves sat up. He tried to speak, but his throat hurt. Connie handed him a beer and told him to drink it. His drinking gloves were sticking out of Connie's pocket. Connie was wearing latex gloves.

It hurt to swallow. When he finished the beer, Connie gave him another.

"Jesus, Connie, give me a break. I can't chug beer like I used to."

"Just drink the beer, detective," Connie said coldly.

Alves took a swallow and set the bottle down on the bench. He'd better savor the beer. The beers were his hourglass. When they were gone, so was he.

"Detective, I didn't tell you to enjoy the beer. I told you to drink it. Pretend you are eighteen and trying to win a drinking contest at a frat party."

Alves took another swallow. The mac and cheese rose in his throat. He finished the bottle and Connie made him drink two more. Alves was feeling the effects of the beer. He usually only drank one or two to get a good buzz. After five beers he was drunk.

When the last beer was gone, Connie took a step away from him. "So you want to know about Mitch Beaulieu?"

Alves didn't want to know the truth. Not now. Not like this. He needed to be sober. He wanted it to be in an interrogation room with Mooney. He wanted it to be on tape. Video, if possible. He knew that if Connie told him everything now, then he would not live to tell it to anyone else. "I think I already know everything," Alves said.

"You don't know shit," Connie said.

"I know you killed innocent people for no reason."

"That's how you see it? Not me. I always kill for a reason. I kill out of necessity. I kill for the good of all men."

A wave of nausea swept over Alves. He tried to shake it off.

"Who have you killed?"

"Don't pull that shit on me. You know who I killed. That's why we're out here tonight, isn't it? You thought you could get me to slip up and say something I shouldn't. Maybe get a confession. Guess what, pal? You hit the jackpot."

"Who have you killed, Connie?"

"Oh, I get it. You want that full confession you came looking for. I know you're not wearing a wire and you're never going to leave this place, so I'll give you that."

"That's good of you," Alves said.

Just that morning he'd made pancakes for Marcy and the twins. When he was getting ready to leave for work, Marcy had told him to wait a second, then she'd kissed him, told him to be careful, to "drive nice," like she always used to. Alves needed to find a way out of this. He needed to lure Connie close enough to catch him with a sucker punch, get his gun back.

"Don't be a wiseass or I'll just kill you right now. Then you would have died for nothing, without any of the answers you came looking for." Connie paused. "Detective, I know you're upset about Robyn Stokes. I never would have killed her if I had known she was your friend."

The randomness of victims, the crazy logic of killers, the way everything had to fall just right for the right detective to put everything together at just the right moment. It sickened and frightened Alves. "Why, Connie?"

"I showed you why. You've been to my house. You still haven't figured this out, have you? I had to practice."

An image of Connie's basement flashed into his mind. The mock courtroom. The judge's bench. The prosecutor's table. The witness stand. And the jury box. Seats for eight jurors. There were only six confirmed victims of the Blood Bath Killer. Six bathtubs filled with blood. But if you added Emily Knight, the woman who disappeared walking home from work, and Nick Costa, Connie's fellow prosecutor, that made eight. But he'd gone over every square inch of Connie's house. How had he preserved eight human bodies in his basement courtroom?

Then he knew. That's what that massive laundry table was. An antique embalming table. Alves had seen them at older funeral homes. It was a gruesome thought. If the victims had been preserved, embalmed, they could have sat in that basement courtroom. They could have listened as the great prosecutor delivered his opening and closing statements.

But the bodies were gone. If only he could, he'd get a search warrant, dig up the yard and take the entire house apart, plank by plank, until he found them.

The idea of those bodies in the basement courtroom, the pain in his shoulders, the meal and the beer—all of it was too much. The gorge rose in his throat, and he couldn't hold it back.

CHAPTER 108

When Alves could focus again, Connie started talking. "You can't understand why I do what I do. You're too caught up in the little details to see the big picture."

"Try me," Alves said. Not caring about an answer, but stalling for time, for something.

"Detective. Think about all the gangbangers that have been killed with the community .40 that was floating around. The one Greene and Ahearn found under the front seat of Stutter Simpson's Toyota Tercel the night they arrested him. The very piece of evidence that I'm going to launch him with, in spite of Ray Figgs. Your problem, and Figgs's problem, Detective, is that you both get caught up in the crying mothers and grandmothers, the friends who set up sidewalk shrines for their fallen brothers, the value of each human life. I can look beyond that and see that the neighborhood is safer without those gangbangers."

Alves felt his stomach lurch again. This time he knew it wasn't the beer and the heavy meal. He couldn't begin to get his mind around what Connie was telling him. "You killed kids on the street, too? How many people have you murdered?"

"I wouldn't call it murder, detective. Murder is the *unlawful* killing of a human being."

"You think it's lawful to kill innocent people?"

"Don't be so surprised, Detective. You gave me the idea. You're the one who talked about how we could reduce the murder rate if we could catch the serial killer targeting the gangbangers who had just 'turned their lives around.' You know, like every good defense attorney argues, 'But judge, my client was just about to turn his life around, he's thinking of going back to get his GED, his girlfriend has a baby on the way, he's good to his mother.' "

"Connie, for God's sake, I was joking."

"Okay, Detective. If that makes you feel better. I was trying to give you credit for a brilliant idea. Sure, the homicide rate was up a little over the past year with everyone that was taken out by that one gun, but it should be way down next year. And not with long, drawn-out prosecutions, but with quick hits. How much time and money was wasted trying to put Jesse Wilcox in jail? How many people died in the meantime? Problem solved. And it didn't cost anything. No one else has been hurt."

"You killed Jesse Wilcox?" It was almost incomprehensible. How could one horror build on another? Where was the end of this twisted and tangled, knotted rope of a confession?

"He was killed with the .40, wasn't he? He would have been the first, but I thought it would be safer to bury him somewhere in the middle. No pun intended," Connie smiled. "The best part is that, despite Ray Figgs, I'm going to convict Stutter Simpson for Jesse's murder. Wrap things up nice and neat."

"You're sick. You're going to send an innocent man to jail for the rest of his life?"

"He might be innocent of Wilcox's murder, but we both know that he's committed others. I knew you didn't have the balls to do it. You just come up with the ideas and get me to do your dirty work. I can see this is upsetting you, Detective, but I wanted you to have the answers you came looking for."

"Connie, please. Think about Marcy and the kids."

"I have, and it really is a shame. All the stress of investigating homicides finally got to you, Detective. It became a burden for you. Sadly, tonight, after discussing this stress with your good friend Connie over dinner, you bought yourself a six pack and came out to the stadium you hung out in as a kid. You got drunk and decided to put an end to everything.

"Don't worry. All your buddies in the department will have a fundraiser for Marcy and the twins. I'll be there. Maybe they'll have an annual golf tournament and raise money for a couple of years before a new cause comes along and everyone moves on with their lives. Marcy will move on, too. She'll find herself a new husband, maybe one of your cop buddies. I'm still single, you know," he winked at Alves. "And Marcy is a fine looking woman. The kids are young. Their memory of you will fade. In time they will learn to love their new father. Everything will work out just fine. It always does."

"You're not going to get away with this, Connie. I've got a call into a Detective Mike Decandia in Tucson, Arizona."

"Sorry, detective. Won't work. I've beaten him before. He's not that good. And think about it. Mitch is still the Blood Bath Killer. Richard Zardino is the Prom Night Killer. And those gang kids just keep killing each other with that 'stash gun.' You need to be a man about this. It will be over in a second. In fact, as the saying goes, I think this is going to hurt me more than it hurts you."

Connie laughed. He moved in closer, the gun pointed at Alves's head.

This was it. He had one crack at Connie. Should he aim low? Maybe hit him with an elbow in the nuts? Or the jaw? A square shot to the jaw could stun him, maybe knock him out. Alves waited until Connie stood close to him on his right side. Connie was much taller than he. He sized Connie up and made his decision. He swung his right elbow at Connie's midsection. Caught him in the ribs. Heard a crack. At the same time he grabbed the barrel of the gun with his left hand, turning it away from his body. He tried to stand up as he hit Connie with a few more elbows, but the alcohol was having its effects. Alves lost his footing and Connie pulled the gun out of his grasp. He felt Connie's powerful arm wrap around his neck, choking him.

"Any last words?" Connie asked, loosening his grip slightly.

Alves began to pray. "O my God, I am heartily sorry for having offended Thee, and I detest." He raised his voice. "All my sins, because I dread." He was almost yelling. "The loss of Heaven and the pains of hell . . ."

Connie placed the gun against Alves's right temple. Alves closed his eyes.

The quiet of the stadium was interrupted by the sound of a single gunshot.

CHAPTER 109

Alves kept his eyes closed for a moment.

He felt no pain.

"Motherfucker," Connie shouted.

Alves was not dead. He felt more alive than he had felt since Connie first choked him out. Had Connie missed with the shot? No. Alves's ears weren't ringing. He opened his eyes. Connie had backed away from him.

Connie was bent over, holding his side. "You are going to die for this." He raised the blood-soaked Glock toward Alves.

A second shot.

This time Connie dropped the gun and stumbled backward, falling onto the hard turf.

Nearly thirty yards away, Sergeant Ray Figgs stepped out of the shadows and moved toward Connie, his gun pointed at Connie. Alves could see that Connie was barely breathing. A pool of blood was glistening in the moonlight. Figgs kicked the Glock away from Connie's reach.

"How did you find us?" Alves shouted at Figgs.

"I've been watching him," Figgs said. "I never bought that thing with Stutter Simpson and the .40. And ADA Conrad Darget is the only one who could have planted that gun."

"Well, you could have got out here sooner."

"I lost you when you came in close to the stands. I had to move slowly.

I never had a very good angle. But I had no choice when he put the gun to your head. You okay?"

"Yeah." Alves could feel his head spinning. Maybe it was the beer. Maybe it was how close he had come to dying. Maybe it was the knowledge of what Connie had done.

Figgs put his gun down on the bench and helped Alves to his feet. It felt good to have the blood flowing again.

Another shot went off.

Alves had never been shot before. The bullet hit his left arm, near his shoulder. It burned as if a red hot poker and been driven through him. Figgs pushed him down. Both of them managed to roll behind a steel trash can. Alves held his shoulder, trying not to make any noise. God, it hurt. He could see Connie up on one knee. He had a small gun in his hand. The two-shot derringer. Alves reached for his ankle, praying that his lifesaver was still there. He got a firm grip on his snubby. He handed the gun to Figgs.

Figgs stayed close to the ground. "Don't move," Figgs said.

"It isn't supposed to end like this," Connie called. "I have been chosen to do this work."

"Drop the gun or I'll shoot."

"I can't let you do this," Connie said, struggling to stand and aim.

Figgs fired a shot into Connie's chest and Connie fell onto his back. He didn't move. Figgs walked over and kicked the derringer away.

Alves stopped to adjust the sling. No matter what he tried, he couldn't get his arm into a comfortable position. But he felt guilty thinking about his discomfort, considering what Mooney was going through. Alves continued down the corridor until he reached the cul-de-sac of recovery rooms in the ICU. He paused outside and watched Mooney lying with his eyes closed. Should he bother him? Would a visit agitate him?

Mooney opened his eyes. "What're you, a Peeping Tom, skulking around outside people's rooms?"

"Yeah. Actually, I got bored checking out the hot babe in the room down the hall who was getting a sponge bath from two sexy nurses. I thought it'd be more fun to watch a cranky, old-fart cop taking his afternoon nap."

Mooney smiled. That was all Alves needed to get out of him.

"How're you doing, Sarge? Hey, Leslie." She was sitting in a chair by the window.

Mooney raised his thumb.

Not bad, Alves thought, considering Sarge had lost a section of colon and a chunk of his liver. And he'd lost a lot of blood. Those small-caliber bullets did more damage than a big gun.

"The twins are having fun feeding Biggie," Alves said. "He's quite the mac and cheese fan."

Mooney almost managed a smile.

"I'm just glad you're okay," Alves said.

Leslie stood and came forward to give Alves a hug. "I could use a cup of coffee. I'll leave you two alone, but no work talk. Doctor's orders."

Leslie hadn't even disappeared down the hall when Mooney managed to ask, "What about Darget? Figgs was here earlier, told me what happened. Said Darget took two in the ten ring."

"Connie's in critical. Paramedics on scene said he was nothing but body parts."

Mooney tipped his chin up, tubes and all. "Figgsy. From Department sharpshooter to barstool and back again."

"Sarge, I shouldn't be talking about the case. Leslie said you can't have any stress. How about the Pats? Big game this weekend, huh? They're saying it's going to be a blizzard by game time."

With his dry, raspy voice Mooney asked, "Execute search warrants?"

"Yeah. His house, office, parents' house. We even hit his grandparents' farm. We got the embalming table. Luminol came up positive for human blood, but that doesn't tell us anything. Could have been there since the table's funeral home days. There was no actual blood for us to test for DNA. Nothing much else in the house."

Alves stopped talking and smiled. A young nurse with a big blond ponytail came in to check Mooney's blood pressure, oxygen and temperature. The second she was out the door, Alves continued. "We didn't find any trophies from the victims. I was hoping to find the suits, underwear, jewelry, something. No newspaper clippings or TV coverage. Darget kept a very neat house."

"Car?" Mooney croaked.

"Hasn't owned a car in a while. Got stolen a few years ago, just after we closed the Blood Bath case. Oddly enough, they found it torched down by Tenean Beach in Dorchester. Never bought a replacement. He's been riding around in the DA's office minivan ever since his promotion. We didn't find anything in the van. But it wouldn't matter if we did. Each of the kids he killed had been in that van when they got picked up for court by his investigators. He got to know each of them personally before he put two in the hat."

Mooney gestured for the cup of ice water on the bedside table. Alves put one of the tiny blue sponges into Mooney's mouth like a lollipop. It would be a while before Sarge would be enjoying his Schlitz. "Parents," Mooney mumbled. "Grandparents."

"Nothing at his parents' house. His grandparents own thirty acres in Bridgewater. Used to be a working farm, now it's pretty much over-grown. Grandmother is up there in years, but she still manages to take care of the house and all. Grandfather's pretty bad with Alzheimer's. Just stands there and shouts out passages from the Bible."

"Evidence?"

"No. But we did find something interesting out in the woods behind the barn. An old oil tank with the top third cut off. Apparently, the old man used to burn brush and trash in there. He had a blower hooked up to it. Once he got the flame going nice and hot, he'd kick on the blower, and it heated up like an incinerator. It would eat up pieces of wood as fast as you could feed them in."

"Bone fragments? Anything?"

"Been cleaned out. Recently. I asked the old woman when her hus-band last used it. Not for years. She said Connie was the last one to use it a few years ago when he came out to get rid of the ark."

Mooney raised his eyebrows.

"You heard me right. She was embarrassed to tell the story. It seems as though grandpa had some mental health issues to go along with the onset of Alzheimer's. The old man's name is Noah Darget. Back in the mid '90s, before the Alzheimer's got too bad, he believed that the world would come to an end at the turn of the century. He was convinced that he was *the* Noah and that he had to build an ark. He starts building this monstrosity back behind the barn, but he never completes it. This half-finished mess sits out there for years, rotting away, until one day Connie volunteers to get rid of it for his grandmother. He tells her he's got some construction debris from his house in Hyde Park and takes it back there in the minivan. He spends the whole weekend out there burning every last bit of that ark and his debris, with the old man watching. Then he hauls the remaining ash to the asphalt batching plant down the road."

They were both quiet for a couple minutes.

"Sarge, I think he incinerated Robyn and the others with that rotten wood. Now all those people, they're part of a highway somewhere."

"Can we tie him in?"

"We can. We've got his statements corroborated by circumstantial evidence tying him to the Blood Bath case. For the gang killings with the .40, we have the confession he made to me. Not to mention motive and opportunity. I've got ATF trying to raise the serial number off the gun. And let's not forget, he tried to kill me with Ray Figgs as a witness."

Mooney tried to smile. "Hope that prick-of-misery Darget dies."

Alves sat with Mooney as the late afternoon sky lit up orange with the setting sun. He watched his sergeant drift in and out of sleep. He wasn't sure if he wanted Connie to live and face justice or to die. He thought about something he hadn't thought about since he was a kid. How a prayer was like a wish. And how you got just one.

In the quiet room humming with the machines that kept Wayne Mooney alive, Alves put his folded hands on the clean, smooth white blanket, bent his head and said a prayer.

ACKNOWLEDGMENTS

Of course, thanks to my writers' group, Lin Haire-Sargeant, Peggy Walsh, and Candice Rowe, for their unflagging encouragement, support and hard work during the early drafts.

Once again, special thanks to Boston Police Sergeant Detective Kevin Waggett for his enthusiasm. Not a day goes by without a call or email from my good friend offering suggestions, insights and tips.

Thanks, too, to everyone who assisted me: my mentors Judge Bob Tochka and Peter Muse; Paul Treseler and Matt Machera, my #1 fans; my friends Sarah Richardson, Terry Reidy, Kevin Hayden and Rahsaan Hall; Boston Police Sergeant Charlie Byrne (Ret.), Deputy Superintendent Earl Perkins, Lieutenant Bob Merner, Detective Mike Devane, Sergeant Mark Vickers, Sergeant James O'Shea, Detective Marty Lydon, Sergeant Michael Fish, Senior Criminalist Amy Kraatz, Criminalist Kevin Kosiorek, Jim Hassan, Kevin Reddington, Truesee Allah, Judge Dave Poole, Frank McCabe, Liza Williamson, Eric Breckner, and Sammy Kamel for their technical assistance.

Thanks to Jessica, Chris, Nolan, Russell, and Castin for keeping me on track.

For their wisdom and guidance, thanks to Mark Tavani and Simon Green.

And thanks to Candice, for without her there would be no Sleep.

ABOUT THE AUTHOR

RAFFI YESSAYAN is the author of *8 in the Box*. He spent eleven years as an assistant district attorney in Boston. Within two years of becoming a prosecutor, he was named to the Gang Unit, ultimately becoming its chief. He recently left the DA's office to go into private practice. He and his wife live in Massachusetts.

ABOUT THE TYPE

This book was set in Requiem, a typeface designed by the Hoefler Type Foundry. It is a modern typeface inspired by inscriptional capitals in Ludovico Vicentino degli Arrighi's 1523 writing manual, *Il modo de temperare le penne*. An original lowercase, a set of figures, and an italic in the "chancery" style that Arrighi helped popularize were created to make this adaptation of a classical design into a complete font family.